P9-DNY-855

MUTATION

MUTA

TION

ROLAND SMITH

SCHOLASTIC PRESS
NEW YORK

Library of Congress Cataloging-in-Publication Data

Smith, Roland, 1951-
Mutation / Roland Smith. — First edition.
pages cm — (Cryptid hunters)
Summary: "Marty and his best friend, Luther, have managed to rescue Marty's cousin Grace from the clutches of the nefarious pseudo-naturalist Noah Blackwood, but their most dangerous mission lies ahead of them. Marty's parents have been missing in Brazil for months, and their trail has all but run cold. With time running out, Marty and the Cryptos Island crew race off for Brazil — where they discover that Noah Blackwood has twisted the natural order of things beyond their wildest, most terrifying dreams" — Provided by publisher.
ISBN 978-0-545-08180-1
[1. Adventure and adventurers — Fiction. 2. Animals, Mythical — Fiction. 3. Jungles — Fiction. 4. Missing persons — Fiction. 5. Brazil — Fiction.] I. Title.
PZ7.S65766Mu 2014
[Fic] — dc23

2014017169

10 9 8 7 6 5 4 3 2 1 14 15 16 17 18

Printed in the U.S.A. 23
First edition, October 2014

The text type was set in Garamond.
The display type was set in Bank Gothic.
Book design by Phil Falco

cryp·to·zo·ol·o·gy (krip-ta-zō-ä-la-jē) *noun* The study of animals, such as the Sasquatch, the Yeti, the Loch Ness Monster, the Chupacabra, kraken, and others, whose existence has not yet been proven scientifically. There are thought to be more than two hundred ***cryptids*** in existence today.
— **cryp·to·zo·o·log·i·cal** (-zō-a-,´lä-ji-kal) *adj.*
— **cryp·to·zo·ol·o·gist** (-´ä-la-jist) *noun*

FOR ALL MY CRYPTOZOOLOGY FRIENDS
WHO HAVE STUCK WITH ME THROUGH THESE
LONG YEARS, WAITING FOR MARTY AND GRACE
TO COMPLETE THEIR ADVENTURE

Marty O'Hara: Wolfe's nephew. Grace's cousin (formerly thought to be her twin). Thirteen years old. Brown hair, gray eyes, a foot taller than Grace. Talented artist. Master chef. Scuba diver. Mountain climber. Skydiver. Has an eidetic memory. He has spent most of his life at the Omega Opportunity Preparatory School (OOPS) in Switzerland. His parents, Timothy and Sylvia (the most famous photographer/journalist team in the world), are missing after a terrible helicopter crash in the Amazon rain forest.

Grace Wolfe: Wolfe's only daughter (although for most of her life she thought she was Timothy and Sylvia O'Hara's daughter and Marty's twin sister). Black hair, blue eyes the color of robin's eggs like her mother Rose's. Born at Lake Télé in the Congo. Thirteen years old. Small for her age, but a foot *smarter* than Marty. The best student to ever "grace" the halls of OOPS. Fluent in several languages. Habitual journal-writer (uses a Montblanc fountain pen and Moleskine notebooks). Lock-picker. Genius.

Luther Percival Smyth IV: Marty's best friend and former roommate at OOPS in Switzerland, where they managed to get into a tremendous amount of trouble. Coauthor/illustrator of Marty's graphic novel. Sleeps like a vampire. Eats like a wolf. Gangly, with wild orange hair. His father (Luther Percival Smyth III) and mother are billionaires and often forget they even have a son. Expert computer hacker and video gamer.

Dr. Travis Wolfe: Cryptozoologist. Veterinarian. Oceanographer. Cofounder and owner of eWolfe with Ted Bronson. Called Wolfe by his friends — and foes. Grace's father. Marty's uncle. Sylvia O'Hara's older brother. Widower. Former son-in-law of Noah Blackwood. A giant of a man — just under seven feet tall. Unruly black hair, bushy black beard, brown eyes. Wears size-fifteen shoes. His right leg was bitten off by a Mokélé-mbembé as he tried to save his wife, Rose Blackwood, in the Congo. He now wears a high-tech prosthesis invented by Ted Bronson.

Dr. Ted Bronson (a.k.a. Theo Sonborn): Wolfe's closest friend and partner at eWolfe. Eccentric genius. Inventor. Recluse. Rumored to have not left the Quonset hut on Cryptos Island (where he develops his marvelous gadgets) in more than three years.

Theo Sonborn (a.k.a. Dr. Ted Bronson): Has been with Wolfe since the beginning. Surly. Pugnacious. Obnoxious. Jack-of-all-trades, master of none.

Dr. Noah Blackwood: Wealthy. Powerful. Owner of several animal theme parks around the world, all called Noah's Ark. Environmental desperate to work her way to the top in Blackwood's organization.

Dr. Laurel Lee: Wolfe's cultural anthropologist. Birdlike. Athletic. Former circus aerialist. Taught Grace to walk on a high wire to help her focus and overcome her many fears. Laurel and Wolfe are sweet on each other.

Ana Mika: Investigative journalist, world traveler, and Ted Bronson's longtime girlfriend.

Mr. and Mrs. Hickock: Caretakers on Cryptos. Wild "Bill" Hickock remains on the island; Melanie Hickock (Ph.D. in Egyptology) is currently curating an Egyptian exhibit at the University of Washington.

Dylan Hickock: Sixteen years old. Caretakers' son. Just got his driver's license. He's new to the Cryptos Island crew, but not new to cryptids.

Dr. Robert "Doc" Lansa: World-renowned biologist. Hot-tempered and tireless. Runs a jaguar preserve in Brazil.

Jacob "Jake" Lansa: Doc's son, and a rain forest enthusiast in his own right.

Flanna Brenna: A botanist at the jaguar preserve, and likely Jake's future stepmother. The mastermind behind the web of zip lines they use to navigate the rain forest canopy.

Special Agent Steven Crow: An FBI agent close to retirement. He's been on the trail of hijacker D. B. Cooper (a.k.a. Buck Johnson) for years, and he thinks he's coming to the end of the road.

Buckley "Buck" Johnson: Hijacked a jet under the alias D. B. Cooper, hoping to use the ransom money to save the life of his son, but ultimately failing. After he returned the money, he disappeared.

CONTENTS

The Cryptid Hunters Saga So Far . . . XII

DAY ONE

Flight 3
One Way or the Other 11
Zip 23
Manaus 40

DAY TWO

The *Rivlan* 49
Chopper 58
Poolside 75
D. B. Cooper 80
The Preserve 86
Raul 93

DAY THREE

Crow 107
Snap! 120
Walking in the Rain 136

DAY FOUR

Dead in the Water 145
Blink 159
Trips 164
They're Coming 176
Model Prisoners 190
Dung Heaps 199
The Compound 202
Bot Hop 211
Inside 223
Doors 234
Chicken 239
Too Far 244
Beneath 255

DAY FIVE

Boots and Bare Feet 267
Caged 271
Bot Spotting 286
Dead Monkeys 298
So Far So Good 307
Click Click Click Snap 316
I Am You 324
The O'Haras 328
It's Been Two Weeks . . . 330

THE CRYPTID HUNTERS SAGA SO FAR . . .

Fraternal twins Marty and Grace O'Hara are attending the Omega Opportunity Preparatory School (OOPS) in Switzerland when they receive shocking and tragic news: Their parents, Sylvia and Timothy, have disappeared after a helicopter crash in the Brazilian rain forest. The twins have to leave OOPS to stay with Travis Wolfe, their mother's mysterious older brother.

Travis Wolfe lives off the coast of Washington State on a volcanic island called Cryptos. Together with his genius business partner, Ted Bronson, Wolfe runs a very profitable tech company, but his real interest is cryptozoology. He spends almost every dime he makes searching the world for mythical animals called cryptids. Now, though, his mission is finding Sylvia and Timothy.

A few days into Marty and Grace's stay on Cryptos, a cultural anthropologist named Laurel Lee shows up unannounced. While living in the Congo, Laurel came into possession of a large egg supposedly belonging to a dinosaur called Mokélé-mbembé. Back in the U.S., Laurel took the egg to be tested at the labs of Dr. Noah Blackwood, the famous wildlife conservationist and TV personality, and his people stole it from her.

Travis Wolfe and Noah Blackwood have been archenemies for years. Noah is rich, famous, and respected, but Wolfe knows that Noah's wildlife parks around the world — his Arks — are fronts for his real purpose, which is to collect rare species and "harvest" them for his endangered taxidermy collection.

Wolfe springs into action. He and Laurel plan to travel to Lake Télé in the Congo to save the last dinosaur on earth before Noah Blackwood and his chief henchman, Butch McCall, get their hands on it. Wolfe decides to send Marty and Grace back to OOPS, but they have to ride along on a supply drop over Lake Télé before returning to Switzerland. Things don't go according to plan, and the twins land in the Congo clinging to a parachute, days before Wolfe and Laurel can get there.

Alone in the treacherous jungle, with Butch McCall stalking them, Marty and Grace take up residence in a gigantic tree house built by Wolfe years earlier. While there, Marty and Grace discover that they are not twins after all, but cousins. They learn that Travis Wolfe, their guardian, was married to the late Rose Blackwood — Noah's daughter. To escape her controlling father, Rose eloped with Wolfe and they hid out in the Congo. Grace, their daughter, was born there. Noah Blackwood is Grace's grandfather.

Marty and Grace find the Mokélé-mbembé nest. The last living dinosaur has died, leaving behind two eggs. The cousins take the eggs and escape by hijacking Noah Blackwood's helicopter, leaving Butch and Noah to make their way out of the jungle on foot.

Back on Cryptos Island, Wolfe decides it's best to leave the country for a while. He knows that Noah is going to come after both the eggs and Grace. Marty's best friend from OOPS,

Luther Percival Smyth IV, joins them aboard Wolfe's research ship, the *Coelacanth*, and they all head to New Zealand to catch a giant squid for Northwest Zoo and Aquarium, the rival to Noah's Seattle Ark. Butch McCall manages to get aboard the *Coelacanth* disguised as a researcher, with two co-conspirators to help him, Yvonne Zloblinavech and Mitch Merton.

The Mokélé-mbembé eggs hatch, producing two baby dinosaurs. Meanwhile, Noah Blackwood pursues the *Coelacanth* aboard his own research ship, manned with mercenaries. As Marty and Ted maneuver the *Coelacanth*'s submersible to catch a giant squid, Noah and his hired hands attack the ship. The crew fends off the assault, but not before Blackwood's scuba divers secretly place explosive charges on board. Below, Marty and Ted discover the explosives and frantically try to disarm them. On deck, Butch, Yvonne, and Noah's mercenaries have bagged the Mokélé-mbembé hatchlings and are holding Laurel at gunpoint.

Noah lands his chopper on the *Coelacanth*'s helipad. Butch threatens to shoot Laurel if Wolfe and his men don't lay down their arms. To protect her father and friends, Grace agrees to go willingly with her grandfather. Marty and Ted disarm all the bombs, and the Cryptos crew heads back to Seattle with the first giant squid ever to be captured alive. But they've lost Grace and the dinosaur hatchlings.

Wolfe heads to Washington, DC, leaving Marty and Luther with the new Cryptos caretakers, the Hickocks, and their son, Dylan. Together with Dylan, Marty and Luther set off for Noah's Seattle Ark to find Grace themselves.

Grace convinces Noah Blackwood that she is happy living in Seattle with him. But she's truly after information about her late mother, Rose, and she's curious about the contents of the sealed-off third level of Blackwood's mansion.

Marty, Luther, and Dylan manage to enter the Ark undetected, but their plans are thwarted by Blackwood's facial recognition technology. Luther is drugged and kidnapped by Butch McCall, and locked away in a lower-level room below the Ark. Noah fears that Wolfe is planning to take back Grace and the dinosaur hatchlings and shuts down the Ark, trapping Marty and Dylan inside the grounds. He plans for the intruders to be killed by his genetically engineered and vicious chupacabra, controlled remotely by his henchwoman, Yvonne.

Grace manages to enter the secret third floor of Blackwood's mansion, where she discovers a horrifying diorama of stuffed endangered and extinct animals, as well as the green screen set where he fakes episodes of his nature TV show. Grace leaves the third floor via a laundry chute that reunites her with Marty and Dylan. Luther makes his own escape by crawling through the duct system of the Ark, disconnecting all of Blackwood's surveillance cameras along the way. Then they capture Yvonne, take the remote that controls the chupacabra, and trick her into thinking she's locked in a dark room with the vicious creature. They also rescue both hatchlings and three baby pandas from the Ark before being picked up by Ted Bronson in a helicopter he's stolen from Blackwood.

Noah is furious and wants Grace, the hatchlings, and his pandas back.

DAY ONE

FLIGHT

Marty O' Hara watched the three panda cubs wrestling in the aisle at thirty-five thousand feet. He was aboard his uncle Travis Wolfe's converted bomber jet, winging his way south to the Amazon basin in Brazil with several other members of Wolfe's Cryptos Island crew. Marty was exhausted and wanted to take a nap, but he couldn't because he was holding Wolfe's growling three-pound teacup poodle on his lap. It was all he could do to keep PD, as the tiny dog was known, from leaping into the fray and getting mauled by the adorable black-and-white bear cubs.

"Panda-monium," Marty quipped.

His cousin, Grace, looked up at him from the aisle where she was supervising the wrestling match. "Punny," she said. "I'm sure going to miss these cubs."

Marty had to admit that the cubs were cute, but he hadn't been around them enough to know if he was going to miss them or not.

Marty's best friend, Luther Percival Smyth IV, and their new friend, Dylan Hickock, were in the back of the jet behind a hermetically sealed bulkhead, to everyone's olfactory relief, feeding the Mokélé-mbembé hatchlings. The two not-so-little dinosaurs were voracious eaters, and they always smelled worse — if that was even possible — after a meal. Travis Wolfe and Ted Bronson were three rows in front of Marty, staring at their laptops and crunching the treasure trove of data that Grace had stolen from Noah Blackwood's computer. It had only been a day since Ted, Marty, Luther, and Dylan had rescued Grace from Blackwood's mansion, where the renowned naturalist had held Grace, his own granddaughter, since kidnapping her several weeks earlier.

"Blackwood," Ted said, pointing to the television screen above his head.

Marty was out of his seat like a shot, clutching PD.

"A rerun from last night," Wolfe said.

A smiling Dr. Noah Blackwood was being interviewed inside the Squidarium at Northwest Zoo and Aquarium. A giant squid was swimming in the background. Standing next to Blackwood was Dr. Michael Loch, the zoo's director. He looked as if he would rather be in the clutches of the giant squid, with its beak piercing his skull, than standing next to Noah Blackwood.

"So, what do you think, Dr. Blackwood?" the eager reporter asked.

Noah amped up his smile to 250 watts. "It's magnificent!" he said, putting a congratulatory hand on Loch's shoulder.

Loch looked like he was going to be sick.

"We will learn a great deal about these mysterious denizens of the deep by having this specimen in captivity," Noah continued. "I couldn't be prouder of Dr. Loch and the NZA staff."

Marty rolled his eyes. Noah was making it sound like Loch and the NZA staff worked for him.

"Doesn't having the giant squid here at NZA affect the bottom line at your wildlife park, the Seattle Ark?" the reporter asked.

Noah's smile dimmed, but only slightly. "A rather crude way to put it," he said. "And the answer is no. I am not interested in the bottom line. My sole purpose in life is the conservation of wildlife. I am not concerned with how many people come through the gates of the Seattle Ark versus Northwest Zoo and Aquarium. My mission can be summed up in two words, 'Wildlife first.'"

My sole purpose, Marty thought. *My mission. My, my, my . . . Lie, lie, lie . . . Liar, liar, pants on fire.*

"I didn't mean any offense," the reporter said, then continued undeterred. "I was interviewing some zoo visitors here at NZA, and they said they'd been planning to visit the Ark today but changed their minds when they found out the panda cubs wouldn't be on display. I was just thinking that the —"

Noah cut him off. "I'm glad you brought up the panda cubs," he said. "They are a perfect example of what I was just saying. We determined that they were becoming slightly stressed by all of the attention they were receiving. We decided to take the cubs off display for their own well-being, knowing full well that it might affect our so-called bottom line, as you put it."

Marty glanced behind him. Grace had stepped forward in order to better see the interview. The cubs were pulling on her shoelaces. If anyone was stressed, it was Grace. She was hanging on to the seats on either side of the aisle, trying not to topple over.

"How long do you think the cubs will remain off display?" the reporter persisted.

"Until we deem it appropriate to put them back on display," Noah said.

Or until Butch has a chance to pop over to China and poach three more cubs for Blackwood to showcase, Marty thought.

Among the files that Grace had "liberated" from Blackwood's computer was a report about how his henchman Butch McCall had "harvested" the cubs from their mothers in the Gansu province of China.

Noah made a big deal out of looking at his watch. "I'm afraid I'm going to have to cut this short," he said. "I have animals to tend to back at the Ark."

"Five less than you did two days ago," Marty said.

Grace laughed. They watched Noah walk out of camera view. A look of relief passed across Dr. Loch's face. The camera panned back to get a view of the crowd watching the giant squid.

"Is that Al Ikes?" Grace asked.

Marty stepped closer to the screen. Grace was right: It was Al Ikes, but he wasn't dressed like the Al Ikes they knew. His typical three-piece suit had been replaced by a black hoodie, jeans, and high-top sneakers.

"That's Al," Wolfe confirmed. "He and his crew are keeping an eye on Blackwood while we're away."

Al must have realized he was being filmed because he quickly stepped out of the camera shot. He was ex-CIA, and he didn't like to be photographed. He and his "crew" were in charge of security on Cryptos Island, Wolfe's headquarters.

Didn't do us any good two nights ago when Blackwood tried to have his chupacabra murder us, Marty thought. *Not that I'm complaining. If Al had known about our plan, he would have stopped us from going to the Ark, and we wouldn't have gotten the hatchlings — or the panda cubs.*

"What about Butch and Yvonne?" Marty asked.

"Al hasn't caught sight of them yet," Wolfe answered. "Which is a little worrisome. But he reported that Blackwood went back to the Ark after the interview and was very visible throughout the day."

"Butch is probably still licking his wounds," Ted said. "I did a number on him the other night. I doubt he'll be moving around much today."

Marty hadn't seen the "number" Ted was talking about, but Grace had told him that Ted was some kind of fiftieth-degree black-belt ninja, as well as a super genius and a hijacker. Ted had managed to rescue them with Blackwood's own helicopter, which was now stowed away in the back of Wolfe's converted bomber.

Wolfe looked at Marty. "I suspect Yvonne isn't moving around too well today, either, after what you did to her with that pig."

Marty grinned. He hadn't hurt Blackwood's other trusted employee, Yvonne Zloblinavech, but she was probably still shaken up. He and Luther and Dylan had locked Yvonne in a dark room with a potbellied pig after convincing her it was the chupacabra she had sent out to kill them.

"I wish I could have seen her face," Wolfe said, returning his grin.

"You wouldn't have recognized her," Marty said. "She looks a lot different without her fake smile. Kind of scary, actually."

One of the pandas wrapped its front paws around Wolfe's right leg and tried to take a playful bite out of it. He laughed and picked it up. "You'll get a mouthful of metal, little guy."

Years earlier, Wolfe's right leg had been bitten off by Mokélé-mbembé, the mother of the dinosaur hatchlings, but his injury wasn't apparent when he walked or ran. Ted had invented a prosthetic leg out of a special metal alloy that Wolfe claimed was better than flesh and blood, but Marty knew his uncle would rather have his real leg back.

"Do they have a good enclosure for the pandas at the jaguar preserve?" Grace asked.

Wolfe looked a little confused by the question, which wasn't unusual. He always looked a little confused when Grace or Marty asked him a question. "I'm not sure," he finally said. "I haven't been there before, but it doesn't matter. The cubs aren't going to the preserve."

"What are you talking about?" Grace cried.

"The pandas don't belong to us," Wolfe said.

"They don't belong to Noah Blackwood, either," Grace said.

"Exactly. Which is why I asked Phil and Phyllis if they would make a side trip to China after they drop us off in Brazil."

Phil and Phyllis Bishop were Cryptos Island's pilots. The father-daughter team were in the cockpit flying them south.

"Kind of a big side trip," Marty said.

"But necessary," Wolfe insisted. "We can't possibly take care of these little guys where we're going. We'll have our hands full with the hatchlings. I've been in touch with the Chengdu panda research center. They've agreed to take the cubs off our hands with no questions asked."

"Is it a good place?" Grace asked.

"The best," Wolfe assured her. "I've been there several times. It's where the cubs belong, and it's the best place to keep them out of the clutches of Noah Blackwood."

"They belong back with their mothers," Marty said.

Wolfe frowned. "I agree, but that's no longer possible."

"Thanks to Butch McCall," Grace said bitterly.

They all knew that Butch had shot the mothers to get the cubs.

"Can't we have him arrested or something?" Marty asked. "Animal poaching. International wildlife smuggling. Violation of the Endangered Species Act. I bet he's broken a dozen laws."

"He and Noah Blackwood have probably broken thousands of laws," Ted said. "But we don't have any solid proof."

"What about the files I stole?" Grace asked.

"It's fabulous information, but it's vague," Ted explained. "We understand what they're talking about because we know what they're capable of, but nothing we have here would stand up in court. For one thing, the information's stolen. For another, Blackwood and Butch have been doing this stuff for decades. They're very careful with the language they use. These records could be interpreted in several different ways."

"And Blackwood's a very powerful man," Wolfe added. "He has a lot of money and a lot of influence. Nobody's going to be eager to prosecute him even if we find something that's actionable." He fixed his dark, intense eyes on Grace's robin's-egg-blue ones. "And then there is you," he said quietly.

"What do you mean?" Grace asked.

"Noah Blackwood is going to come after you."

"Not very likely after I hacked his computer, kidnapped his panda cubs, and stole back the hatchlings," Grace said.

"Actually, it's even more likely now," Wolfe said. "Noah doesn't like to be crossed. He doesn't like to lose. He wants you back."

"And he wants the hatchlings back," Ted added. "And the pandas, although he'll have a hard time getting them once Phil and Phyllis return them to China. He will be coming after all of us."

"What do we do?" Grace asked.

"We have a good head start," Wolfe said. "We have eyes on Noah Blackwood. What we do now is take advantage of the time by trying to find Marty's parents."

Wolfe handed Grace the panda cub. PD growled, but Marty held him tight.

"I'll put the cubs back in their enclosure," Grace said.

"I'll give you a hand," Marty said.

He dropped the tiny poodle in Wolfe's lap. PD continued to growl.

ONE WAY OR THE OTHER

Luther and Dylan were covered in blood.

"Nice timing," Luther said. "Why do you two always show up when we're finished?"

The two Mokélé-mbembé hatchlings were wrapped around each other on a bed of straw, snoring and farting, sleeping off their bloody gluttony.

"Whew!" Marty said, waving his free hand in front of his nose. "I think Wolfe has a shower in back. It'll get the blood off, but not the stink."

"What stink?" Luther asked.

"Let's get this mess cleaned up before we shower," Dylan suggested. There were bits of meat, guts, and bloody knives strewn all over the food prep table.

"Don't worry about it," Luther said. "Marty and Grace will clean up."

"In your dreams," Marty said. "We have our hands full." He was carrying one of the pandas. Grace had the other two.

"We'll take them," Luther said.

"Forget it," Grace said. "You'll get them all bloody."

She headed through a second bulkhead hatch. Marty followed, but not before giving Luther a victorious grin.

"When you're done back there, we need to get moving on our next graphic novel," Luther called after him. "I have some good ideas, and Dylan does, too."

Marty hadn't even thought about writing and illustrating the next installment of their adventures. Right now, he was focused on getting to Brazil and finding his parents.

But we do have a long flight ahead of us, he thought. *Working on a few pages might get my mind off things.*

"We are staying in Brazil for the duration," Wolfe had announced before they took off from Cryptos, adding ominously, "one way or the other." This meant they weren't leaving until they found out what happened to Marty's mom and dad — Sylvia and Timothy O'Hara. Sylvia was Wolfe's younger sister. There was only *one way* Marty wanted to find his parents, and that was alive and well. But he knew he might not get his wish. His parents had been missing for a long time, in one of the harshest environments on the planet.

Worrying about them isn't going to help me find them, Marty told himself.

He took in his surroundings. Wolfe's converted bomber was divided into several sections separated by bulkheads. Up front was the cockpit, or flight deck, where the Bishops were handling the controls of the plane. Behind the cockpit was the seating section, where Wolfe and Ted were huddled over their laptops. Behind that was the galley, which had been converted into the hatchling nursery. Behind the galley, where he now stood, was animal holding.

He put his panda into the cage with the other two cubs and watched as they started to do somersaults in the straw.

"I'm going to miss them," Grace said.

"I'll bet," Marty said distractedly. He hadn't been in this part of the plane since he and Grace had been in the Congo, or more accurately, *over* the Congo.

He pointed to a familiar hatch in the floor. The hatch covered the bomb bay that Wolfe used to airdrop supplies for his expeditions. There were two containers in the bay waiting to be dropped before they landed in Manaus, Brazil.

"Remember that?" Marty asked.

Grace turned around, looked, and gave a visible shudder. "How could I forget?"

Marty laughed. Bo, Wolfe's bonobo chimpanzee, had gotten out of her cage as they'd been flying over the Congo. He and Grace had climbed into the bomb bay to get Bo back at the exact moment Phil Bishop had released the load. At the time, the fall had been the number one most terrifying thing that had ever happened to him. So many other terrifying things had happened to him since that the fall was now down to number six.

Or maybe number seven, he thought.

He walked over to another bulkhead.

"Where are you going?" Grace asked.

"I want to check out what Wolfe brought along for the trip."

Marty had spent their last day on Cryptos Island inside Wolfe's stone fortress, sleeping, cooking, and eating, and he had missed the loading. He opened the bulkhead hatch and switched on the light. Grace followed him in.

"Whoa!"

Marty had expected Wolfe to bring supplies and equipment, but nothing like this. The large section was stacked from floor to ceiling with plastic and wooden crates. They were barely able to squeeze past them to get in.

"What is all this stuff?" Grace asked.

Marty didn't know, but he was certainly going to poke around and find out. The containers were carefully marked. He pointed at a stack marked *Freeze-Dried Food*.

"Wolfe has enough grub to feed an army for a year!"

He continued his poking, discovering medical supplies, four-wheelers, motorcycles, tents, hammocks, two-way radios, rain ponchos, flashlights, batteries, remote-operated cameras, hats, rope, tools, and spare parts for everything.

"Look at this!" He pointed at two large containers marked *Ultralight*.

"What's an ultralight?" Grace asked.

"Are you kidding? An ultralight is an airplane . . . well, more like a go-cart with wings really. I've always wanted to fly one. You can bet if Ted's designed it, it will do things normal ultralights never dreamed of doing."

"I doubt Wolfe is going to let you fly it."

"He let me fly the dragonspy."

"There's a big difference between flying a bot using a remote control and piloting an airplane from inside the cockpit."

"Don't forget that I was inside the Orb about a million miles beneath the ocean when we captured the giant squid."

"Hardly a million miles," Grace said. "And you forgot to mention you were with Ted, who was the one piloting the Orb when you captured the giant squid."

"Minor technicality," Marty said, but she had a good point. If he wanted a shot at flying the ultralight, he would have to get Ted Bronson on his side. He was going to start working on this as soon as he got back up front. Ted was a lot more reasonable about letting him do stupidly dangerous things than Wolfe was.

They wove their way deeper into the stacks of stuff.

"How's he going to get all of this to the jaguar preserve?" Grace asked.

"Blackwood's helicopter, I guess," Marty said, although they hadn't seen the helicopter yet.

"My grand —" Grace turned red. "Noah Blackwood's helicopter is not that big."

"It's not your fault he's your grandfather," Marty said.

"I know that," Grace said. "It's just so . . . Oh, never mind. It would take a hundred trips on Noah's helicopter to get this stuff to the jaguar preserve, and some of these containers won't fit through the door."

Marty let the whole Noah-Blackwood-is-Grace's-grandfather thing go. He'd be sensitive about it, too, if his grandfather was a narcissistic psychopath.

"Well," he said. "They have to get all this stuff there somehow." He opened the final bulkhead door. Blackwood's helicopter was lashed down to the steel floor on the far side of the cargo hold. The rotors had been removed so it would fit into the hold. He walked over to it for a closer look.

"I guess that explains it," Grace said from behind him.

"Explains what?" Marty asked. He was staring at the helicopter, thinking how weird it looked without rotors, and visualizing it with the rotors back on so he could draw their escape from the Ark with the hatchlings and panda cubs.

"This thing," Grace answered.

"What thing?" Marty turned around.

Grace was standing next to what looked like a huge boat. Or maybe a gigantic army tank. It was hard to tell in the dim light. Whatever the massive object was, it took up three-quarters of the cargo hold.

"I guess we know how they're going to move all the stuff now," Grace said.

"The Thing," Marty said, touching the camouflage-painted hull.

"Love the name," Ted Bronson said, stepping through the bulkhead door. "I'm calling it the *Rivlan*, but I like The Thing." He walked over to them. "Volkswagen produced a car in the seventies called The Thing. I wanted one, but of course I was too young to drive back then. *This* thing looks a little like The Thing."

"There's also a horror movie called *The Thing*," Marty said. He and Luther had watched it several times.

"Which was a remake of another movie from the fifties called *The Thing from Another World*," Ted said.

Marty didn't know Ted was a movie buff, but then again, there was a lot he didn't know about Ted Bronson.

"So it's a boat," Marty said.

"Essentially. But it does a couple of things traditional boats can't do."

Marty wasn't surprised. Ted squatted down beneath the hull. Marty and Grace joined him.

"It's made out of the same material as the Orb, although reconfigured a bit for terra firma."

The Orb, formally the Oceanic Reconnaissance Bot, was a deep-water submarine, and a fraction of the size of Ted's boat.

Ted pointed to the large tires protruding from the hull. "I have it in tire mode at the moment, but there's also an all-terrain track mode that turns the boat into a bulldozer that will pretty much knock down anything in its path, though I doubt we'll be using that in the rain forest. That mode is not exactly environmentally friendly. There is also a hover mode. Brings the boat about twenty feet off the surface. It won't do us much good in the rain forest, but it'll work well for avoiding flotsam and jetsam on the river."

"What're *flotsam* and *jetsam*?" Marty asked.

"The Amazon River is the second-longest river in the world," Grace said.

"What's the longest?" Marty asked.

"The Nile," Grace answered immediately. "But the Amazon is the largest river by water flow. The average discharge is greater than the next seven largest rivers combined. It has the largest drainage basin in the world, almost three million square miles, and accounts for approximately one-fifth of the world's total river flow. The width of the Amazon varies between one and six miles at the low stage, but expands during the wet season to thirty miles or more. The river flows into the Atlantic Ocean in a broad estuary about a hundred and fifty miles wide. The mouth of the main stem is fifty miles across. The river is sometimes called the River Sea."

Marty stared at his cousin in wonder. Grace had changed a lot in the past few weeks, but in other ways she hadn't changed at all.

"Thanks for that, Ms. Wikipedia," he said. "But what I asked originally was, what are *flotsam* and *jetsam*?"

"Sorry," Grace said. "*Flotsam* and *jetsam* refer to debris like logs and garbage. With that much water flowing, the Amazonian version of flotsam and jetsam could be hundred-foot trees. You hit one of those and you're sunk."

"Not with this boat," Ted said, giving the hull a slap. "It's impervious to almost everything. Unfortunately, passengers aren't. If we slam into a hundred-foot hardwood tree at a hundred and twenty-five knots, someone is going to get hurt."

Marty did a quick calculation in his head. "That's almost a hundred and fifty miles an hour!"

"The upper end is closer to two hundred miles an hour."

"That's faster than a helicopter!" Marty said.

Ted nodded. "Which is why we're going to have to do our fast runs at night. We don't want to attract too much attention, or scare people to death. But chugging along during the day like a regular boat is going to slow us down. The chopper is going to get to the jaguar preserve before the *Rivlan* does."

"I assume you're driving, or piloting, the boat," Marty said. "Who's flying the helicopter?"

"Wolfe," Ted said.

"How long will it take him to get to the preserve?" Marty asked.

Ted shrugged. "Hard to say. He'll have to stop and refuel at least once, maybe twice if there's a strong headwind."

"Who's flying to the preserve with the hatchlings?" Grace asked.

"That's what I came back here to talk to you about. The chopper's going to be kind of crowded. For obvious reasons, Wolfe doesn't want anyone getting a look at the hatchlings, so he's flying them to the preserve. That means that Luther will be on the chopper because they seem to have taken to him."

That's going to be one stinky trip, Marty thought. "Did you tell Luther?" he asked.

"I just talked to him. He said he'd be happy to stick with the hatchlings." Ted looked at Grace. "You're on the chopper, too. Luther will need help."

"Why me?"

"Because Wolfe doesn't want you out of his sight," Ted answered. "And I agree with him. After the hatchlings, you're Blackwood's primary target."

"He's not down here yet," Grace said. "There's a chance he won't figure out —"

Ted interrupted her. "He's going to figure it out, Grace."

"He didn't find Wolfe or my mom in the Congo."

"True, but they weren't in possession of the last two living dinosaurs on earth. And technology has changed everything. It's a lot easier to find people now than it was fifteen years ago. You're going with him. Wolfe's not budging on that. You might as well go along with it."

Marty looked at Grace. Her blue eyes were completely neutral, which was usually a bad sign. He quickly looked back at Ted. "What about me and Dylan?"

"I know you want to get to the jaguar preserve, and we could probably squeeze you into the chopper, but I was hoping that you and Dylan would give me a hand on the *Rivlan*."

Marty was eager to get to the preserve to find his parents. When someone, or something, wasn't trying to kill him, he had thought of little else. He ran his hand along the *Rivlan*'s hull. He knew from experience that flying over a river in a chopper and riding on a river were two entirely different things. Riding aboard the *Rivlan* might be his only chance to see the real Amazon. And then there were the ultralights. He glanced into the other cargo hold where the crates were. He didn't want to get too far from those.

With Wolfe upriver, I just might be able to talk Ted into letting me take one out for a spin.

"What would I be doing aboard?" Marty asked.

"Like I said, I'll be running fast during the night. Eight hours of that is going to wipe me out. If I don't have someone to pilot the *Rivlan* during the day at regular speed, I'll have to tie up so I can sleep. That's going to slow my arrival at the preserve by days. You and Dylan would be the day pilots."

"But at the speeds you're talking about, the *Rivlan* shouldn't be that far behind the chopper."

"That would be true if we were talking about traveling in a straight line, but the Amazon is anything but straight. It meanders back and forth like a giant anaconda. And I'm anticipating mechanical failures. The *Rivlan* has never been in the water."

"What?" Marty wasn't sure he had heard him correctly.

"You and Dylan would be on the *Rivlan*'s maiden voyage."

"How do you know it will even work?" Grace asked, taking the words out of Marty's mouth.

"It'll work," Ted answered. "But there will be glitches. There always are. I think I've brought enough spare parts to take care of any eventuality, but I'll be honest, if we have a breakdown, it could take me a while to fix it."

"Maybe *I* should ride on the *Rivlan* to the jaguar preserve instead of Marty," Grace said.

"Thanks, but no thanks," Marty said. "You heard what Ted said. Wolfe has a lot on his mind. He doesn't need to be worrying about you along with everything else."

"Are you sure?" Grace asked.

"Positive," Marty answered, but he wasn't positive. He wanted to get to the preserve and start looking for his parents, but with Blackwood on the prowl, Grace would be safer with Wolfe. He changed the subject. "So what's the latest from the preserve?"

"You remember Jake Lansa?"

"Sure," Marty answered. "Dr. Robert Lansa's son."

"Doc" Lansa was in charge of the jaguar preserve. His son, Jake, had been sailing to Australia when Marty and Grace had met him. Jake had taken Ted's girlfriend, Ana Mika, and Laurel Lee out to the *Coelacanth* off the coast of New Zealand, where they'd caught the giant squid.

"Jake's back in Brazil now," Ted explained. "He got to Manaus about the same time as Laurel and Ana. The three of them headed upriver with one of Doc's biologists. They got to the preserve last night. Laurel and Doc are heading out into the forest as soon as they can get their gear together, to find that uncontacted tribe that might know about your folks."

"What do you mean by *uncontacted*?" Grace asked.

"A group that has never had contact with the outside world. And finding them is not going to be easy. Uncontacted tribes are usually uncontacted because they don't want to be contacted. When Wolfe gets there, he'll head out with a guide who works for Doc. Everyone else will be sticking around camp, including me, as support for the expedition. If they get into trouble, we're the cavalry."

"But instead of horses, we'll have an ultralight," Marty said.

Grace gave him an eyeball roll, which he completely ignored.

Ted smiled. "So you saw the crate."

"I sure did," Marty said. "And I wouldn't mind taking it out for a spin."

"You know how to fly?"

Marty nodded. "I've had lessons."

"When?" Grace asked.

"Skydiving camp."

"That hardly counts," Grace said.

Ted laughed. "It actually *does* count. The most important skill for an ultralight pilot is to know how to use a parachute."

"Until you hit the top of the canopy," Grace pointed out.

"That's a problem," Ted admitted. "And it can hurt."

"Speaking of parachutes," Marty said. "When do we make the supply drop?"

Ted looked at his watch. "Several hours. Early evening in Brazil. We'll try to drop the supply canisters as close to camp as we can, then head into Manaus to unload. You two might want to get some rest. Once we get there, we won't have much time for that."

ZIP

Jake Lansa was amazed at all the additional lines Flanna Brenna had strung through the canopy during his time away from the jaguar preserve.

"You could go at least five miles in any direction from camp without touching the ground once," Jake said.

"Seven point five miles," the redheaded woman replied, jumping off the platform and disappearing into the thick green tangle.

Jake had been following his father's botanist girlfriend along her web for the past several hours, trying to get his "canopy legs" back by taking short runs on the zip lines. He was now standing on a platform readying himself for a two-hundred-yard run, trying to remember everything he knew about long zips.

"It's just like riding a bike," he whispered as he waited for Flanna to let him know that she was offline.

"All clear!"

A flock of blue-and-gold macaws exploded from the tree to his right, screeching off into the canopy. He snapped his harness on to the line and looked down. He could barely see the ground through the broad leaves and thick vines.

"Just like riding a bike," he repeated, and stepped off the platform into a void.

He knew immediately that it was nothing like riding a bike.

Too fast!

He was completely out of control. Flanna had a bungee block breaking system at the end of each long run. He hoped it would slow him down. It didn't. He hit the block. The bungee snapped like a piece of twine. He slammed headfirst into a branch as big around as he was. He heard his helmet crack. He dropped like a rock. Everything went black.

Stars, he thought. *How odd. You don't see stars in the rain forest. The canopy blocks the sky. And why am I hanging here? Where am I? What happened?*

He shook his head trying to clear the fog. He regretted the move immediately. It felt like someone had inserted a hot poker into the center of his brain. He threw up, which was a little awkward, and messy, upside down. At least he thought he was upside down. He couldn't see. There was something in his eyes, which he hoped was not vomit.

"Oh my God! Jake! Are you okay?"

He could hear Flanna shouting somewhere above him, but he couldn't see her. He reached a gloved hand up to his face to wipe away whatever was blinding him. He looked at his glove. It wasn't vomit; it was blood. A blurry-looking Flanna was working her way down to where he was dangling like a spider monkey.

"You're tangled," Flanna said.

What was that phrase Marty O'Hara and his friend Luther had used?

"Duh *du jour*," he said.

"At least your sense of humor works." Flanna was now perched ten feet above him on a landing platform. "I'm going to throw you a line. Can you manage to tie it to your harness?"

"I think so."

She dropped the line. After a couple of awkward attempts he managed to snag it, but it seemed to take him forever to attach it to the harness, as if he'd somehow forgotten how to tie a knot.

"Secured," he was finally able to say.

"Are you sure?"

He stared at the knot for several seconds before he was able to confirm that the knot was indeed secured.

What's the matter with me?

"I'm going to right you so you can grab the zip line." Flanna sounded like she was speaking to him from the bottom of a steel barrel. "Once you have the line, you'll have to untwist yourself to free up the pulley. I can't tell if it will be clockwise or counterclockwise."

Jake wasn't quite clear on the clockwise/counterclockwise thing, but he did understand that in order for her to reel him in he had to free the pulley. He began twisting himself around.

"That's the right direction," Flanna said. "Keep going."

Every couple of rotations, he had to stop and wipe the blood out of his eyes.

"I guess the helmet didn't do me much good," he said.

"The helmet saved your life," Flanna said. "A couple more twists."

Finally, the pulley popped free. Flanna reeled him in like a fish and helped him onto the platform.

He sat down with his feet dangling over the edge. "Feels good to have something solid under me."

"I bet. Do you know what happened?"

Jake shook his head. "Ouch!"

Flanna smiled. "Better use your words."

"I'm not sure what happened," Jake answered, keeping his head very still. "I guess I started out too fast and snapped the bungee brake."

"Too much time on the ocean and not enough time in the trees?"

"I guess. How bad is it?"

"I need to take off what's left of your helmet. Hold your head steady."

He did, but it still hurt as Flanna popped the helmet off. She took out a package of antiseptic wipes from her backpack. "Head wounds always look worse than they are."

"That's comforting."

"This is going to sting."

She was right. The gentle dabbing felt like a blowtorch on his forehead. When she finished, she leaned back and squinted at the wound.

"Well?" Jake asked.

"The bleeding has stopped for the most part. I don't see any gray matter leaking out. No permanent disfigurement. You're going to live. But I'm going to have to put in a stitch or two."

"You're a botanist," Jake pointed out. "Not a plastic surgeon."

"I'm all you have, unless you want to stitch it up yourself."

"Have you done it before?"

"Yep, and I'm pretty good at it, too, but we can't do it up here. My medieval medical instruments are back at camp."

Flanna got out her first aid kit and bandaged his forehead while a group of golden lion tamarins watched from a safe distance. Jake's head still throbbed, but by the time Flanna finished he was feeling better. He pulled himself to his feet, swaying a little.

"Is that the tree or me?" he asked.

Flanna laughed. "Probably a little of both."

"Are we taking the zips back?"

Flanna shook her head. "We'll go the old-fashioned way. On our feet. You don't have a helmet, and it might be best for you to stay on the ground until the gash heals. If you're not careful, it will go septic. The rain forest is the perfect environment for infection."

Jake grinned. "So you're grounding me?"

Flanna returned his grin. "That's right, mister."

Jake's mother had died a couple of years earlier in a tragic accident. It had taken a while for him to get used to his dad having a girlfriend, but now he assumed she would one day be his stepmom, that is if she and Doc could ever get out of the rain forest and end up in the same place at the same time. Flanna and Jake were always teasing each other about her being Jake's stepmom — a situation that was going to be a little weird for both of them when it finally happened. Flanna was about ten years younger than Doc. She would always be more of an older sister to Jake than a mom.

What would have been an hour-long trip on the zip lines was going to take them three or four hours on foot.

Flanna got an odd look on her face and scanned the surrounding canopy as if she were looking for something, or someone.

"What's the matter?"

"I don't know," Flanna said. "I'm sure it's nothing, but the past couple of days I've had this feeling that there is somebody else out here. That we're being watched. Ridiculous, I know. A case of the jungle willies, but I can't seem to shake it."

Jake hoped that if there was someone watching, they hadn't seen his bonehead collision with the tree.

"Are you feeling okay?" Flanna asked.

Jake rubbed his head. Aside from the throbbing, he felt fine. "I'm good to go."

"Well, go slow so your head doesn't start bleeding again."

They roped down to the ground and started the long trek back to camp.

Aboard the sailboat, on his way to Australia, there had been nothing but open sky and 360 degrees of horizon. In the rain forest there was no sky, no horizon, and little light penetrating the thick canopy. He'd missed the shadowy rain forest, and he was glad to be back, but he wasn't sure being on foot right now was the best way to get back to camp. Every step he took hurt his head. He was lagging farther and farther behind his future stepmom.

About an hour into the painful walk, Flanna came to a sudden stop. She was fifty yards ahead of him. At first he thought she was waiting for him to catch up, but there was something in her posture that told him it was something else.

"What the matter?" he called out.

"Jararaca," she answered quietly.

Jake froze. One thing he hadn't encountered at sea was venomous snakes. The *jararaca*, or fer-de-lance, was one of the most venomous snakes on earth. It was also one of the most aggressive. Flanna took a very slow and deliberate step backward, then paused. Jake wanted to rush forward and help her, but there was nothing he could do for her. If he ran up and disturbed the snake, it might strike.

Flanna was wearing long pants, but they weren't snake-proof pants. Everyone at the preserve had them, but they rarely wore them because the pants were too hot. She wasn't wearing boots, either. Sneakers worked a lot better when you were zip-lining and climbing the slippery canopy. Flanna took another tentative step back. Jake couldn't see the snake from where he was, and there was a good chance she couldn't see it clearly, either. The fer-de-lance blended in almost perfectly with its surroundings. It was lucky she'd seen it before it struck.

If she'd seen it before it struck.

The horrible possibility moved him up the game trail closer to her. "Are you hit?"

Flanna stopped in midstep. "No, but there are two of them," she said, her eyes forward. "Aggressive, ready to strike. I'm just trying to get out of range. Make sure there's nothing behind me. I don't want to trip."

Jake quickly scanned the path behind her. "You've got two roots coming up four steps behind you. A big one and a little one. I'll tell you when you're on them." He zeroed in on her muddy tennis shoes. "Step!"

Flanna hesitated and felt the root with the heel of her shoe.

"That's the small root," Jake said. "The bigger one is about eight inches behind it."

She carefully negotiated the second snag.

"It's clear all the way to me," Jake said.

She continued moving backward, then turned around about ten feet before she reached him.

"That was close," she said, perspiration pouring down her face. "A fine pair we make. You smash into a branch, and I nearly step on a pair of mating fer-de-lances."

"They were mating?"

"I think so, and they weren't too happy about being interrupted."

Jake pulled out his water bottle and handed it to her. She took a couple of sips and passed it back.

"Guess we'll have to circle around," Jake said.

"A wide circle," Flanna said. "I'll take lead. I have a pretty good idea of where they are."

The snake encounter slowed Flanna way down. Jake was easily able to keep up with her now. They got around the area where the snakes were and found the path back to camp.

"Have you noticed anything odd about Raul since you got back to camp?" Flanna asked after a while.

Raul was a native they had picked up on their first trip upriver. He had helped them track and capture their first jaguar. His entire body was covered in jaguar rosettes.

"He's always been a little odd," Jake said.

"The past few days he's been unusually quiet and a little surly."

Jake shook his head and regretted it immediately. "He seems okay to me," he said after the throbbing subsided. "Maybe he's upset because he has to stay in camp and wait for Wolfe, instead of going ahead with Doc and Laurel."

"Maybe. But he must have understood the reason for it. This Travis Wolfe can't be expected to head off into the rain forest by himself."

Jake laughed, and added that to the growing list of things he shouldn't do. His head felt like it was going to fall off his neck.

"You okay?"

"Yeah."

"What's so funny?"

"If that's Raul's problem, it's not going to go away when he meets Wolfe. Wolfe appears to be completely capable of going anywhere by himself."

"I'd forgotten that you've met him."

"Briefly," Jake answered. "Aboard his research ship."

"What's he like?"

"Nice enough. Big guy with a black beard. I heard he's missing a leg, but you wouldn't know it to see him walk. I think he and Laurel are together. At least that's the impression I got."

"Did he say anything about cryptozoology?"

"You mean Bigfoot, Loch Ness Monster stuff?"

"Yeah."

"No. Why would he? We talked about his sister and brother-in-law."

"Sylvia and Timothy O'Hara."

"Right."

"Did you know that Wolfe's a cryptozoologist?"

"You're kidding?"

"Nope."

"Do you believe in that stuff?"

"It's fringe science to be sure, but the rumor is that Dr. Wolfe has made some astounding discoveries, most of which he keeps to himself, which is admirable and unusual for any biologist. When we make a discovery, we can't wait to get it out there."

"Publish or perish," Jake said.

"Exactly. But this doesn't seem to apply to Dr. Wolfe."

"Or my dad," Jake added. As far as he knew, Doc hadn't finished writing up his elephant research from a few years earlier.

"You've got that right," Flanna agreed. "He'd much rather be in the field making discoveries than in front of a computer screen writing about them."

"Do you think there are cryptids out there?"

"There are certainly a lot of undiscovered animals. Scientists find hundreds of new species every year. Most of them are insects of course, but there are always a handful of mammals among the newbies. But not mega-vertebrates, which are Dr. Wolfe's area of interest. The world has been mapped by satellite, but it hasn't been fully explored. Your dad and Laurel are headed to one of those unexplored areas right now."

Laurel and Doc were at a complete standstill. They had been hacking their way west with machetes all day, making pretty good progress until they'd run into a river that wasn't on their map or GPS.

Doc rechecked his GPS for the sixth time, shaking his head. "This river isn't supposed to be here."

"And yet here it is," Laurel said. She looked up at the canopy. For as far as she could see, the tree branches on both shores touched in the middle of the river. "What are the chances of this river being completely covered for its entire course?" she asked.

"I would have said completely zero until we stumbled into this obstacle," Doc answered. "I've searched a two-hundred-mile radius on the map and GPS, and this river doesn't show up anywhere. It's deep and has a significant flow. It has to dump into the Amazon, but I don't see where."

"Maybe it goes underground," Laurel said.

"Maybe," Doc said. "But I'm beginning to think I misinterpreted his map. It's hard to believe he would forget that we had to cross a major river. It must be fifty yards across here."

The "he" Doc was referring to was the indigenous man who had approached their camp in the middle of the night a few days earlier. Using sign language, the man had suggested that he'd seen Sylvia and Timothy O'Hara. He had drawn a crude map in the dirt near the fire before disappearing back into the dark forest.

"I should have just followed him into the forest," Doc said.

"Why didn't you?" Laurel asked.

"I was exhausted. I'd been out doing a survey for nearly two weeks. If I hadn't returned to the jaguar preserve first, Flanna would have sent the Brazilian army out after me. And then there was the map. Why would he have drawn it for me if he wanted me to go with him right then? I might have misunderstood, but it seemed pretty clear at the time that he didn't want me to follow him."

Doc pulled out the map he had transcribed to paper and showed it to her. "Up to this point, all the landmarks have been spot on. There's supposed to be a swampy area due south, which according to this map would be on the other side of the river. Can you swim?"

"Like a dolphin."

"Well, I swim like a stone. If we crossed here, my bloated corpse would end up in the Atlantic. I think we should head upriver and find a narrower place to cross." Doc unsheathed his machete and started hacking his way upriver.

Laurel followed at a distance so she didn't get hit with the blade or the debris. Doc was an enthusiastic bushwhacker, but he needed to pace himself. It was late afternoon, the temperature was in the upper nineties, and the humidity was close to a hundred percent. Doc was strong, but Laurel gave him about forty-five minutes before he collapsed. He lasted an hour and ten minutes, or two and a half miles. When he finally stopped, he was drenched in sweat and out of breath, as if he'd been swimming in the river against the current.

"Hot," he wheezed.

She handed him a water bottle. He drank the entire bottle without taking it away from his lips. She gave him a second. He finished half of it, then walked over to the river and put his head underwater for about twenty seconds. He shook the water out of his hair and said, "I'm good to go."

"If you keep going like that, you're not going to get anywhere." Laurel held her hand out. "Mind if I give it a shot? We won't get there as fast, but at least we'll both get there."

"Wherever we're going," Doc said, handing her the machete. Before she started, she took a sharpening steel out of her pack.

"You've got to be kidding," Doc said.

Laurel Lee quickly swept the steel back and forth a dozen times across the nicked blade. Then she handed back the machete, along with the steel. "Keep the machete sheathed. I'll use mine until it goes dull, then I'll switch with you. Have you ever used a steel?"

"Not while I'm walking."

Laurel smiled. "I'm sure you'll figure it out." She started walking and swinging her machete. "For me, the trick to doing this all day long is to use my voice," she said. "If I can talk without getting breathless, I know I'm moving at the proper pace. . . ."

She kept this banter up as she hacked her way through the dense cover growing along the river, switching machetes with Doc when needed. After a couple of hours, Laurel stopped to get a drink of water and switch machetes again.

"Want me to take over?" Doc asked.

"You can if you want, but I'm fine."

Doc looked across the river. "Not much change." He looked at his watch. "It'll be dark soon. I'll take over until we find a place to set up camp."

An hour later he came to a stop. "Listen," he said, out of breath, sweating.

Laurel closed her eyes and listened. "Waterfall?"

"Either that or rapids." He took the fresh machete and redoubled his efforts. Forty-five minutes later, they broke out of the tangle onto a football-stadium-sized pool of fast water fed by a sixty-foot waterfall.

Doc stuck the machete into the soft sand along the shore and pulled out his GPS. "This pool isn't here," he said.

Laurel understood GPS technology, and at times had actually used it, but she didn't have a lot of faith in it, and this was a good example of why. She walked down to the edge of the pool and peered through the mist to get a closer look at the falls. She could see how the satellite might have missed it. The tree branches above the falls were touching in the middle of the stream.

Doc joined her. "It's stunning, isn't it? If I could find a navigable way to the Amazon, I think I'd move our base camp here." He looked up at the falls. "We won't have time to get to the top before dark."

"We could do some island hopping to get across," Laurel suggested.

"The water's pretty fast in between. We'd have to rope across so we don't get washed away. But is that the right move? Did our friend cross here? And if he did, how did he manage it without ropes?"

"Vine ropes?"

"Maybe."

"Let's look around."

They didn't find any vine ropes, but they did find footprints in the sand leading to the waterfall.

"They're fresh," Doc said.

Laurel squatted down for a closer look. "Bare feet," she said. "Splayed toes. Typical indigenous print. I'd say there are at least three people."

The prints ended at the base of a pile of giant moss-covered boulders running down the right side of the waterfall.

"You game?" Laurel asked.

Doc looked up at the sky through a small opening in the canopy. "We'll have to hurry before we lose our light."

It took them more than an hour to clamber over the slippery rocks, which came to an abrupt end about halfway up the waterfall. A sheer wall towered above them. This close to it, they couldn't see the top in the waning light.

"We could climb it," Doc said. "But not without proper gear."

"Do you think our barefoot friends climbed the wall?"

Doc shook his head. "A monkey couldn't climb that wall without climbing gear." He got out his headlamp and slipped it over his forehead. "We'll rope down, make camp, and take another look at the wall in the morning. I just need to find a place to anchor the . . . Wait a second . . ." Doc squatted down and shined his headlamp on the ground.

The footprints had reappeared, then disappeared into a crevice in the rock wall. Doc shined his light into the narrow opening. "Tight squeeze, but it looks deep. You up for some spelunking?"

The opening had been created by the separation of two massive rocks. Laurel wriggled into the crevice sideways. Doc followed, but it was a much tighter squeeze for him. The fissure led to a good-sized cave behind the roaring waterfall. The sandy ground before them was covered with footprints. In the center of the cave were the remains of a campfire.

Laurel felt the ashes. "Warm."

They followed the prints to the far side of the cave, where they found another fissure, shorter than the first, but wider.

"Great place to spend the night away from biting insects and venomous snakes," Laurel said.

"Good point," Doc said. "But I think we should keep moving. They can't be that far ahead."

They crossed the river that wasn't there.

"Almost done," Flanna said.

Jake was lying on a camp cot in one of the huts. His face was covered with a surgical drape to keep the gash sterile, which was ridiculous because Flanna had numbed the area around the gash with a concoction she had put together from rain forest plants. Whatever the numbing agent was, it wasn't working. It felt like she was using a tent spike to stitch the wound.

Flanna removed the surgical drape with a dramatic flourish and gave him a smile. "You are back to your handsome self."

"Is my forehead on fire?"

Flanna blew on it. "Sorry about that. It's out now."

"Ha."

Flanna handed him a mirror. Jake had looked at the gash just before lying down and had thought he'd have to wear his hair like Harry Potter to cover up the jagged wound. Now there was nothing more than a thin red line that would probably disappear in a couple of weeks.

"Where are the stitches?"

Flanna laughed and held up a small tube. "I'm not much of a seamstress so I used surgical glue. Better known as superglue, but this is the sterile variety. I'm going to put a bandage on to protect it, but you'll need to change it several times a day because of the humidity. I'd take it off while you're sleeping or just sitting around to let the wound air out."

As she applied the bandage, they heard a jet roar overhead.

"Wolfe's supplies," Flanna said.

Jake looked past her through the hut's open doorway. Ana Mika, Travis Wolfe's journalist friend, and Buck Johnson, one of the biologists at the preserve, were standing in the center of the small clearing staring up at the darkening sky. Raul stepped out of the forest and joined them. They hadn't seen him since they'd returned to camp.

"What's Wolfe dropping in?" Jake asked. "We have enough supplies to last us for months."

"Ana said he was dropping in a cage, which Wolfe wants us to assemble before he gets here tomorrow."

"A cage for what?"

"She said Wolfe was bringing in a couple of dinosaurs."

Jake laughed. "Ana's a little strange."

"You've got that right. Although I do like her, in spite of her odd sense of humor."

Jake and Flanna joined the others in the clearing in time to see the second supply chute deploy. Ana was looking down at the smartphone thing she called a Gizmo. When she and Laurel had arrived at camp the night before, they'd asked all of them to put on tracking tags. Buck had been reluctant to comply, but they'd talked him into it by pointing out that if Sylvia and Timothy O'Hara had been wearing them, they would have been found within minutes of the helicopter crash that had resulted in their disappearance.

"I take it that the supply canisters have tracking tags," Jake said.

Ana nodded. "I have locations on both of them. The farthest is about a quarter mile away." She pointed. "The second is a hundred yards east."

"Hung up in the canopy no doubt," Flanna said.

"No doubt," Ana agreed. "We'll have to cut them down and haul them back."

Flanna looked up at the sky through the small clearing. "If we hurry, we should be able to get them cut them down and hauled back to camp before it gets dark."

Jake looked at Ana. "A dinosaur cage, huh?"

"That's right," Ana answered.

Jake laughed and followed Flanna into the woods.

MANAUS

Marty was out of his seat, leaning across Grace and looking out the tiny window at the city lights of Manaus, Brazil. "Smog," he said.

"Smoke," Grace corrected.

"Same thing."

"No, it isn't."

Marty was glad she was bickering with him. He'd missed that.

They were on their final approach to the Eduardo Gomes International Airport.

"Manaus is a lot bigger than I thought," he said.

"Two million people," Grace said. "The city was built on rubber."

"Huh?"

"Rubber for things like tires. The rain forest used to be the only place on earth where rubber trees grow. The rubber barons made millions and millions of dollars. They were so rich they sent their laundry to Europe to be washed, then had it shipped back to them."

"You're kidding me."

Grace shook her head.

"I have to admit, your annoying factoids are sometimes interesting," Marty said. "So this is where rubber comes from."

Grace shook her head again. "Not anymore. A Brit by the name of Henry Wickham smuggled rubber tree seeds out of Brazil in 1876. The British set up rubber plantations in Malaysia, Sri Lanka, and Africa that eventually put the Manaus rubber barons out of business."

"No more dirty underwear to Europe," Marty said.

"Exactly. Manaus fell on hard times, but it managed to survive by knocking down the rain forest for timber, harvesting Brazil nuts, making soap, refining oil, and manufacturing cell phones."

"Buckle up," Phil announced over the intercom.

Marty sat back down, craning his neck to peer out the window. "How about switching seats?"

"Forget it," Grace said, buckling her belt.

Begrudgingly, Marty buckled up, too.

"Now that I have you trapped," Grace said, "I've been meaning to ask about my mom's trunk."

Back at Lake Télé in the Congo a few months earlier, Marty and Grace had found Rose Wolfe's trunk in the Skyhouse, Rose and Travis's former home there. Grace hadn't had the courage to open the trunk herself, so she'd asked Marty to go through it for her, hoping there was something in it that would shed light on Rose's relationship with her father, Noah Blackwood. As Rose was dying, she'd made Wolfe promise to keep Grace away from Blackwood, and Grace wanted to know why.

"I didn't find anything useful," Marty said. "There were photos of Wolfe and your mom, pressed plants, daily logs of their search for Mokélé-mbembé, plans for the Skyhouse, photographs of tracks and animal poop. Nothing about Noah Blackwood or your mom's past. I'm not sure what you thought we'd find. It's obvious that your mom wanted to keep you away from Blackwood because he's a homicidal maniac."

"What about the Moleskines?" Grace asked. "There were dozens of them."

"You might find some of the journals interesting," Marty said. "But I didn't. They were filled with poems, observations about Lake Télé, sketches of animals, and stuff about you when you were a baby."

"What kind of stuff?"

"I don't know," Marty said. "She was afraid you were going to toddle off and get yourself killed. They had to tie you up like a dog on a long leash. Apparently, you had a constipation problem. I was kind of interested in that."

"Be serious!" Grace scolded.

"I am being serious. WTMI. There was a bunch of mushy stuff about Wolfe and her. It's no wonder she didn't want him to get his hands on the Moleskines. She was really over the top in the romance department. I had to skim most of it." He leaned over, picked up his pack, and opened the flap. "I didn't have time to read these two, so I brought them along in case we bumped into each other."

He pulled them out. They didn't look like Moleskines. They looked like small dictionaries. They were swollen to three times their normal thickness. Grace took one and almost gagged.

"What happened to them?"

"They got a little wet."

"They stink!"

"I fell into a moat!" Marty complained. "I could have broken my back. Lucky I had the pack on to cushion my fall."

"That doesn't explain the smell."

Marty sniffed the second Moleskine and his eyes started to water. "Rhino pee," he said.

Grace held the Moleskine out at arm's length, but it didn't do much good. "You're kidding me."

Marty took a second sniff. "Definitely rhino pee, maybe with a dash of pond scum thrown in. I don't know what you're complaining about. While you were lounging around the pool at the mansion, I was risking my life trying to save you."

"I didn't need saving," Grace said.

"You didn't *know* you needed saving," Marty said. "If you don't want it . . ." He started to put the other Moleskine back into his pack.

Grace stopped him. "I'll take it," she said. "I just wish I had rubber gloves and a clothespin for my nose so I could read it."

The landing gears dropped, and the Moleskines and Rose's trunk were forgotten as Phil brought the former bomber in for a perfect landing. As they began their slow taxi, they were joined by a car with flashing blue lights and *Aduaneiro Internacional* written on the side.

"Cops," Marty said.

"International customs," Grace corrected.

"I can read Spanish," Marty said.

"It's Portuguese. That's what they speak in Brazil."

"Spanish, Portuguese, customs, cops, what's the diff? A cop is a cop, and it'll be interesting to see their faces when we tell them we're carrying three kidnapped panda cubs and two baby dinosaurs."

A look of shock and dismay crossed Ms. Smarty-pants-I-speak-a-dozen-languages's face. Marty unbuckled and stood up. Luther and Dylan were sitting in the two seats across the aisle from them. Marty leaned over and looked out their window. An identical car was on their side.

"Cops," Luther said.

"Customs," Marty said. "Can't you read Portuguese?"

"Whatever language they speak, and whoever they are," Luther said, "we're busted. I wonder what Brazilian prisons are like."

Marty looked up toward the bulkhead where Wolfe and Ted were sitting. Their seats were tilted back, and it looked like they were asleep. He hurried over to them. Wolfe had the aisle seat; Ted had the window seat. They both had their eyes closed as if they didn't have a care in the world.

"Uh . . . we've landed," Marty said.

Wolfe opened one eye. "And?"

"And we're sandwiched in by customs agents."

Wolfe opened his other eye, brought his seat into the upright position, then leaned over Ted, who didn't budge, and looked out the window.

"What do you want us to do?" Marty asked.

Wolfe stretched and yawned. "What do you mean?"

"We could empty a couple of crates and hide the hatchlings and pandas inside. You think they'll check the crates?"

"Unlikely," Wolfe answered.

Marty had traveled all over the world and had been interrogated by dozens of customs agents. He knew the routine.

Wolfe has lost it, he thought.

"They'll want to check our passports and our visas," he said. "They'll want to go through our stuff and make sure we aren't smuggling things into the country."

"They won't be asking for your passport, or your visa," Wolfe said. "They won't be getting on the airplane, and you won't be getting off the airplane until after they leave the hangar."

"What hangar?"

"The empty hangar they're escorting us to." Wolfe reached under his seat and pulled out a duffel bag. He unzipped it and took out a bundle of hundred-dollar bills.

Marty could see there were a lot more bundles where that one had come from.

"You're going to bribe them?"

"I guess you could call it that," Wolfe admitted. "But I prefer to think of it as purchasing very expensive private visas. We can't let them see the hatchlings or the pandas. We can't advertise the fact that we're here. Blackwood may still be at the Ark, but he's going to come after us. I don't want to make it too easy for him."

The window darkened as they taxied into the hangar. Wolfe unbuckled, stood up, and stuffed the cash into his pocket.

A half hour later he came back on board and said the coast was clear. They had the hangar all to themselves.

DAY TWO

THE *RIVLAN*

It took them until well after midnight to unload the jet, reassemble the helicopter, then reload everything into the helicopter and the *Rivlan*. While they worked, Phil and Phyllis slept on a couple of cots in the corner of the hangar so they would be rested for their long flight to China. Marty wished he could join them on a cot. He regretted not catching some shut-eye like Wolfe and Ted had. The short nap seemed to have done them good. They buzzed around the hangar like bees around a hive.

"Guess that does it," Wolfe said. "Gather around, everyone. I have some things to report before we head out on our different paths."

Marty and Dylan jumped down from the *Rivlan*, where they had been stowing the last of the equipment. There was so much stuff aboard that they would probably sink when they got the *Rivlan* to the Amazon. Grace stepped out of the jet, where she had been saying good-bye to the panda cubs. Luther came out the helicopter, peeling off a bloody pair of disposable gloves and oblivious to the smell coming off him. Phil and Phyllis wandered over holding steaming cups of coffee. Ted was the last to join them, at least in body. He was so completely absorbed in something on his Gizmo that he bumped into Phil, causing him to spill his coffee.

"First of all, thanks for all your hard work," Wolfe said after everyone had settled down. "It's not easy getting an expedition together this quickly. As soon as I'm done here, Ted, Marty, and Dylan will get the *Rivlan* on the Amazon and head west. They're mostly moving the *Rivlan* under cover of darkness so it doesn't attract too much attention. The last thing we want is attention." His gaze lingered on Marty and Luther.

"What?" they both said simultaneously.

"Just be cool," Wolfe said. "We all need to get to the jaguar preserve without incident. We have important work to do there."

Marty and Luther gave him a firm nod.

Wolfe rolled his eyes as if he didn't believe them and continued, "Grace, Luther, and I will take off at first light in the chopper. If all goes well, we should be at the preserve this afternoon." He looked at Phil and Phyllis. "Are you two ready to head to China? Did you get enough sleep?"

"Plenty," Phyllis said. "Where do you want us to go after we drop the cubs off?"

"Fly back to Cryptos. You'll need to be on standby 24/7. If Noah shows up in Brazil, we may need a lift out of here in a hurry." He looked at Ted. "Want to share your news?"

"It's good news," Ted said with a grin. "And it might keep Noah busy and off our backs for a while. Looks like Grace's outtakes of *Wildlife First* hit the airwaves, at least in some markets. Noah Blackwood is in full-on damage control mode, which should keep him close to home, talking to the press for the next several days. He's pulled the bogus episode from distribution, claiming that he was hacked and that the *fake* footage was put together by an anti-environmentalist group, not mentioning who this group is, of course. The outtakes have gone viral on the Internet, and there isn't a thing he can do about it. Bottom line, he'll slither out of this, but until then it'll be fun watching him squirm."

Wolfe nodded and looked at his watch. "Time to go." He shook Ted's hand, then gave Marty and Dylan short hugs. "See you in the jungle. Good luck."

Under the bright lights of the hangar, the *Rivlan* looked like a bucket of corroded scrap metal.

"We are going to die," Marty said under his breath as he followed Dylan and Ted up the rusty ladder to the deck.

"I heard that," Ted said. "Ugly is only skin deep."

"Don't judge a book by its cover," Dylan said.

"A stitch in time saves nine," Marty said.

"What does that have to do with anything?" Dylan asked.

"Not a thing," Marty said.

The deck was stacked with battered crates. Ted had made them string hammocks between the crates to make the boat appear more Amazonian. "The *Rivlan*'s distressed look is intentional," he told them. "So we don't attract too much attention on the river."

Marty started up the short steps to the pilothouse, or bridge, but Ted stopped him. "Wrong way. We're going below deck. You're headed up to the fake bridge, which is actually functional, but we'll only be using it during daylight hours." He walked through a hatch and down a short set of steps.

Marty and Dylan followed. They had both been below to check it out, and if anything, it was in worse shape than the deck.

Ted led them through the greasy galley to the chart room, which consisted of a single table piled with mildewed navigational charts that looked like they'd been last used by Magellan, and a rickety chair that didn't look like it would support a glass of water.

"This is the *real* bridge?" Marty asked.

"Hardly."

Ted tipped the chair backward, then set it straight. A second later the wall in front of them slid open, revealing a brightly lit room that looked like it belonged on a starship.

"Whoa!" Dylan said.

Marty wasn't nearly as surprised, having been in the Orb Ted had built to pursue the giant squid. But he was still impressed, and relieved they weren't heading up the Amazon in a complete bucket of bolts. The room looked nothing like the other parts of the *Rivlan*. It was shaped like a dome, and the walls, ceiling, and floor looked like they were made of black glass. There were four high-tech leather chairs equipped with seat belts and shoulder harnesses — one chair in front and three behind. The front chair, with the flashing buttons, switches, and levers, was clearly the captain's chair.

"Dibs on the captain's seat!" Marty called out.

"In your dreams," Ted said, settling into the front chair. "Buckle up. Let's get this show on the road, or rather, on the water."

Marty took the right chair, Dylan the left, leaving the seat in the middle empty.

"Ready?" Ted asked.

Marty and Dylan braced themselves. The lights dimmed and the dome came to life with a 360-degree high-definition view of the inside of the hangar.

"If you want to see what's behind us, all you have to do is lean left or right or back," Ted said.

The boys leaned . . . a little too far. The chairs whipped completely around several times before they were able to get them under control. Marty thought he was going to be sick. He glanced over at Dylan; he didn't look much better.

Ted had swiveled the captain's chair around to face them. "Takes a little while to get the hang of it. The technology is similar to what they use in the Segway, but more responsive. All you really have to do is *think* right, left, up, down, stop, and it will happen. There are sick bags in the right-hand pockets of the chairs if you need them."

"Thanks for letting us know that before we sat down," Marty said.

Ted grinned. "No problem. Ready to go?"

Marty and Dylan nodded.

Ted hit a button. There was a slight humming noise, then complete silence.

"Is it working?" Dylan asked.

"Perfectly," Ted answered. "The engine runs silent. In fact . . ." He hit another button on the panel. The *chugga-chugga-chugga* of an old diesel engine echoed through the bridge.

"Fake sound," Marty said.

"Yep, and take a whiff of this." He hit another button. The bridge was filled with the smell of diesel fumes.

Marty and Dylan started choking.

Ted laughed. "That's your brain telling you that you're breathing in diesel fumes. It smells like diesel, but it's harmless." He hit another button and the air cleared, as if the noxious smell had never been there. He pointed to the top of the dome.

The exhaust pipe on top of the fake bridge was belching out nasty black smoke.

"I take it that that's not diesel smoke," Dylan said.

"Fake fumes," Ted said. "Smoke and mirrors," Ted said. "The *Rivlan* has virtually zero environmental impact."

"Unless it's in bulldozer mode," Marty pointed out.

Ted nodded. "Which I hope we don't have to use."

They watched Wolfe walk over to the huge hangar door and slide it open. The streaming video surrounding them was so clear, it looked like they could reach out and touch everything in the hangar.

"We'll wheel out of the hangar, then move into hover mode. The tricky part will be getting to the river without anyone seeing us."

Actually, the tricky part turned out to be getting over the airport's fence. Ted switched to hover mode right out of the hangar, keeping the *Rivlan* low to the ground. Aside from its being slightly quieter, Marty didn't feel much difference. Ted stuck to the shadows, maneuvering the *Rivlan* behind the hangar, across an access road and a secondary runway, then following the fence along the west side of the airport. The engines, or fans, or whatever Ted had invented to make the *Rivlan* fly, kicked up so much debris in front of the cameras it was hard to see where they were going.

"What are you looking for?" Dylan asked.

"Some place to get over the top. The highest I've had this thing is about eight feet. The fence along here is about twelve — topped by three feet of razor wire. The higher we go, the more power we'll need. With the added cargo, I don't think we're going to make it over."

“We could dump Dylan off,” Marty said.

“Very funny,” Dylan said.

“Just an idea.”

“Uh-oh,” Ted said, pointing. Flashing blue and red lights were racing up behind them. “We must have tripped a motion sensor along the fence. They aren’t close enough to see us yet, but that’s going to change in about twenty seconds. Hang on.”

Marty felt his stomach drop to his knees as Ted pushed the throttle to its limit. The bow jerked up at a forty-five degree angle, then fell like a rock. The *Rivlan* bounced on the ground with a loud bang.

“No worries!” Ted said, although he sounded pretty worried.

He backed the *Rivlan* fifty feet away from the fence, then shot it forward again twice as fast as before.

“That’s more like it!” Ted shouted. “Get ready!”

Before Marty could ask what he was supposed to get ready for, the bow tilted up again, but instead of stopping it kept going and going and . . .

Ted swore, then shouted, “Lean forward! Lean forward! Lean forward!”

Marty gave it his best shot, but he discovered that leaning forward while tipping backward and being buckled in with a seat belt and harness was impossible. He glanced over at Dylan. His face was bright red, his jaw was clenched, and every muscle and tendon in his neck looked like it was going to burst. For a second, the *Rivlan* froze in space as if it were making up its mind about which way to go, then it began to tilt forward again.

“That’s what I’m talking about,” Ted yelled. “Go, baby, go!”

There was a loud scraping sound underneath them.

“What was that?” Dylan shouted with alarm.

"The top of the razor wire," Ted answered, frantically pushing buttons and pulling levers. "We're over the top."

The bow dipped sharply. Marty felt like his seat belt was going to cut him in two. A millisecond before the *Rivlan* buried itself nose-first into the dirt, the bow popped back up, and they shot across open ground at 132 miles an hour. The flashing lights behind them disappeared. Ted slowed the *Rivlan* down to 50 so everyone could breathe again.

"That could have gone a different way," he said.

"Yeah," Dylan said. "We could have all been killed."

"Nah," Ted disagreed. "Maybe a couple of broken bones and some bruises, but you wouldn't have died. If we had slammed into the ground, the airbags would have deployed. It's not often you're given the opportunity to test the upper limits on a new device like this right out of the box."

And to live through it, Marty thought. His heart was slamming in his chest, but he couldn't help but grin at the mad inventor. Ted's cup was always half full regardless of the circumstances.

Ted slowed the *Rivlan* to a crawl. Then he maneuvered it down a dark street in an upscale residential area, through an alley, and past a swimming pool in someone's backyard.

"If they're looking out their window right now, they're going to report a UFO," Dylan said.

Beyond the pool was a dock with sailboat tied to it. Ted headed for the water, flipping switches and pushing buttons. Fifty feet past the sailboat, he set the *Rivlan* onto the water. A couple more switches and the *chugga-chugga-chugga* sound effects started. Fake gray smoke belched from the rusty stack, from a diesel engine that wasn't there.

The sun was just coming up.

"The Amazon," Dylan said with awe.

"Not quite," Ted said. "This is a tributary. We'll be on the Amazon in about half an hour, at which time I'm going to turn piloting duty over to you two while I get some shut-eye."

"We'll pilot it from down here?" Marty asked.

"I guess *piloting* isn't exactly the right word. At slow speeds the *Rivlan* pilots itself. You'll run the show from up top to keep an eye on things and, more important, to be seen. It would look a little strange if the *Rivlan* was heading upriver with no one behind the wheel."

Ted got out of the captain's chair, stretched, and looked at Marty. "I'm hungry. How about some breakfast?"

Marty unstrapped himself. "I'll have to clean the galley first so we don't die from toxic waste exposure, but yeah, I can whip something together."

The galley wasn't nearly as dirty as it looked. In fact, it was perfectly clean. The dirt and grime were all smoke and mirrors, just like the fake engine sound and fumes. Ted's technicians on Cryptos had painted the grunge on the stovetop, counters, and fridge.

Tainted paint, he thought with a laugh.

As he waited for the butter to melt in the omelet pan, he checked everyone's location on his Gizmo. Phil, Phyllis, and PD were headed west toward China at forty thousand feet. Ana and the others at the jaguar preserve were moving around in a tight cluster, no doubt putting together the hatchlings' new enclosure. Doc and Laurel looked to be about ten miles west of the preserve. And Grace, Luther, and Wolfe were flying up the Amazon in the stolen chopper.

CHOPPER

When Wolfe had announced that it was time to board the helicopter, Luther had immediately shouted "Shotgun!" and climbed into the right-hand seat next to him.

Grace didn't mind being in the back — even with the crated hatchlings directly behind her, snoring and passing gas — because it gave her a chance to be alone. As much as one *could* be alone in the cramped confines of a helicopter.

She had put on a headset to dampen the noise of the engine and muted the volume so she didn't have to listen to Luther peppering Wolfe with questions. Her intention had been to spend her time in back reading her mother's soggy journals, but not realizing how tired she was, she'd fallen asleep within minutes of taking off from the airport. She awoke suddenly with the sun in her eyes, a crick in her neck, and a terrible smell in her nostrils. At first she didn't quite know where she was, but one look at the back of Luther's head, with his flaming red hair just growing back in, and Wolfe's black shaggy beard, brought it all back to her. She was on her way to a jaguar preserve, on the run from her grandfather Noah Blackwood.

Mother's Moleskines, she thought. She unzipped the pack on the seat next to her and pulled out the swollen journals. One advantage of being so close to the hatchlings was that she could no longer smell the damp mildewed paper.

She set the first Moleskine in her lap and stared down at the black cover. She had asked Marty to go through the trunk because she'd been afraid to do it herself, afraid of what she might discover, afraid of her past.

Ridiculous! she thought, and opened the cover.

Like Rose, Grace had written in Moleskine journals since she'd learned how to write, even though she had only been a toddler when her mother died. She wondered if she had watched her mother write in these journals without a conscious recollection of seeing it, and copied her, like kids do.

The first thing Grace noticed was that her mother had been smarter than Grace was with her journaling technique. Grace used a fountain pen to write. Her mother used a pencil. If Rose had used a pen, the contents would have been ruined when Marty dunked the Moleskine in rhino pee.

The first page was dated fourteen years earlier, six months before Grace's birth. Below it was a single sentence . . .

> *I've been having vivid dreams the past several nights. Rather than write about them, I am going to attempt to draw them.*

The first drawing was a two-page spread of Lake Télé in the Congo. Her mother had drawn a large island in the middle of the lake. Grace had spent several horrifying days at Lake Télé with Marty, and she was certain there was no island there. But she reminded herself that the drawing was from her mother's dreams, not reality. She turned the page. The next drawing was a bedroom, but again it wasn't the bedroom from the Skyhouse that Rose and Wolfe had built on the lake's shore. It was smaller and more utilitarian: almost more a box with a bed, a dresser, a desk, and a window covered with bars. The windows in the Skyhouse did not have bars. They were simple cutouts covered with fine mesh screens to keep the insects at bay.

The next drawing was a view from the bedroom window, presumably from her mother's dream island on Lake Télé, because in the picture there was a village on the lake. The real lake had no such thing. Lake Télé was one of the most hostile, isolated places on earth, which is why Mokélé-mbembé had survived there for so long.

Grace wondered if her mother's dreams had been caused by that isolation. Lake Télé was a lonely place. Regardless of how much her mother had loved Wolfe, having only him to keep her company had to have been difficult. Grace didn't know Wolfe that well, but she suspected he was the kind of man who could spend long stretches of time alone without ill effect.

She glanced up at Wolfe, who was staring straight ahead through the windshield without so much as a nod to the jabbering Luther.

He may prefer to be alone, she thought. *Cryptos Island certainly lends itself to that kind of life. But what about my mother? Was she cut out of the same cloth?*

The Congolese rain forest was beautiful, but it was also dark and claustrophobic. After a while it pushed in on you, making your chest ache for open sky.

She continued flipping through the pages.

Sketches of villagers farming, children playing . . .

Her mother was a good artist, something Grace had not inherited. She could draw a picture with words and sentences, but not with lines and shading.

Marty should have looked through this Moleskine. He would have been impressed.

She finished reading the first journal and picked up the second. The drawings inside this one were more architectural in nature. Each page seemed to be a different room, or a design for a room. There were laboratories, bedrooms, kitchens, hallways, closets, bathrooms, utility rooms, electrical diagrams, heating diagrams, conference rooms. . . .

It was clear to Grace that these rooms were a different type of dream. Rose must have wanted to build a sophisticated research facility at Lake Télé. A place where scientists and researchers from all over the world could gather to study the unique ecosystem.

Rose never got a chance to see her dream come true.

Grace felt a hot tear run down her cheek. She wiped it away quickly, and was glad she had, because at that moment Luther turned around and said something she couldn't hear through the muted headset. She turned it back on.

"What?"

"Fuel stop," Luther said.

Grace looked out the window. Sure enough, they were descending. She hadn't even noticed. Five hundred feet beneath them was a floating fuel barge. Before they had left the hangar, the helicopter had been fitted with pontoons for water landings. The chopper touched down on the river's surface like a feather. Wolfe shut the engine down. A couple of men on the barge readied lines. Luther started to open his door.

"Hold it," Wolfe said.

"What? I'm just going to jump out and catch the lines."

Wolfe shook his head and glanced back at Grace. "You both need to stay put. No need to advertise we have two kids on board. If the bargemen see you, word will spread up and down the Amazon faster than we can fly."

Grace wanted to get out of the helicopter, too, and stretch her legs, but she knew Wolfe was right. The more quietly they got to the preserve, the better.

"Can we at least crack the windows open?" Grace asked.

"Sure," Wolfe said. "But use the window on the river side so no one can see you." He climbed out onto the pontoon, caught a line thrown by a bargeman, and tied it off.

Grace opened the window and took a couple of deep breaths of gas fumes, which smelled sweet compared to the hatchlings' exhaust inside.

"Do you think the hatchlings will sleep until we get to the preserve?" she asked.

"Geez, I hope so," Luther said. "Kind of hard to feed them midair inside a crowded chopper."

The hatchlings' crate took up half the cargo space. The other half was stacked with boxes of frozen meat. Enough to feed the hatchlings for weeks.

"I wonder what will happen to them?" Grace asked.

"To who?"

"The hatchlings."

"Haven't you been listening?" Luther asked. "Wolfe's been gabbing about that almost the entire flight."

Grace seriously doubted Wolfe had been *gabbing*, but didn't argue the point. "I had my headset off. What did he say?"

"Wolfe would like to take them back to the Congo and let them go, but he can't do that until he takes care of the Noah Blackwood situation. He thinks Noah would just send Butch or another of his minions to recapture them. The other alternative is a small island Wolfe has in the South Pacific. It's uninhabited and has a good prey base. He thinks they could make a living there, but there are logistical problems. The island is isolated and a long way from anywhere. Finding someone to live on the island with them would be nearly impossible."

"Robinson Crusoe," Grace said.

"Who's that?" Luther asked.

"Apparently you weren't paying attention during literature at OOPS," Grace said.

"So?" Luther said.

Omega Opportunity Preparatory School, or OOPS, was the private school in Switzerland that Marty, Grace, and Luther had all attended since kindergarten. Luther was heading back there at the end of summer unless he could talk his parents out of it.

"*Robinson Crusoe* is a book about a guy named Robinson Crusoe who gets stranded on a deserted island," Grace said. "It was written in 1719 by Daniel Defoe."

"Useful information," Luther said, rolling his eyes. "I'm certain it will come in handy someday."

Grace shook her head in pity.

Luther looked out the window. "Uh-oh."

Grace followed his gaze. Wolfe was surrounded by a half-dozen uniformed men carrying guns. She was out of the helicopter in a flash, disobeying her uncle's order. She didn't care if she was seen or not. Luther was right behind her. By the time they reached Wolfe, another man had joined the guards, but he was not wearing a uniform.

Wolfe gave Grace and Luther a disapproving look, but said nothing about them disobeying him. The man reached into his sweaty shirt pocket, pulled out a leather wallet, and flipped it open.

"Special Agent Steven Crow, FBI."

"As in Federal Bureau of Investigation?" Luther blurted out.

Wolfe gave Luther another disapproving look, then nodded at Agent Crow. "What can I do for you?"

"Scuttlebutt is that you're heading to Doc Lansa's jaguar preserve upriver. I need a lift."

"I don't know who Scuttlebutt is," Luther said. "But you have it wrong. We're —"

Wolfe grabbed Luther's arm. "Can you excuse us for a minute, Agent Crow?" He took Grace's arm, too, and escorted them both to the end of the barge, where they couldn't be overheard.

"I thought I told you two to wait in the helicopter."

"That was before the Brazilian army surrounded you," Grace said.

"They're police," Wolfe said. "But that's beside the point."

"How did he know we were going to the jaguar preserve?" Luther asked.

Wolfe gave him a small grin. "Scuttlebutt," he said. "The jungle vine. And now they know you and Grace are on board."

"Maybe he works for Blackwood," Luther said.

"Maybe," Wolfe agreed. "But his credentials look real, and it's best not to lie to the FBI."

"He looks kind of old to be in the FBI," Grace said. "He must be in his seventies."

Wolfe nodded. "And by the photo on his credentials, and the way his clothes are hanging on him, he looks like he's lost a lot of weight. I'm guessing probably recently. But none of that matters, either."

"The FBI doesn't have jurisdiction in Brazil," Luther pointed out.

"Are you an attorney now?" Wolfe asked.

Luther shook his head. "Saw it on a TV show."

"Perfect," Wolfe said. "He may not have jurisdiction, but the police he's with do. Look. We need to be really cool about this. The one thing we don't want is for Agent Crow or his friends to discover what we have on board the helicopter. We need to get our cargo to the preserve. What we don't need is to be detained in a Brazilian jail."

"Why don't we just take off?" Luther asked. "No way they're going to catch us in a boat."

"Because we have about eighty miles of fuel left," Wolfe answered. "This is the last fuel stop before the preserve. And they may not be able to catch us, but they'll be able to *catch up* with us. They know where we're going. We don't want to become fugitives and have the federal police after us." Wolfe looked off in the distance for a second, then turned back to Luther. "But you might have hit on something with the boat. I'm going to try to talk him into using alternative transportation. But in case he doesn't go for it, I want you to figure out a way to mask the hatchlings so there's no chance of him seeing them. I'll put him in the copilot seat, which will put him farther away from the back."

"What about when we get to the preserve?" Grace asked.

"We'll deal with that when we get there," Wolfe said. "Right now we need to get out of *here*." He pointed at the banks of the river. Both sides were now lined with curious onlookers staring at the helicopter and the police boat. "This is exactly the opposite of how I wanted to get upriver." He turned to Grace. "You come with me." He looked at Luther. "Put some stuff in the backseat to make it look like there's no room. And do what you can to hide those hatchlings."

"The first thing you should do is open the windows so Agent Crow doesn't gag to death," Grace said.

Luther started toward the helicopter. Grace followed her father over to Crow and the policemen, who were standing by the pumps. The fueling crew hovered a few feet farther away, waiting for permission to do their job.

"Sorry about that," Wolfe said. "Kids."

Crow nodded. "Do you work for Noah Blackwood?"

Grace nearly fainted.

"What?" Wolfe asked.

"Noah Blackwood," Crow said. "I ran the tail number on your helicopter, and it's owned by Ark Enterprises. CEO, Noah Blackwood."

Grace waited for him to say, "And you are under arrest!" But Crow just stared at Wolfe, waiting for an explanation.

"I don't work for Noah Blackwood," Wolfe said. "I borrowed his helicopter."

"Nice guy, this Noah Blackwood," Crow said. "I don't really care how you acquired the helicopter. All I'm interested in is a lift to the jaguar preserve."

Grace tried to hide her relief. He obviously didn't know, or care, that the helicopter was stolen, or who Noah Blackwood was, which surprised her. She thought everyone knew Noah.

Agent Crow looked fit despite his recent weight loss. His face and arms were deeply tanned. Instead of the dark suit and tie that were the unofficial uniform of most FBI agents, he was wearing jeans, snake-proof boots that went halfway up his calf, a light cotton shirt, and a sweat-stained baseball cap advertising one of the local beers. He had a couple of days of white stubble on his face, and there were dark circles under his brown eyes, as if he hadn't slept, or slept very well, for a while. He was a little shorter than Wolfe, which still put him well over six feet tall.

"What's the FBI's interest in the jaguar preserve?"

Crow shook his head and smiled. "Sorry, but I'm not at liberty to say."

"How much do you weigh?" Wolfe asked.

"I beg your pardon?"

"Your weight," Wolfe repeated, taking his Gizmo out of his pocket. "I need it to figure out our load."

"I'm not sure. I haven't seen a scale in months."

Wolfe squinted at Crow. "Two ten? Two twenty?" He started tapping on the Gizmo. When he finished he shook his head.

"What?" Crow asked.

"By my calculations, if we take you on board, we'll crash, which wouldn't help any of us."

"Why should I believe you?"

"Why would I lie?"

"Because you don't want to take me upriver for some reason, and I suspect the reason is inside that helicopter."

"We're not up to anything illegal."

"Then you wouldn't mind my friends here giving the helicopter a little search."

"I *would* mind," Wolfe said. "We're way behind schedule, and we have perishable and fragile cargo aboard that I don't want your friends manhandling." He nodded toward the policemen. "Why don't you have them take you up to the preserve?"

"Because this is the end of the line for them. They aren't authorized to go any farther. It could take me weeks to get there hopping little boats."

"Better than dying in a helicopter crash," Wolfe said.

"Like your sister and brother-in-law, Dr. Wolfe," Crow said.

Grace's breath caught in her throat. She glanced at Wolfe. If he was surprised, there wasn't a trace of it in his expression.

"Their deaths have not been confirmed," Wolfe said evenly.

"You could do worse than having a veteran FBI agent's help in determining what happened to them. I've had a lot of experience finding people."

"I'm sure you have," Wolfe conceded. "But we can't accommodate you on this flight."

"Too bad," Crow said. "We'll just have to take a look at what you're hauling."

"Be my guest," Wolfe said. "But the delay will force me to take my other offer off the table."

"What offer?"

"We have a boat coming up behind us. It should be here in a few hours. I'll have them stop and pick you up. If the boat takes longer than twenty-four hours to get you to the preserve, I'll fly back and pick you up myself. Either way, you'll get there."

"You really don't want them checking what you have on board, do you?"

Wolfe looked at his watch. "What I don't want is to be delayed a second longer. It's critical that we get these supplies upriver."

"What assurance do I have that you'll do what you say?"

Wolfe looked him in the eye. "You have my word."

Crow shook his head. "Sorry, Dr. Wolfe. That's not good enough."

"Do you know Albert Ikes?"

"Everybody in the FBI knows Al Ikes. He's a legend in the intelligence community."

"Have you met him?"

"Several times."

"Would you take his word?"

"If he was here, yes."

Wolfe held his Gizmo up. "I can have him here in five seconds."

It took three seconds for a tired-looking Al Ikes to appear on the Gizmo screen.

"How's it going?" Al asked over speakerphone.

"I'm with a friend of yours," Wolfe said quickly, making it clear that they weren't alone. "FBI agent Steven Crow."

"What's he doing down there?"

"I'll let him tell you himself. But the reason I'm calling is that I need you to vouch for us. Apparently, he doesn't trust me."

Al laughed. "Occupational hazard. He's a cop just like me. We don't trust anyone. Let me talk to him."

Wolfe gave Crow the Gizmo. Crow looked at the cell-phone-like device curiously, but didn't say anything.

"You've lost some weight, Steve," Al said.

"A little," Agent Crow said. "You still with the company?"

"Yeah. Special assignment. I'm running protection for Travis Wolfe and Ted Bronson."

"Why?"

"Sorry," Al said. "National security. Need-to-know only. I thought you'd retired from the bureau."

"They put me back on the payroll."

"After you found that money?" Al asked.

"Something like that."

"That was quite a coup."

"Got lucky."

"What brings you down to Brazil?"

"Need-to-know only," Agent Crow said.

Al laughed. "Fair enough. What does Dr. Wolfe have to do with whatever you've got going on down there?"

"I need a ride upriver. Simple as that. He won't take me on his helicopter but says he'll give me a lift in his boat, which is allegedly coming along in a few hours."

"If Wolfe says he'll get you upriver in the boat, you can take it to the bank," Al assured him. "But I need you to do a favor for me."

"What's the favor?"

"You need to keep quiet, and I mean completely quiet, about whatever you see aboard the boat, and at the jaguar preserve. Travis and Ted have come up with several gadgets the U.S. government is very interested in. You're holding one in your hand right now. It's all top secret stuff, which is one of the reasons he doesn't want you on his helicopter."

"I know how to keep my mouth shut," Agent Crow said. "But in fact, it isn't his ride. I ran the tail number and it belongs to a Noah Blackwood."

"I'm aware of that," Al said. "It's a complicated and fluid situation. I'll let you go, but I have to ask one more time. What are you doing down there, Steve?"

Agent Crow shook his head. "Sorry, Al."

"Okay. Hand me back to Wolfe."

Crow gave Wolfe the phone. "I'll tell the captain to start the refuel."

"Thanks."

"And the boat will be here in a few hours?" Crow said.

Wolfe nodded. "I'll give Ted Bronson a call as soon as I finish with Al. Do you have a sat phone?"

Crow nodded.

"Give me your number and I'll tell him where you'll be."

Crow scribbled the number on a card, then walked over to the refueling crew. Wolfe waited for him to get out of hearing range, then looked back at the Gizmo screen. "So, what's Crow's story?"

"Good agent. Been around forever. In fact, I'm surprised he's *still* around. His claim to fame is the recovery of the money in the D. B. Cooper hijacking case. I heard he'd retired after that. Are his creds current?"

"They look to be," Wolfe answered. "Did he actually find D. B. Cooper?"

"Nope, which I'm sure annoyed him to no end. He spent a good part of his career trying to run D.B. down. I'll make some inquiries, see if anyone knows what he's doing down there."

Grace looked over at Crow. He was saying good-bye to the policemen as they boarded their boat.

"What's going on with Blackwood?" Wolfe asked.

Grace looked back at Wolfe.

"He's still here conducting media interviews at the Ark," Al said. "And he seems to be making some headway. The talking heads are sympathetic. 'Poor Dr. Blackwood is the victim of an elaborate hoax. . . . The perpetrators are said to be a radical hunting group. . . .' Blah. Blah. Blah. I'll upload the so-called doctored *Wildlife First* episode. The only thing you have to watch is the last thirty seconds. Blackwood has really thrown down the gauntlet this time. He's committed."

Grace closed her eyes. She had seen the original video Al was talking about. She could hear every word — every lie — of those last thirty seconds.

"I'm recording this from somewhere deep in the Congo, and it very well may be the last time you see me . . ." Noah Blackwood had flashed his trademark grin, tinged with a little sadness and regret. *". . . but don't despair. I've had a good run, and I've managed to save some animals along the way, for which I'm grateful. I came out here to rescue a dear colleague and I may have killed myself in the attempt, but looking back on my life I have no regrets — except one: that I won't be alive to see the impact of this, my greatest discovery ever. . . ."* The camera moved jerkily to his right. A close-up of the two Mokélé-mbembé hatchlings appeared. *"Dinosaurs exist!"* The camera returned to Noah's feverish face. *"Two of them, anyway. The last of their breed. I will try to get them to safety, but if I can't, the last thing I will do before I die will be to let them go. . . ."* The scene switched to a close-up of a now well-groomed and healthy-looking Noah Blackwood.

"To quote Mark Twain, the reports of my death have been greatly exaggerated. But what has not been exaggerated are the dinosaur hatchlings I showed you while I was lost in the Congo. I managed to get my friend and the hatchlings to safety. Right now, for security reasons, we are keeping the hatchlings at an undisclosed location. They are thriving, but they need a little more time to adjust to their new circumstances. I will have more information for you on next week's show. Until then . . . Wildlife first!"

"What about Butch and Yvonne?" Wolfe asked, snapping Grace out of the terrible replay in her head.

"No sign of those two, which can't be good," Al answered. "They got a little banged up at the Ark, but not enough to keep them down. And I can't think of any reason why Blackwood would keep them under wraps. They're not implicated in his current woes."

"What about his jet?"

"Parked in Blackwood's hangar along with his two pilots, but that's not to say Butch and Yvonne aren't on the move in another private jet we don't know about. There's something strange going on."

"What do you mean?"

"I'm not sure. I've had some of my people looking into Blackwood and Butch's recent travels. They kind of appear and disappear from places without any official record of their arrival or departure. My point is that Butch and Yvonne could be anywhere, so you need to stay diligent. There's a chance Blackwood has figured out where you are, and they are either on their way or they are already there."

"We'll keep our eyes open." Wolfe signed off.

"Who's D. B. Cooper?" Grace asked.

“A hijacker from a long time ago. He boarded a passenger jet in Portland and announced that he had a bomb. When they got to Seattle, he let the passengers go but kept the pilot, copilot, and a flight attendant. Cooper demanded a couple hundred thousand dollars in cash and four parachutes, which the FBI gave him, thinking that he just might have the hostages bail. This assured him of getting four working parachutes. The plane then took off from Seattle and headed for Nevada. Cooper locked the crew in the cockpit and gave the pilots the exact route and elevation he wanted them to fly. Somewhere over Mt. Saint Helens, he opened the back door and jumped with the cash strapped to his body, but no one realized it until they landed in Nevada and found he wasn't on the jet. D. B. Cooper, not his real name of course, was never heard from again.”

“You know a lot about it,” Grace said.

“Everyone who lives in the Pacific Northwest knows a lot about it.” Wolfe looked over at the helicopter. “Looks like we're ready to go.” He paid the bargemen and climbed into the pilot's seat.

Grace got into the right-hand seat. She looked back at Luther. He had done a good job of hiding the hatchlings. He was literally buried under supplies in the backseat.

“Hey, where's Crow?” Luther asked. “What going on?”

Grace smiled. “Shotgun!” she said.

Wolfe started the engine.

POOLSIDE

Butch walked out to the pool to check in with Noah one more time before he left. Noah was sitting under a patio umbrella watching himself being interviewed at the Seattle Ark.

"Is this live?" Butch asked.

"Yes," Noah said impatiently. "Quiet! It's almost over."

"So the whole thing was a hoax," the reporter was saying.

"An elaborate and very well-executed hoax," a smiling TV Noah said. "It's sad really to see this much money being spent on efforts to undermine what we're trying to do for wildlife. Think of what that time and money and effort could have done to actually help animals."

"The YouTube video has over five million hits. Have you seen it?"

"I haven't looked at the so-called outtakes. I never will. And I'm confident that our millions and millions of supporters have not been taken in by this malicious slander. They are smarter than that." The TV Noah looked at his watch. "I'm afraid that I have animals to tend to. If you'll excuse me. But please come back anytime. I promise that the next time you do, we will have bigger and better things to discuss."

The reporter smiled. "Dinosaurs?"

The TV Noah returned the smile and walked away.

Butch stifled a shudder. The smiling man walking away from the reporter was not Noah Blackwood. He was known as Mr. Zwilling, and he was exactly like Noah Blackwood in every way. Mr. Zwilling gave Butch the creeps.

"Perfect!" Noah said, taking a sip of his iced, freshly squeezed mango juice. "I told him to be cagey if asked about the dinosaurs. That smile he gave the reporter was sublime." He switched the television off with the remote and stared at Butch with cold blue eyes for a full minute.

Butch hated it when he did this.

"You still look a little banged up," Noah finally said.

Butch felt banged up. It had only been a couple of days since Ted Bronson had beaten the crap out of him at the Ark. Even so, Butch wanted to go another round with Ted. A fair round. One where he wasn't blindsided on a dark path.

"I'm fine," Butch said, and changed the subject. "So you showed the footage of the hatchlings on the *Wildlife First* episode?"

"Of course I did," Noah said. "We're all in on this. And as soon as you get them back for me, you're headed to China to pick up three new panda cubs. All will be as it was except that we will no longer have to worry about Travis Wolfe and his Cryptos Island crew sticking their noses in our affairs. Is everyone in place?"

"Just about," Butch answered. Noah had given him very detailed instructions about where to send their teams. "How do you know where the Cryptos crew and Lansa's staff from the jaguar preserve are?"

"This," Noah said. He reached into his starched safari coat pocket and pulled out a device that was a little bigger than a smartphone.

Butch had seen firsthand how much the Cryptos crew depended on those things when he was aboard the *Coelacanth.*

"Dear old Mitch." Noah smiled. "At least he was good for something. I think you said they call it a Gizmo? A beautiful piece of technology."

Mitch Merton, or Mitch the Snitch, as Butch liked to call him, had been working on Cryptos for years, feeding them information, but he'd blown his cover aboard the *Coelacanth.* He had taken refuge beneath the Ark to become Noah's next personal taxidermist, but the job hadn't worked out. The last time Butch had seen Mitch, Dr. Strand, Noah's creepy geneticist, had been spiking his drink. Noah had planned to put the same brain implant they'd used on the chupacabra into Mitch's brain. There had been no love lost between Butch and Mitch, but Butch had almost felt sorry for him.

"How's Mitch doing?"

"He died on the operating table," Noah said, with no more emotion than if he were informing Butch that he had stepped on an ant.

Butch realized he was *really* looking forward to going to China on his own to poach more panda cubs.

"But back to this Gizmo thing," Noah said. "It took a while for my technicians to figure out exactly how it worked, but they did. And, more important, they've figured out a back door into the entire eWolfe network. I can hack into everything they have with this tiny unit. Remarkable." He began swiping his finger through the menus.

"Do they know we still have it?" Butch asked.

"I don't think so," Noah answered happily. "Or else they would have tried to take it offline. Of course that's not possible now. My techs have put up an impregnable firewall. They can't touch this one." He smiled. "But we can touch them. I can shut down all of their communications, including their ability to track each other, with a swipe of the finger, which I will do at the appropriate moment."

"After we have all of them in hand," Butch said.

Noah gave him a sour look and shook his head. "What would be the point of shutting down their communications *after* we have them all in hand? This is a divide-and-conquer operation, Butch. We'll take them down in ones and twos. The first two have already been cut from the herd. Is the team in place?"

"We have an eye on them," Butch said.

"It's time to move," Noah said. "Take them. They'll be wearing tags around their necks like this." He reached into his pocket and pulled out a plastic tag that had been broken in two. "This was Mitch's. Destroy their tags before the team brings them here."

"And if they resist?"

"Have them killed."

"What about the others?" Butch asked.

"I'll let you know." Noah's blue eyes narrowed. "And keep your two-way radio on."

A couple of days earlier at the Ark, Butch had briefly turned off his two-way, and Noah blamed their loss of the hatchlings and the panda cubs on Butch's failure of protocol. Clearly, he was still in the doghouse, but he wasn't alone. Yvonne Zloblinavech was in the doghouse, too.

"Where's Yvonne?" Butch asked.

"She's headed upriver," Noah responded. "More than likely on her way to her death."

D. B. COOPER

Marty and Dylan were in the fake pilothouse acting like they were piloting the *Rivlan* up the Amazon. *Acting* because the *Rivlan* was in fact piloting itself. It was as if it had eyes — slowing down and speeding up as needed, veering left and right to avoid flotsam and jetsam, shoals, and other boats.

"I think Ted was exaggerating when he said he needed our help," Marty said. "We could probably be below deck sleeping right now, like he is."

"You think?" Dylan laughed.

Marty looked out the window. The Amazon was wider than he'd expected. In some places it looked to be a mile across, and there was a lot of boat traffic. The banks were crowded with shantytowns and ramshackle houses that looked like they had been pieced together with junk snagged from the muddy river.

"It's like a slow-motion interstate freeway," Dylan commented.

"I'm going down to get my sketchbook," Marty said. "Might as well start drawing up what happened at the Ark."

"Can you grab me a bottle of water?" Dylan asked.

"Sure."

As Marty started out of the pilothouse, his Gizmo buzzed. He pulled it out of his pocket and looked at the screen.

"Wolfe!"

He put it on speakerphone.

"Where's Ted?" Wolfe asked. "I've been trying reach him for a half hour. He isn't answering."

"Hello to you, too," Marty said.

Wolfe gave him a sheepish grin. "Yeah, sorry about that. But I thought something must have happened."

"We're fine," Marty said. "Ted's asleep. He must have turned his Gizmo off. Where are you?"

"Final leg. We just refueled. We'll be at the preserve in a couple of hours. You doing okay?"

"Chugging along. At this rate, we should be there sometime next year."

"Don't worry, you'll make up the time after sundown, but you'll have a stop to make. Tell Ted he needs to pick up a passenger at the fuel barge. He's an FBI agent."

"You're kidding."

Wolfe shook his head. "I don't have time to give you the details right now. Just pick him up and take him to the preserve. His name is Steven Crow."

"Did you say Steven Crow?" Dylan asked, yanking the Gizmo from Marty's hand.

"Yeah," Wolfe said.

"Impossible," Dylan said.

"What are you talking about?" Wolfe asked.

"What's he look like?"

"Old guy."

"Heavy?"

"No, but if I had to guess I'd say he's lost a lot of weight recently. His clothes were a couple of sizes too big for him. Are you saying you know him?"

"I think so," Dylan said.

"From where?"

"It's a long story," Dylan answered. "Why does he want to go to the preserve?"

"He wouldn't say," Wolfe answered. "I guess we'll find out when he gets there. Just pass it on to Ted when he wakes up. I've told Crow to be on the lookout for you. And tell Ted that Al Ikes thinks Butch McCall and Yvonne are either down here or on their way down here. They haven't been spotted since the night you broke into the Ark. You need to keep your eyes open for them. Also, Blackwood appears to be weaseling his way out of the outtake problem. They ran the real *Wildlife First* episode. At the end of it, after he repels the pirates that actually work for him, there's a short scene of him in the Congo supposedly lost and dying while trying to save Butch. It ends with a glimpse of the hatchlings, which he claims to have discovered."

"Oh, brother," Marty said.

"Ted has satellite TV on board," Wolfe said. "So you should be able to catch it. But my point is that he's going to be coming after us hard. He needs the hatchlings back or he's ruined. Without them, he'll be a laughingstock. Don't let your guard down. I'd better go. See you at the preserve."

Dylan still looked a little shell-shocked as he passed the Gizmo back to Marty.

Marty pocketed the device. "Want to tell me about it?"

"It's complicated," Dylan said. "Do you like to read?"

"Of course," Marty said. "Why?"

"Because I wrote down the whole story."

"That's right," Marty said. "You said something about that back in Seattle. But I thought it was a story about Bigfoot. What does this Agent Crow have to do with that?"

"He's not after Bigfoot," Dylan said. "But I do know what he *is* after, and that can't possibly have anything to do with what *we're* doing down here . . . but then why *is* he down here? I never thought I'd see him again, but it looks like . . ."

"I hope the story you wrote down makes more sense than what you're saying now," Marty said.

Dylan pulled out his smartphone. "I typed it up a while back. I've never let anyone read it."

"Fire it up." Marty held out his hand. "I don't have anything else to do."

Dylan gave him the phone. "Open the file called *Sasquatch*."

Marty took it down to the main deck, got himself comfortable in one of the hammocks, and started to read. He read straight through over the next several hours without even getting up to pee.

Dylan had not only had several personal encounters with Bigfoot, but he had survived a volcanic eruption on Mount St. Helens. He had also stumbled across two hundred thousand dollars in cash stolen in an airplane hijacking by a man calling himself D. B. Cooper. Agent Crow had been after the hijacker, whose real name was Buckley Johnson. "Buck," as everyone called him, was a retired wildlife biologist with a bum leg. He had injured his hip bailing out of the hijacked jet.

"What do think?" Dylan asked.

Marty nearly fell out of the hammock. He had been so engrossed in Dylan's story he hadn't noticed him sitting three feet away.

"How long have you been there?"

Dylan shrugged.

"It's fantastic!" Marty said. "Buck Johnson's cabin with Pandora's box and the lava tubes are real?"

"Yep."

"Have you been up there since the eruption?"

"Once. My dad and me took my mom up there. She thought we were making the whole thing up."

"Did you see any Sasquatch?"

Dylan shook his head. "There was enough physical evidence to convince her that we weren't lying, but we didn't see any of the animals. Like I said in the story, they're pretty shy. I think we'd have to spend quite a bit of time up there before they'd let themselves be seen."

"When we get back to the States, can you take me up there?"

"Sure."

Marty got out of the hammock. "I think we should try our hand at turning your story into a graphic novel. Of course, we'd have to change all of the names and locations so people don't come up there looking for the Sasquatch. The cabin would be a perfect place to work on the sketches." Marty paused for a moment, then asked, "So what do *you* think happened to Buck Johnson?"

"After he returned the money, I never heard from him again. My dad tried to find him, but it was like he'd disappeared off the face of the earth."

"You think this Agent Crow is still after him?"

"It wouldn't surprise me, but I can't imagine why he'd be looking down here. It's been decades since the plane was hijacked, and Buck returned the money, and he saved Crow's life up on the mountain. What's the point?"

"I think the point is that the FBI doesn't give up."

"What's this about the FBI and fugitives?" Ted appeared on deck, stretching and yawning.

Marty told him about picking up Agent Crow at the barge, then started to fill him in about D. B. Cooper and Sasquatch. Ted listened for a minute, then held up his hand for him to stop. "We knew about most of this," Ted told Dylan.

"How?" Dylan asked.

"Al Ikes did a background check on your family and interviewed your dad. Standard operating procedure for anyone trying to get a job on Cryptos Island. But I don't remember him saying anything about the D. B. Cooper hijacking." He smiled. "That would have stuck in my mind."

"That's because he didn't know about it," Dylan admitted. "I didn't tell him."

"Doesn't matter," Ted said. "We'll pick up this Agent Crow and see what happens." He looked at the sky. "It won't be long before it gets dark. Just enough time for us to eat before we rev up the *Rivlan*."

THE PRESERVE

Wolfe landed the helicopter in a narrow inlet next to a wooden dock. Luther was out the door and on the pontoon before the rotors stopped, but Wolfe didn't seem to care.

"Can't blame him for wanting to get out and stretch his legs," Wolfe said. "Long flight."

Grace looked out the window. Jake Lansa was the first to reach the dock, followed by an older man she didn't know. Next came a woman with red hair, who had to be Dr. Lansa's girlfriend, Dr. Flanna Brenna. Ana Mika and an indigenous man covered with tattooed jaguar spots followed closely behind.

"Raul," Wolfe said.

Grace turned and looked at her father. "You know him?"

"No. But I'm sure we're going to become good friends. He and I are leaving as soon as I climb out of here."

"What?" Grace thought he would at least stick around camp for the night before heading off into the jungle.

"We had a good tailwind coming upriver. Made better time than I thought. There are still a few hours of daylight left, and I want to take advantage of them."

"What about the hatchlings?" Grace asked.

"You and Luther know more about taking care of them than I do. My priority right now is to catch up with Laurel and Dr. Lansa and help them look for Sylvia and Timothy. I want to make a side trip on the way. When I was down here before, I didn't have time to visit the helicopter crash site. I want to see it for myself. Ted and Marty and Dylan will be along soon to give you and Luther a hand. I'll stay in touch on the Gizmo and let you know how I'm doing. I'll call in tonight, I promise."

He gave her a hug, grabbed his backpack, and barely said hello to the people on the dock before disappearing into the jungle with Raul, limping.

Driven, Grace thought, worried about the limp, and wondering if she would ever get used to her father's abrupt departures and his one-track mind.

It took them nearly two hours to unload the helicopter and haul the supplies to camp. The crated hatchlings were the last boxes they moved. Grace and Jake carried one crate. Luther and Buck, the older man who had met them on arrival, carried the other. They set the crates down inside their new enclosure.

Buck leaned down and looked into one of the air holes on the top of the crate. There was a loud bang and a growl from inside. Buck reeled backward.

"I wouldn't be getting too close unless you want to lose something valuable like your nose," Luther said.

"Thanks for the warning," Buck said. "When do we get to see the mystery creatures?"

"As soon as I check out their new digs and make sure they can't escape," Luther said.

The enclosure looked perfectly fine to Grace. In fact, it was the nicest enclosure the hatchlings had ever had. Certainly better than the high-tech dungeon Yvonne had set up beneath the Ark. This one had an indoor holding area and an outdoor corral. The holding area was ten by twenty feet and could be split in two with a gate if they needed to separate the hatchlings. Next to the holding area was a food prep area with a giant freezer, refrigerator, cupboards, stainless steel counters, tools, cleaning supplies, and an immersion tank to thaw out the meat. Ted had shipped in several hundred pounds of precut beef in five-pound freezer bags. All they had to do was take out a couple of bags, thaw them in the bath, and feed the meat to the hatchlings.

"No more butchering," Luther said, putting two bags in the immersion tank.

Ted had also supplied some kind of generator that had enough power to light up the whole base camp.

"This generator doesn't make much noise," Buck observed. "And I can't for the life of me figure out how you get fuel into it."

"I think it runs on —" Luther started.

Grace gave him an elbow. It wasn't their place to tell people about Wolfe and Ted's inventions. "Ted will be here later," she said. "I'm sure he'll explain it."

They walked out to the circular corral, made from four-foot-tall fence sections seamlessly fastened together with some kind of magnetic locking mechanism. The corral was five times bigger than the holding area.

"They're going to love this," Grace said. "They've never been outdoors."

Jake and Flanna were standing outside the corral, each resting a foot on the rail as if they were waiting for a rodeo to begin. Buck and Ana joined them.

"This fence looks like it's made out of stainless steel," Buck said. "But it's lighter than aluminum."

Luther looked at Grace. Apparently, he didn't want to get another elbow in the side. "Some kind of special alloy," Grace said.

"Right," Buck said. "Ted will explain when he gets here."

Grace smiled. She liked Buck. In fact, she liked everyone she'd met at the preserve so far and was looking forward to getting to know them better.

"Time to blow their minds," Luther whispered with relish. "You want to let them out, or should I?"

Grace knew this wasn't really a question. "Go ahead," she said, and joined the others outside the corral.

Luther strutted over to the two metal crates, glanced at the small crowd, then slid open the doors. The hatchlings had been banging around the crates for the past half hour, and Grace thought they would pop out like a couple of jack-in-the-boxes, but nothing happened. Grace was sure Luther was disappointed by the "reveal" and would try to prod the hatchlings out, but to her surprise he waited a few seconds, shrugged, then calmly joined them on the other side of the fence.

"I'm sure they're a little spooked after the helicopter ride," he quietly. "And this is the first time they've been separated since they hatched."

"Hatched?" Flanna asked. "They're birds?"

"Not exactly," Luther said. "You'll see."

And they did. After a couple of minutes, one of the hatchlings snaked its long purplish neck out of the opening and looked around. There was a collective gasp from the preserve crew. At the sound, the second hatchling popped its head out and hissed.

Grace had never heard them hiss before.

Cautiously, they inched out of their crates, their heads bobbing nervously left and right at their new surroundings. They were as big as Shetland ponies now, but looked small within the enormous corral.

"Oh my God . . ."

"Impossible . . ."

"They're fantastic . . ."

Grace barely heard their exclamations as she stared in awe at how the hatchlings were moving. Prior to this, the only two modes she had seen were sleeping and snapping. She glanced at Luther, who appeared equally surprised.

"You think they're okay?" she asked.

"Pretty sure," he said worriedly. "Hopefully, they'll *snap* out of it when we feed them."

"Ha," Grace said.

"Amazing," Flanna said. "I didn't expect . . ." She shook her head. "I mean . . ."

"I didn't, either," Jake said. "Who would have thought. Where are they from? How did you get them?"

Grace had just started to explain when Ana's Gizmo buzzed.

"Wolfe?" Grace asked hopefully. He'd promised to check in when it got dark.

"It's Laurel," Ana said.

The last time Grace had seen Laurel was aboard the *Coelacanth*. Butch McCall had held a gun to Laurel's head, threatening to kill her if Wolfe didn't let Grace go with Noah

Blackwood. Wolfe had refused. Grace had broken the impasse by voluntarily going with her grandfather.

"Can you put her on speaker?" Grace asked.

"Of course." Ana switched the Gizmo to speaker and held it out so Grace could see Laurel on the little screen.

"So you made it!" Laurel said with a broad smile. "Where's Wolfe?"

"He's on his way to you," Grace said. "He left with Raul as soon as we got here."

"He has a long way to go."

"Where are you?"

Laurel laughed. "The truth is that we don't exactly know where we are. The maps are wrong, and this Gizmo of Ted's has been going in and out. I've been trying to check in for a few hours now. Doc's setting up camp for the night. I finally talked him into a few hours of rest. He's as bad as Wolfe."

"I heard that!" someone said offscreen.

"Is that Doc?" Grace asked.

"Who else?" Flanna said. "If you can hear me, Doc, you need to slow down!"

"Yeah, yeah, yeah," Doc said.

Everyone laughed.

"The hatchlings arrived safe and sound?" Laurel asked.

Ana pointed the Gizmo at the corral. The hatchlings had gotten over their initial fear and were now running around the perimeter like a couple of prehistoric puppies. Everyone laughed again but stopped abruptly when they heard the scream.

"Who was that?" Ana asked.

"Is everyone okay?" Flanna scanned the area around the enclosure.

Suddenly, Luther shouted, "The Gizmo!"

Ana stared at the image on her Gizmo's screen. Laurel's Gizmo was pointed up at the canopy, obviously lying on the ground.

"Laurel?" Ana said.

A rock came down on Laurel's screen and the video call ended.

RAUL

Raul was a man of few words, which didn't bother Wolfe in the least. He wasn't one to waste time on idle chatter, either. And even if he'd wanted to talk to Raul, there wouldn't have been time. Raul was leading him through the sweltering rain forest at a brutal and breathless pace. At the rate they were traveling, they would likely reach the helicopter crash site before dark.

If I survive, Wolfe thought as he sipped from his canteen without stopping.

His prosthetic leg was really bothering him. Ted had done a great job on the design, but one factor he hadn't taken into account was the correlation between exertion, sweat, and chafing. The prosthesis wasn't chafing yet, but it was starting to itch, which could lead to crippling problems if Wolfe didn't take care of it soon. He was about to shout ahead to Raul to stop, but it turned out he didn't have to. They had arrived at the helicopter crash site.

The damaged trees had healed and the vines had grown back, but there were still a lot of debris scattered around: the charred fuselage, the twisted rotors, and other pieces too big to haul away and repurpose. Wolfe dropped his pack to the ground, fished his flashlight out of a side pocket, then limped over to the fuselage for a closer look. Raul silently gathered wood for a fire.

Soon after Sylvia and Timothy had disappeared, Wolfe had heard a rumor that the helicopter had been shot down, which he'd discounted at the time. His sister and brother-in-law were journalists, but they rarely covered anything controversial enough to make them targets for assassination. Their specialty, their niche, was adventure travel. They covered the most exotic, hard-to-reach places on earth, Sylvia with her cameras and lenses, Timothy with his journals and Montblanc pens. After the crash, the local authorities had sent him Sylvia's damaged camera and a couple of Timothy's singed journals. There was nothing in the images or the scrawled words to indicate that anything was amiss, except for a cryptic note that they had new information about Noah Blackwood. This wasn't entirely surprising. He, Ted and Ana, Sylvia and Timothy . . . all of them had been keeping tabs on Noah for years and sharing information with one another, but none of it had been enough to take Noah down.

The fuselage was a blackened, charred hull. Vines and plants were already taking it over. In a year it would be completely absorbed by the rain forest. Wolfe examined the outside inch by inch with his flashlight but saw no sign that it had been shot down.

His Gizmo buzzed. It was Ana.

"Something's happened to Laurel and Doc," she said, and gave him the bullet points like the great journalist she was.

"Are their tags working?" he asked.

"No," Ana said.

"Hang on." He opened the tracking app on his Gizmo and found everyone's location except for Laurel's and Doc's. This was bad. The only way to block the signal was to snap the tag in two. Glancing down at the screen again, he saw that Jake Lansa and Flanna Brenna were moving quickly through the forest. Ana said they had left camp fifteen minutes ago with the intention of rescuing Laurel and Doc.

"Do they have a sat phone with them?"

"Yes. I'll send you the number, but Flanna said that the signal has been going in and out all day . . . mostly out."

"Great," Wolfe said. "The smashed Gizmo doesn't worry me. That could have been an accident. But both tags going out is an entirely different matter. How would a group of uncontacted indigenous people know what the tags do?"

"And how would they know how to stop the signal?" Ana added.

"Exactly. I don't like this. Have you talked to Ted?"

"No."

"Call him. Tell him what's going on. I'll try to catch up with Flanna and Jake, but it will be a while. I need to get some rest, or I'll be no good. On top of that, I'm having a leg malfunction."

"Do you want me or Buck to come to you?"

"Negative. You and Buck stay in camp and keep an eye on Grace and Luther and the hatchlings. I'm at the crash site. I'll keep you posted."

He ended the call. He wished now that he had told Laurel and Doc to wait in camp for his arrival. He wished he had stayed in camp and done something about his leg before stomping off into the jungle.

Stop! he told himself. *It is what it is. Laurel is resourceful, and I'm sure Doc is, too.*

Raul had gotten the fire going. Thick smoke rose up into the canopy, which would keep the insects at bay, but Wolfe didn't plan to be around long enough to be bothered by bugs.

Two hours, maybe two and a half.

The first thing he needed to do was check out the inside of the ruined helicopter, which had some risks. The fuselage was a perfect home for dozens of types of animals, many of which were lethal. Wolfe got Raul's attention and pantomimed that was going to crawl inside. Raul looked at him like he was a fool, then held up a finger for him to wait. Raul found a long limb on the ground, quickly turned it into a pole with his machete, and handed it to Wolfe.

Smarter than me, Wolfe thought. "Thanks."

Wolfe started poking around to see if something nasty popped out. He stirred up a family of agoutis. The cat-sized rodents blasted by him, squealing. He was happy to see them. It meant there were no venomous snakes or predators in residence. But one of them didn't make it. Wolfe heard a loud whack behind him and turned around. Raul was holding his trophy by its hind legs, grinning. It was the first time Wolfe had seen him smile.

Big rat for dinner. Not the first time.

Wolfe crawled into the fuselage. It smelled like burnt rubber, rotting vegetation, and what he assumed was agouti urine. The instrument panel had been pried off and taken away along with everything else that could be removed, including the seats. It didn't look like the fire had spread to the inside. He examined the skin inch by inch and came to a blackened rip in the metal that was clearly not caused by the crash.

"It *caused* the crash," he said under his breath as he ran his fingers along the gash.

Wolfe was far from an expert in these things, but it looked like the chopper had indeed been shot down. But by who? And why? He spent a few more minutes looking around inside. The authorities had taken the remains of the two pilots, and except for the camera and journals they'd sent to Wolfe, there had been no sign of Sylvia and Timothy. It had been clear to the authorities that animals had been at the pilots. They theorized that Sylvia and Timothy had probably been dragged deeper into the forest and eaten. Nothing was wasted in the rain forest. Protein was consumed.

Wolfe had seen the grisly photos of the two dead pilots still strapped into their seats. But he didn't understand why Sylvia and Timothy hadn't been strapped into their seats. They did crazy and dangerous things, but neither one of them would have failed to buckle up. Did they unbuckle themselves, or did someone else do it for them?

Wolfe crawled out of the fuselage. Raul had gutted, skinned, and spitted the luckless agouti. Wolfe was hungry, but a large rat was not what he had in mind for dinner. He grabbed his pack and leaned against a tree, shifting his weight off his prosthesis.

The agouti was beginning to sizzle and smelled a lot better than he expected. It felt good to get off his feet, but it was going to feel even better to take his leg off. He glanced at Raul. He wasn't sure if the other man knew about his leg. He rolled his pant leg up, took out his tool kit, and disassembled the various screws, straps, and Velcro. He looked up again. Raul was staring at him. Clearly, Raul hadn't known. Wolfe wished he still had his leg, but he was years beyond being embarrassed about it. He set the prosthesis to the side, took the sock off his stump, and began massaging it with the concoction Ted had come up with to ease the pain and treat the chafing.

Raul stepped a bit closer to watch.

"Do you speak English?" Wolfe asked. Raul hadn't uttered a single word since meeting him at the preserve.

"A little." Raul pointed. "The leg."

Wolfe smiled. "Yeah, it's inconvenient not having one." It was obvious by the look on Raul's face that he didn't understand. "I lost it," Wolfe said.

Raul nodded and went back to the fire to tend to the roasting rat meat.

Ideally, it would have been best to give the stump a rest until morning, but that wasn't going to happen now. Instead of using the Gizmo's GPS, Wolfe slipped on his headlamp, took out a map, and spread it on the ground, thinking it would be easier to explain to Raul what they needed to do on paper.

"Raul?"

Raul held up a finger for him to wait a minute. He was testing his culinary masterpiece to see if it was done. Apparently it was, because he pulled off a hind leg and brought it over.

"Thanks," Wolfe said, forcing a smile. He took a bite and found it surprisingly good. The joke in the field was that when eating exotic camp meat, whether snake or bird or mammal, everyone said it tasted like chicken. The roasted agouti tasted more like rabbit — a little gamey, but not bad. He took another bite and wondered what Marty could do with agouti meat if given a chance.

Wolfe pointed a greasy finger at the map. "We are here," he said, then moved his finger. "Flanna and Jake are here." He traced a line to where they would have to travel to intersect with the others. "We go here to catch them." He didn't bother to try to explain where Flanna and Jake were going, or why they needed to catch up with them.

Raul nodded as if he understood.

"Two hours," Wolfe said, holding up two fingers and pointing at his watch.

Again, Raul nodded.

Once they were under way, Wolfe's plan was to send Raul ahead, because with his bum leg there was no way he could keep up with the smaller man. He would explain this to Raul after they started out.

"Are we good?" Wolfe asked.

Raul answered by grabbing the stick he had carved earlier and brandishing it as if he were going to clobber Wolfe with it.

Wolfe could not have been more shocked. Without his prosthesis, he was completely at Raul's mercy. And Raul did not look to be in a merciful mood.

Wolfe glanced at his pack. He had a pistol and knife inside, but the pack was five feet away. It might as well been a mile. He'd never reach it.

After everything I've faced in my life. All the dangers, diseases, having my leg chewed off by a dinosaur, I'm going to be murdered by a berserk indigenous Brazilian in the middle of nowhere with a stick.

The situation was so ridiculous, there was nothing Wolfe could do but laugh. The laugh seemed to disarm Raul to some degree. He was still holding the stick at the ready, but his fierce expression had softened.

"I kind of hope we can work this out," Wolfe said quietly. "I'd prefer not to be killed if it's all right with you."

He wasn't certain Raul understood the words, but he hoped he understood the nonthreatening tone. To his surprise, Raul now seemed to understand everything he said, and much more.

"Not kill," he said. "Capture. This is the place."

"What place?"

"The place I told them I would bring you."

"Who did you tell this to?"

"Os três."

Wolfe's understanding of Portuguese was rudimentary, but he could decipher this. "Who are the three?"

"Forest men."

Wolfe stared at Raul for a few moments, trying to absorb what he was saying. "What do you mean by 'capture'?"

Instead of answering, Raul hit the stick on the ground three times. Three men stepped out of the forest into the light of the fire. They held blowpipes to their lips. The pipes were as tall as they were, and all of them were pointed at Wolfe's head. The men were naked except for loincloths held around their stout brown waists by leather strings. Hanging on the strings were wooden clubs, dart quivers, and two-way radios. Like Raul, their brown skin was tattooed with jaguar spots.

"Os três," Raul said quietly.

"I see that," Wolfe said calmly, trying to disguise his own fear, which was not caused by the blowpipes, the clubs, or the sudden appearance of the three men. What was most disturbing were the two-way radios. Uncontacted tribes did not carry sophisticated communications equipment.

Wolfe was usually the tallest man in the room, and the strongest. But without his leg he was the shortest and the weakest. He hadn't felt this vulnerable, this exposed, since he had been dragged one-legged out of the Congo on a litter more than a decade ago. He didn't like the feeling.

"What do they want?" he asked.

"They want us to go with them," Raul told him.

Wolfe forced a smile. "What if I refuse?"

Raul shrugged.

One of the men lowered his pipe and approached. He reached down and picked up Wolfe's prosthesis, backed away, and looked at it in the light of the fire. A second man joined him, leaving Wolfe covered by only one man. They started talking to Raul about the leg in their native tongue, pointing to the boot still attached. Raul seemed to understand them and responded in kind. Wolfe didn't understand a word of it. It occurred to him that with one man guarding him, this might be his best shot of getting out of the situation, but it wasn't a good enough shot.

Raul walked back over to him, carrying the leg. He dropped it on the ground in front of Wolfe. "I need the tag on neck."

Wolfe wanted to say no, but there was little point. With one leg he was virtually helpless. He took off the tag and tossed it to Raul. Raul removed the tracking tag from his own neck, snapped both tags in two, and tossed them into the fire.

"Phone," Raul said.

"Why?"

Raul darted in and grabbed Wolfe's backpack. He found the Gizmo in the side pocket, smashed it repeatedly with his stick, then threw it into the fire with the tags.

Wolfe was not completely discouraged. For years he had functioned perfectly fine in the woods without a Gizmo or a tracking tag. He took some comfort in the fact that they hadn't just killed him outright. This meant they wanted him alive for some reason.

"They want us to go with them," Raul said. "You need to put the leg back on your . . ." He hesitated.

"The word is *stump*," Wolfe finished for him. "What if I say no?"

"I think they will kill you."

"Thanks for the clarification," Wolfe said.

"I don't know that word."

"Not important."

Wolfe began the elaborate procedure of putting his prosthesis back on. The jaguar men stepped closer to watch every complicated move. If they were going very far, which he assumed they were, he was going to have a problem. The stump was still very tender.

Raul rifled through Wolfe's bag, taking his gun and knife and anything else that might be used as a weapon. He put these in his own pack and dropped Wolfe's back in front of him.

"I need to tie your hands," he said.

"How about we skip that part?"

Raul shook his head.

Before getting to his feet, Wolfe picked up the agouti meat and took his time eating it, trying to exert some semblance of control over the situation. They let him finish.

A small victory.

He tossed the bone into the dark and got to his feet. He tested the prosthesis, keeping a close eye on the three blowpipes, which were again pointed at his him. Raul tied his wrists together with zip ties.

Zip ties and two-ways. Not good.

"Hard going in the dark," Wolfe commented.

"Cats see at night," Raul said.

They started off into the dark forest.

DAY THREE

CROW

It was just after midnight. Marty and Dylan were belted into their seats as the *Rivlan* veered around a bend in the river at well over a hundred miles an hour. There was a long straight stretch of river in front of them without any boat lights.

"It's kind of like flying," Marty said.

"Hang on," Ted said. "I'm going to open her up and see what she can do." He pushed the throttle forward.

Marty was slammed back into his seat and thought his lungs were going to collapse from the pressure. At 210 miles an hour, the *Rivlan* started to shudder. Ted eased back on the throttle until they got to 130 miles an hour.

"Not bad," Ted said, slowing down the *Rivlan* even more. "We have a lot of boat traffic coming up around the next bend." He pointed to a live satellite feed on one of the monitors. "Looks like we'll have to chug along for a couple of miles before we can let her rip again. If you two want to unbuckle and stretch your legs up top, go ahead. I'll let you know before I step on it."

"Good idea," Marty said, getting out of his seat.

Ted grinned.

Dylan stood up and stretched. "I think I'll stay down here with Ted. I have some questions about how this thing works. When will we get to the fuel barge?"

"Half an hour or so," Ted said.

"I'm still not sure why we're stopping at all," Marty said. They had gotten word from Ana that something had happened to Laurel and Dr. Lansa, and now Wolfe's signal had gone offline.

"Because we said we would," Ted said.

"Yeah, but that was before everyone disappeared."

"All the more reason to pick up reinforcements," Ted said. "It will only take a minute to snag him from the barge."

Every minute counts, Marty thought. He went up top and breathed in the fresh night air. It had cooled down some and the sky was clear, no moon, but a million stars. The riverbanks were dotted with small campfires and dim electrical lights powered by generators that echoed across the water. Marty climbed into a hammock, put his hands behind his head, looked up at the sky, and thought about his parents. They had been missing for months now. Every day that had gone by, it had looked more and more unlikely that they had survived. His parents had spent more time outdoors under the stars than they had indoors under roofs. They were both experts in wilderness survival.

If they were alive, they would have found their way out of the rain forest by now. If they were injured and couldn't travel, they would have found a way to get the word out by now.

"You okay?" Ted had stepped out onto the deck.

"I was thinking about my parents," Marty said.

Ted sat down on a crate near the hammock. "We're all thinking about them."

Most of the time, Marty could keep the heartache at bay, but it was back, and so heavy he thought the hammock would break. "It's been too long," he said.

"I don't know about *too* long," Ted admitted. "I wouldn't give up hope. Sylvia and Timothy are tough and resourceful. If anyone could survive a helicopter crash, it's them. As you know, the four of us grew up together. Sylvia and Timothy always thought Wolfe and I were wimps. And compared to them, we were."

"Do you think Blackwood has anything to do with this?"

"Whenever something goes south on us, Blackwood is usually behind it, but I don't know how he's managing it this time around. To snatch Laurel and Doc so quickly, and maybe Wolfe, he'd have to have an elaborate network of people already in place. And I'm not just talking about Butch and Yvonne. He'd have to have a dozen people or more down here, and there aren't a dozen people within a hundred miles of the jaguar preserve. It's in the middle of nowhere. We have an extensive dossier on Blackwood. As far as we can tell, he has no contacts in Brazil."

Marty thought about it for a minute. "Why not?"

"What do you mean?"

"Noah has contacts everywhere. Why not in the fifth-largest country in the world, with the largest concentration of wildlife on the planet?"

Ted stared at Marty in the shadowy light. "I'm sure he's done *Wildlife First* shows down here."

Marty shook his head. Except for the most recent episodes, he had seen every *Wildlife First* ever produced. He had watched the show all the time back when he was at OOPS, long before he learned Noah Blackwood was a serial liar and homicidal maniac.

"Your eidetic memory," Ted said.

"There have been two hundred and sixteen episodes," Marty said. "Want me to list where they've all been filmed?"

Ted smiled. "That won't be necessary. I believe you. And you're right. It's very strange that he's never done a show down here." He pulled his Gizmo out, thumbed something into it, and read for a couple minutes. "Here's another strange thing. *Wildlife First* airs in every South American country except Brazil, which is the biggest market down here. There are dozens of comment strings complaining about it. Brazilian networks say that they've tried to air it, but have failed to reach an agreement with Blackwood's production company."

"Why?" Marty asked.

"That's a great question. And we should have asked it a lot earlier than this. We've been looking for things that are there. You thought outside the box by finding something that *wasn't* there."

Ted was always talking in riddles like this. "Is that a compliment?"

"Of the highest order." Ted started tapping on the Gizmo again. "I'm emailing Al. He needs to look into this."

Marty swung out of the hammock and walked up to the bow. An array of bright lights twinkled about half a mile ahead. "I think we're coming up on the fuel barge," he called back.

"So we are," Ted said. "I guess I better climb up to the bridge and act like I'm actually driving this thing. Do you feel like whipping something together for a midnight snack? After we pick up Crow, we'll be going full speed ahead and we'll have to stay buckled in."

"Sure," Marty said. Cooking would help him get his mind off his parents. He went down to the galley.

Dylan was getting a drink of water when Marty slid down the galley ladder behind him, nearly scaring him half to death.

"Jeez!"

"Jumpy," Marty said. "How do you like your eggs?"

"Over easy."

"I'm making cheese omelets."

"Then why did you ask? And why are you making breakfast at one in the morning?"

"Because Ted is hungry and we're not going to get a chance to eat because he's putting the pedal to the metal after we pick up your friend Crow."

"He's not exactly my friend."

"Whatever he is, he'll be on board in a couple of minutes. We're coming up on the fuel barge."

"You need help making breakfast?"

"Nope," Marty said. "You better get up top. I'm sure you and Agent Crow have a lot of catching up to do."

Dylan hurried up the ladder.

"You handle the lines," Ted shouted from the fake pilothouse.

Dylan wove his way through the crates to the bow, watching the well-lit fuel barge get bigger and bigger as they chugged closer and closer. He wondered if Agent Crow was on the barge watching. He wondered what Agent Crow's reaction would be when Crow saw him. A man on the dock tossed him a line. He caught it, wrapped it around the cleat, then hurried to the stern and caught the second line. The man who threw the line shouted something to him in Portuguese, which Dylan didn't understand. Ted came down from the pilothouse. Dylan thought he would be in disguise as the dumpy Theo Sonborn, but he was just the James-Bond-look-alike genius Ted Bronson. He shouted something in Portuguese back at the man. The man shrugged and walked away.

"What did he want?" Dylan asked.

"He wanted to know how much fuel we needed. I told him we were just picking up a passenger."

"What does the *Rivlan* run on anyway?"

"Nothing they have on the barge, that's for sure."

A man stepped out of the shadows. He had a large duffel bag slung over his shoulder. If this was Agent Crow, he had lost at least a hundred pounds.

"Are you Ted Bronson?" the man asked without looking in Dylan's direction. The gravelly voice hadn't changed. Dylan would have recognized the sound of it anywhere.

"Yes, sir," Ted said. "At your service."

"You're earlier than I expected."

"The boat is faster than she looks."

The boat is faster than any boat on earth, Dylan thought. *Crow is in for several surprises before the night's out.*

"Grab his bag, Dylan."

And here comes the first surprise.

Dylan reached over the gunwale. Agent Crow stopped him, staring in complete shock.

"Dylan Hickock?"

"You've lost a lot of weight," Dylan said. "You look good."

"What are you doing down here?"

"I guess I could ask you the same thing. My dad's working for Ted here, and for Travis Wolfe. How I got down here is kind of a long story."

"Your dad's aboard?"

Dylan shook his head. "He and Mom are up in Washington."

"Maybe we could continue this reunion after we get under way," Ted said. "They're waiting for us upriver, and I'd like to get going."

"Aren't you going to refuel?" Crow asked. "As I understand it, this is the last refueling barge for miles."

"Tank's full," Ted said. "Come aboard. Untie the lines." He climbed back up to the pilothouse.

Dylan took Crow's duffel and set it on the deck. There obviously wasn't much in it.

Crow climbed over the gunwale. "I'll get the stern line."

"Great."

Dylan walked up to the bow and undid the line. As soon as it was free, Ted started maneuvering the *Rivlan* away from the barge.

"I can honestly say you're the last person I expected to see down here," Crow said, walking up to bow.

"I could say the same thing for you," Dylan said.

"What do you hear from Buckley Johnson?"

"Nothing," Dylan said. "I haven't seen him since Mount St. Helens erupted."

"Why do I find that hard to believe?"

Dylan shrugged. "Because you're a cop and you don't believe anybody."

"There's some truth to that," Crow admitted, giving him a slight smile. "I'll tell you why I'm here. Buckley Johnson is working at Robert Lansa's jaguar preserve."

It was Dylan's turn to be shocked. "What makes you think that?"

"I've been tracking him for months. He passed by here a couple of days ago ferrying Jake Lansa and a couple of Travis Wolfe's people upriver. And if you're thinking about warning him that I'm coming, go ahead."

"Go ahead?"

Crow nodded. "He can run, but he can't hide. I'll run him to ground eventually."

"He's an old man," Dylan said. "He returned the money."

"I'm an old man, too. And it doesn't matter that he returned the money. He hijacked an airplane. It's a serious crime."

"He needed the money to save his son."

"Is that what he told you?"

"Yeah," Dylan said. "And I believed him." Buck's son had been dying of cancer when Buck hijacked the airplane. He needed the money for an experimental treatment, but his son had died before Buck could get the money off the mountain.

"Might be true," Crow admitted. "But that doesn't alter the fact that he broke the law."

"He saved your life on the mountain."

"That is true," Crow said. "Although I don't know how he did it. We were buried under a ton of burning trees."

Dylan didn't exactly know how Buck had done it, either, but he suspected the Sasquatch had something to do with getting the men out of the smashed car. Crow had been unconscious with a broken leg and hadn't seen them.

"However he managed it," Crow continued, "it still doesn't take away the hijacking."

"What are you going to do when you catch up to him?"

"Arrest him."

"Then what?"

"What do you mean?"

"You've been after Buck for years."

"Decades."

"Okay, decades," Dylan conceded. "What will you do after you arrest him?"

"Retire, I guess."

"Go fishing?"

"I don't fish."

"Travel?"

Crow shook his head.

"Collect stamps? Learn a foreign language? Buy an RV and see the country? Go cruising? Write your memoirs? Get married and have a family?"

Crow shook his head to all of them.

"So what are you going to do all day?"

Crow stared at him for a long time, then said, "The truth is, Dylan, I don't know."

Dylan knew what *he* was going to do. "I'm going to call Buck."

"Be my guest."

Dylan caught Marty in the middle of flipping an omelet.

"I wish there was more than one omelet pan," Marty said. "By the time I get this one finished, the first three will be ruined." He looked at Dylan. "Agent Crow is aboard?"

"Yeah."

"We'll give him the coldest omelet."

"I need to use your Gizmo."

"Back pocket," Marty said.

Dylan fished it out and looked at the screen. "How do I make a call?"

"Depends who you want to call," Marty answered, flipping the omelet again.

"I need to call Buck Johnson. Crow says he's at the jaguar preserve."

"Buck Johnson, from your story?"

Dylan nodded.

Marty slipped the omelet onto the fourth plate. "I'd call Ana. She'll put him on if he's there."

Dylan handed the Gizmo back to him.

"Uh-oh," Marty said.

"What?"

"Blank screen."

"Battery?"

"I don't think so. We better get Ted."

They found him sitting in the pilothouse with Agent Crow. He was staring at his Gizmo, looking perplexed.

"Did you get ahold of Buck?" Crow asked.

"No, the Gizmo is —"

"Dead," Ted said. "Mine, too." He looked at Crow. "Can I borrow your sat phone?"

Crow handed it to him. Ted dialed a number on speaker and let it ring for a long time before ending the call.

"That was Ana's sat phone. She would have answered if she had gotten the call."

He dialed another number, and a voice answered after the first ring.

"Yeah," Al Ikes said.

"It's Ted. I'm using Agent Crow's phone."

"Because your Gizmo is out," Al said. "So are ours. Your tech team on Cryptos is working on the problem, but so far they haven't cracked it. Looks like you've been hacked. Where are you?"

"Just leaving the fuel barge."

"What about the *Rivlan*'s sat feeds?"

"The *Rivlan* was never set up with communications because we have the Gizmos for that," Ted said. "The *Rivlan*'s sat feeds are on a different server, different partition, and they're working fine. I might be able to switch the partition, but that would take time, which we don't have. We need to get to the preserve and find out what's going on. If you find anything out, give Crow a call."

He handed the phone back to Crow.

"I'm not sure what all that meant," Crow said, pocketing the phone. "But I take it that there are some outside forces working against you."

Ted laughed. "You've got that right."

"Noah Blackwood?"

"No doubt." Ted looked at Marty. "You have our grub ready?"

"Our grub is ruined," Marty said.

The grub was not ruined, but it was colder than Marty would have liked. As they all stood and ate in the crowded galley, Ted gave Agent Crow an abridged rundown of the recent skirmishes between Noah Blackwood and Travis Wolfe, leaving out several important details, such as the baby dinosaurs and grand theft helicopter.

Crow listened carefully as he ate his omelet — and half of Marty's — finishing the last bite just as Ted concluded his story.

"Delicious," Crow said, dabbing a bit stray egg from the corner of his mouth with a paper towel. "The best meal I've had since I got down here."

By the way your flesh is hanging on your bones, Marty thought, *it looks like the only meal you've had down here.* "It would have been better to eat fresh from the pan," he said.

"It was still good," Crow said. He looked at Ted. "So this Noah Blackwood is a bad guy."

"That's putting it mildly."

"He hides it well," Crow said. "I've seen his show a couple of times."

"The show is part of the elaborate scam," Ted said.

"So what do you think his intentions are?"

"He'll try to take back what we took from him, then he'll try to kill us," Ted said with a smile on his face.

"The helicopter," Crow said

And his granddaughter, and a couple of dinosaurs, Marty thought.

"Right," Ted said. "You might not want to get mixed up in this."

"Nothing else to do," Crow said.

"Except to arrest Buck Johnson," Dylan said harshly.

"That, too," Crow acknowledged calmly. "I have no real authority down here, but I do have good contacts with Brazilian law enforcement, which could be helpful to you." He put his empty plate in the sink. "Since I'm along for the ride, you might as well introduce me to the rest of your crew."

"This is the rest of the crew," Ted said.

"What? Who's piloting the boat?"

"No one," Ted answered.

A look of alarm crossed Crow's face.

"No worries," Ted said. "The *Rivlan* drives itself at this speed."

"What about logs and river debris?"

"You mean flotsam and jetsam," Marty said. "The *Rivlan* has an automatic garbage detector."

"I hope you're right." Crow looked out the porthole. "Your friend Dr. Wolfe told me this thing was fast. At this rate, we won't get to the jaguar preserve for three days."

"We'll get there a bit faster than that," Ted said. "Do you get motion sickness?"

"I haven't yet, and I've been on the river for months."

Ted looked at his watch. "We better get below and strap in."

"Strap in?" Crow asked. "On this old tub?"

Marty and Dylan just grinned.

SNAP!

Snap!

Grace moved her hand out of reach of the sharp teeth just in time.

"Close one," Luther said. "But look at it this way. If you lose a digit, you still have nine left."

Grace was fond of her fingers and wanted to keep them. It was a little after nine in the morning, but already her black curly hair was matted with sweat. She wasn't sure if it was due more to the heat or her fear of losing a finger. Luther had several scrapes on his hands from near misses. Every time the hatchlings nicked him, he gave a crazy grin, a fist pump, and shouted, "Missed!"

Grace hadn't quite gotten used to Luther's new skinhead look. His bright red hair was starting to grow in around the scabs from his clumsy shave job. Back in civilization, if she had seen him walking down the street toward her, she would have turned and run. In the rain forest, for some reason, he wasn't quite as frightening.

Buck Johnson stood outside the corral watching the feeding. He'd barely taken his eyes off the hatchlings since their unveiling the day before. But he wasn't just watching them, he seemed to be studying them. Ana, on the other hand, was paying scant attention to the hatchlings. Early that morning, when everyone in camp had woken from their fitful sleep, they had discovered that all of their communications were down, including Ana's sat phone. She had spent the entire morning pacing around the small camp trying to find a signal, and was still pacing around, with no luck.

Snap!

"You better watch out," Luther warned.

Grace was worried about the communications being down, too, but she needed to stop thinking about it before she lost a finger. She took a deep breath to clear her mind.

"I don't want to overstep my bounds," Buck called out from across the enclosure. "But I wouldn't mind trying my hand at feeding your friends."

Grace looked at Luther. As head dinosaur keeper, it was his call, not hers.

"Fine with me," Luther said. "As long as you don't *lose* your hand while you try your hand at it. How are your reflexes?"

"I guess we'll find out," Buck said, coming around to their side.

Luther gave him about five minutes of instruction. Buck listened carefully, then said, "You know, I've been watching you for the past half hour, and it seems to me there might be a better way to get the food into them without bloodshed or loss of limb."

"The important thing is for them to get an equal share," Luther said.

"Understood," Buck said, slipping on a pair of disposable gloves.

Grace stepped back and made room for Buck at the rail next to Luther.

"You want the one on the right or the one on the left?" Luther asked.

"I kind of want both of them, if you don't mind."

"I don't mind, but don't blame me if you get bit. They're as fast as cobras."

"I noticed that," Buck said. "I actually don't think you're taking advantage of how fast they are. It might be easier if I just show you."

Luther shrugged. "They're your hands to lose. Go for it." He joined Grace at the rail.

The hatchlings were clearly agitated by the delay. Their heads were bobbing up and down, and their tails were whipping back and forth furiously.

"I'm not sure this is a good idea," Grace whispered.

"It'll be okay," Luther said, but he looked worried.

Buck took two hunks of thawed red meat out of the bucket, one for each hand. The hatchlings got excited thinking they were finally going to be fed, but instead of offering the meat to the hatchlings, Buck held on to it.

Luther shook his head. "If you don't give it to them in the next five seconds, they're going to break down the barrier and eat you!"

Buck shook his head without taking his eyes off the hatchlings' bobbing heads. "I don't think so. Watch."

At the moment the hatchlings' heads were the farthest apart from each other, Buck tossed the meat up into the air.

The hatchlings snapped at the meat like a pair of falcons

snatching pigeons on the fly. The meat disappeared down their long throats.

"Wow!" Grace said.

Luther scowled. "Lucky toss."

Buck threw two more hunks of meat.

Snap! Snap!

Gone.

The hatchlings appeared to love the new feeding technique. Their heads weren't bobbing around, they weren't trying to bite each other, they weren't smashing themselves against the barrier anymore, and Buck's fingers were still intact.

Ana walked up. "What's going on?"

"Dino breakfast," Buck said, tossing two more chunks.

Snap! Snap!

"Can I try?" Grace asked.

"Sure," Buck said. "They're your dinosaurs."

Grace stepped up, grabbed some meat, and gave it a toss.

Snap! Snap!

"This is going to make the feedings a lot faster," she said.

"And safer," Luther pointed out as he gave the new technique a try.

Snap! Snap!

"Feeds will be twice as fast," Luther said. "The other great thing about feeding on the fly is that we'll only need one person to do the feeds now. That will give me a chance to look around, maybe do some canopy zip-lining."

"You're not doing any zip-lining until Flanna gets back," Ana said.

"Okay," Luther said.

Grace narrowed her eyes at him. It wasn't like Luther to give in so easily.

"What?" Luther said.

"Flanna may not be back for days."

"I guess I'll just have to wait."

Grace knew Luther had no intention of waiting.

The worst part of going fast was slowing down.

If you were going to puke, this is when it would happen. Ted pulled back on the throttle, slowing the *Rivlan* down from nearly two hundred miles per hour to ten miles per hour in about five seconds, sending everyone's stomachs to the tips of their toes. Marty looked at Crow. The agent's tropical tan had turned a pale shade of green. Marty knew exactly how he felt. It probably hadn't been the best idea to serve cold omelets slathered in congealed butter just before takeoff. Dylan was out of his chair, mouth covered, rushing up to the deck. Crow was fumbling with his seat belt. It didn't look like he was going to make it before something embarrassing happened, but he managed to get himself free and hurried up the steps behind Dylan.

Ted swiveled around when he heard the retching from above. "Oops! Guess I should have slowed down a bit more slowly. You okay?"

Marty was about to say something about land lubbers and their weak stomachs, but then he heard Crow's heaves joining Dylan's. Marty barely made it to the gunwale before he lost everything.

A few minutes later, Ted joined them on deck, carrying three bottles of water. "You need to rehydrate," he said.

Crow, Dylan, and Marty clung to the rail and shook their heads. Ted leaned over the side. The surface looked like it was boiling.

"Piranhas?" Marty managed to ask between retches.

"Definitely," Ted affirmed.

The *Rivlan* steered itself around a bend, and they saw why Ted had slowed down. There were at least a dozen boats on the water in front of them. Beyond the boats was a good-sized town belching out a ton of smoke and pollution. The rain forest had been cut down for as far as they could see on both sides of the wide river.

"I didn't see this town on the map," Dylan said, taking one of the bottles.

"It hasn't been here long enough to be put on a map," Crow said. "I'm not even sure it has an official name. I was here a couple of months ago. The locals call it Sorrow. And there's plenty of that onshore. Someone discovered gold here eight months ago, and from what I understand it's almost tapped out now." Crow took a tentative sip of water, belched, but managed to keep the sip where it belonged.

"Sorry about the abrupt slowdown," Ted apologized. "I'll try to ease into it next time, but it will be a while before we can speed up again. There's a lot of boat traffic the next ten or fifteen miles. It opens up after that."

"What kind of boat *is* this exactly?" Crow asked.

"Experimental," Ted answered. "Fast."

"Fast?" Crow said. "It's impossible. I've never . . ."

Marty was barely listening, and it wasn't because of his stomach. It was sorrow. He'd read about rain forest destruction and had watched documentaries about it, but that hadn't prepared him for the devastation before him. It looked like the Grim Reaper had mowed the trees down with a giant scythe, then set them on fire. The smoke burned his eyes. He walked over to his hammock, took the binoculars out of his pack, and rejoined the group at the rail. The devastation looked worse close-up. People were cooking food over fires. Dozens of half-naked little kids ran around with oozing sores on their arms and legs. Ramshackle stores displayed unrefrigerated baskets of meat and fish. Other people were selling what looked like used camp supplies, such as tents, picks, and shovels — no doubt from gold diggers who had gone bust. There were a lot people hanging out on the muddy streets. Most of them were men. Most of them were drinking. Marty gazed at the dock along the river in front of the town. Ted had been wrong about the barge being the last place to gas up. The dock was stacked with fifty-gallon barrels. They were refueling a large boat called the *Anjo* that was clearly a cut above all the other boats on the river, including the *Rivlan*, at least on the outside. He glassed the people on board. The men were dressed in jungle fatigues and looked fit. They were carrying sidearms, but somehow he didn't think they were with the Brazilian Army or police. A woman came up from below deck and began talking to one of the camo guys. Marty almost dropped the binoculars in the river.

"Yvonne," he said.

Dylan grabbed the binoculars, nearly taking Marty's head off with the strap.

"Where?" Ted asked.

"On that boat getting fuel," Marty replied.

"Who's Yvonne?" Crow asked.

"I see her," Dylan said. "Who are those guys with her?"

"May I?" Ted held his hand out for the binoculars. Marty ducked out of the strap, and Dylan handed them over.

Ted checked out the boat. "Mercenaries," he said. "Probably some of the same guys that attacked the *Coelacanth.*"

"What's a Coelacanth?" Crow asked.

"A prehistoric fish," Marty answered. "A cryptid. Rediscovered in 1938 in South Africa. By —"

"It's the name of our research ship," Ted interrupted. "The one Noah Blackwood tried to sink off the coast of New Zealand, where we were capturing a giant squid."

Crow took a look through the binoculars. "They do seem to be military. And one of them is looking at us through his binoculars."

Marty took the binoculars from him. Crow was right. One of the camo guys was zeroed in on them. He said something. Yvonne walked over to him and peered through the binoculars. "Busted," Marty said. "Yvonne's spotted us. What do we do?"

Ted smiled. "The only thing to do is to give her a friendly wave."

Marty was happy to oblige. Yvonne returned the wave with a gesture of her own, and it wasn't exactly friendly.

"Time to go below," Ted said. "We're just about through the boat traffic. When we get around the bend, clear sailing for about five miles. Someone will need to keep an eye on them."

Marty handed the binoculars to Dylan and grinned. "Hang on tight up here."

"I think it's Agent Crow's turn," Dylan said.

"Knock it off," Ted said. "The Gizmo comm is down, but the dragonspy should be working. It's on a different partition. Launch it."

"Dragonspy?" Crow asked.

"It'd be easier to show you." Marty pulled the Gizmo out of his pocket and pushed the WAKE icon. A tiny drawer slid open, revealing a golden insect the size of a dragonfly. Its wings unfolded. He pushed another button, and the dragonspy rose into the air on two sets of wings. He flew it around the cluttered deck, then brought it to a hover just above Crow's head.

"Amazing," Crow said. "What powers it?"

"Light," Marty answered. "The wings double as solar panels."

Crow looked at Ted. "It's like a miniature drone. I can see now why the CIA is keeping an eye on you. They don't want anyone else to get this technology."

"You're right," Ted said. "If they had their choice, they'd keep us restricted to Cryptos Island, surrounded by the navy." He reached into his pocket, pulled out a pair of glasses, and handed them to Marty.

"What are these?" Marty said.

"Put them on."

The glasses had straps on the arms to keep them from falling off. Marty slipped them on and was rewarded with a perfect dragonspy's-eye view from the corner of each lens. "Whoa! Google Glass?"

Ted shook his head. "Spyglass. Why limit your vision to what your eyes are looking at? There's audio as well. Try not to lose them. They're the only pair in existence."

Meaning they're probably worth a million dollars, Marty thought. "What does *Anjo* mean?" he asked aloud.

"It's Portuguese for 'angel,'" Crow answered.

"Oh, brother," Marty said. "That boat should be called *Satan* instead."

He flew the dragonspy over to the *Anjo* and they went below.

Yvonne pulled out her sat phone and called Blackwood as she watched the *Rivlan* limp its way upriver. Noah answered on the first ring.

"Yes."

She told him about the *Rivlan*.

"Where are you?"

"Some godforsaken river town getting refueled."

"What does the *Rivlan* look like?"

"It's a junker."

"Right, just like the *Coelacanth* was a junker," Noah said. "Their boat may look like junk, but I can assure you, it isn't. Who's on board?"

"Marty, Dylan, Ted, and an old guy I've never seen before. There could be other people below that I didn't see."

"Tell me more about the old guy," Noah finally said.

"In his seventies. Tropically baked. American, I'd guess."

"What else?" Noah asked.

"They have a lot of gear strapped to the deck. Can't tell what it is."

"Just follow them," Noah said. "We don't want to make a move on them until we have everything in place. Make sure they don't spot you. Got it?"

Yvonne's stomach lurched. She thought about lying to him, but it was too late. Her hesitation gave her away.

"Don't tell me they saw you," Noah said.

"They spotted us before we spotted them," she admitted.

"How could you let that happen?"

"I thought we were way ahead of them."

"Apparently, that 'junker,' as you call it, is faster than you think," Noah said.

"What do you want us to do?"

"Can you take them out?"

Yvonne looked out at the river. The *Rivlan* was two hundred yards ahead, and it didn't seem to be in any hurry. "Not here," she answered. "Too many witnesses. We should be able to catch them upriver, though."

"Get on it," Noah snapped. "Everything and everyone aboard is expendable."

"What about Grace and the hatchlings?"

"They're not aboard the *Rivlan*," Noah answered.

"How do you know?"

"Do you think you're the only person working for me in Brazil?" Noah asked.

"I guess not," Yvonne said, wishing she could take the question back.

"Apparently, you haven't used the telemetry gear I gave you," Noah said.

"You didn't tell me what it's for."

"It's for the hatchlings," Noah said.

"Oh, the —"

"Exactly," Noah interrupted. "The hatchlings and Grace are already at the jaguar preserve. Your job is to make sure the *Rivlan* and its passengers don't join them there."

"What are the rules of engagement?"

"Make it look like a tragic accident. If you fail to make it look like an accident, I will have you killed. How does that sound?" Noah ended the call.

Yvonne kept the phone to her ear as if Noah was on the still on the phone talking to her. The three men with her, whom she hadn't met until she arrived in Manaus, stared at her with hard eyes. She forced herself to smile as if Noah were saying something humorous to her — as if he hadn't just threatened to kill her if she failed. Noah had told the men that she was in charge, something that did not sit well with them. Now she wondered if she really was the one running the show here. Noah said he would *have* her killed. Were these her executioners?

"Okay, then," she said cheerfully. "I'll let you know. Bye-bye."

The men continued to stare at her.

"What's the story?" Spike said.

They all had ridiculously stupid nicknames. Spike, Blade, Point. Spike seemed to be the one in charge. When they weren't leering at her, they were doing sit-ups and push-ups, sharpening their knives, and cleaning their guns.

"We have the go to take them out," Yvonne said.

"*The go*, huh?" Spike said.

The three men laughed.

Yvonne ignored them and reminded herself not to use military terms again. "We're supposed to make it look like an accident," she said.

"Guess that negates using rocket-propelled grenades," Edge said.

"Yeah, and machine guns. Bummer," Blade said.

Another round of laughter.

"What's your plan?" Spike asked.

"I'm an animal trainer, not a soldier," Yvonne said.

"Yeah, I got that," Spike said. "We need a dog trained or something, we'll let you know. How about we follow them upriver, catch 'em along a lonely stretch of water, board 'em, kill 'em, then scuttle their boat, making it look like they ran into something, or exploded. That sound good?"

Yvonne nodded.

"Cast off!" Spike shouted, and climbed up to the wheelhouse.

Yvonne made her way to the bow.

Spike backed the *Anjo* away from the dock and swung it around. When he reached the main channel, he pushed the throttle to full bore. The powerful engines roared and the bow lurched up. Yvonne stumbled, but caught the rail before she fell backward. She turned and looked up at the wheelhouse. Spike gave her a nasty grin and a sarcastic salute.

Yvonne could hardly wait to get off the boat and out of Brazil, but not before she reunited with Marty and Dylan for a little payback. First, they had stolen the hatchlings from under her nose, humiliating her in front of Noah Blackwood. Then they had nearly scared her to death by shoving her into a pitch-black laboratory with the chupacabra. It didn't matter that the chupacabra had turned out to be a harmless pot-bellied pig. She had been in that room for over an hour on top of a lab bench, convinced that the chupacabra was going to tear her throat out at any second. The fear she'd felt then still haunted her, but it wasn't the worst part. The whole experience was made infinitely more humiliating by the fact that it was Butch McCall who had saved her. He'd burst into the room with his gun drawn. She had never been so happy to see someone in her life . . . until he switched the light on and they saw the pig wearing the chupacabra's harness. Yvonne had screamed in rage. Butch had collapsed onto the floor in a fit of laughter. She had never heard Butch laugh before; she had barely seen him smile. The pig had run over Butch and out the door, squealing. This had made him laugh even harder. Making it worse, when Butch told Noah what the boys had done to her, Noah had laughed, too, in spite of the fact that he'd wanted to kill both Yvonne and Butch for costing him the hatchlings, his panda cubs, the four children, his helicopter, and his pride.

Yvonne had to hang on tightly as Spike brought the *Anjo* around the bend. In front of them was a stretch of straightaway that went on for miles. There wasn't a single boat on the water for as far as they could see.

Spike slowed the *Anjo* to a crawl. Yvonne turned and looked up at the wheelhouse. He had handed control of the boat over to one of his men and was coming down the gangway carrying two pairs of binoculars. He passed her a pair.

"They either found a tributary, or they're hiding in the cover along shore," he said. "It'll take some time, but we'll flush 'em out."

Yvonne shook her head. They hadn't found a tributary. They weren't hiding. "They're gone," she said.

Marty and the others smiled down at the Gizmo screen at Yvonne's frowning face. Marty had taken off the spyglasses so that everyone could see what the dragonspy was tracking.

"We're not gone," he said. "We're thirty miles upriver from you."

"Thirty-two point six," Ted corrected. They were all back on deck again as the *Rivlan* slowly chugged its way through another logjam of boats. "Checking the tributaries is going to slow them way down. There are hundreds of them along the Amazon. It's incredible how difficult it can be to find someone along the same river."

"Tell me about it," Crow said. "I've been down here for months looking for Buckley Johnson. And I don't think he's been trying to hide from me."

"How did you find him anyway?" Dylan asked.

"Luck," Crow said. "I tracked him from Arizona to Mexico. Lost him in Mexico, then picked his up his trail again in Costa Rica. Lost him again in Rio, then picked the trail back up in Manaus, then lost him again. I wandered from town to town, village to village, for months. I was about ready to hang it up when I ran into a guy who wholesales carrots."

"Carrots?" Marty asked.

"Oh, man!" Dylan said. "Caught by his carrot addiction."

"What are you talking about?" Ted asked.

"Buck lives on raw carrots," Dylan explained. "It's almost all he eats."

"Bucks Bunny," Marty said.

"That's really bad," Dylan said.

"Anyway," Crow continued, "the carrot wholesaler said that a guy named Buck shows up at his warehouse once a month like clockwork and loads up. Said he was a biologist working at Lansa's jag preserve. And that I had just missed him. He came through a few days before I got there with two women and a young guy. I got ahold of the local police, and they gave me a lift upriver after I gave them a bucket of cash. They wouldn't take me any farther than the fuel barge. That's when Travis Wolfe flew in on Noah Blackwood's helicopter." Crow looked at Ted. "What exactly is your beef with Noah Blackwood?"

"It's a long and sordid story," Ted said.

Crow pointed upriver at the heavy boat traffic. "Looks like we have some time."

Ted began, "It started out with Noah hiring Wolfe and me to catch a great white shark for him . . ."

WALKING IN THE RAIN

Luther was at the edge of camp watching a thick line of army ants destroying and eating everything in their path.

The hatchlings had been fed. Buck was trying to pick up radio signals from the collared jaguars — with no success because every communication device in the camp was down. Grace and Ana were sitting outside their hut having an intense girls-only conversation, which Luther had absolutely no interest in.

He looked at his watch. I would be several hours until the next feeding.

Or food toss, he thought. Buck's new feeding technique was efficient, taking a fraction of time as his own, but it was also boring. Ana had said that they should all stay in camp until there was word from Wolfe or Laurel.

It was more of a suggestion than an order, Luther thought. *And who put her in charge anyway? Time to check this place out.*

He went into Jake's hut and found an old climbing harness and a cracked helmet.

Now all he had to do was find a way up into Flanna's web. He thought about telling Ana he was going to do a little canopy exploration, but he was pretty sure she wouldn't be on board, so he decided to use the *don't tell, don't hear no* technique, which had worked well for him most of his life. He took the path farthest from the huts.

Several things struck him about the rain forest. He had known it was going to be hot and humid, but knowing it didn't prepare him for how it actually felt. The air was thick and stifling, making it hard to breathe. His T-shirt, pants, socks, and underwear were drenched in sweat. The other thing that surprised him was the noise. The rain forest echoed loudly with buzzing, clicking, chirping, squeaking, screaming, chattering, rustling, and other creeping sounds. Luther walked down the narrow path feeling like there were a thousand eyes on him.

Something bit him on the neck. He slapped it and in the process cut the back of his hand on a razor-sharp leaf, which hurt worse than the bug bite. It seemed like everything in the rain forest was out to get him.

Death by a thousand cuts.

He tried to stay in the middle of the path to avoid getting sliced or poked. The ground was squishy and covered with centipedes, beetles, spiders, and other mean-looking crawly things he couldn't identify. Above him, the canopy was so tightly woven that light barely reached the ground. He was starting to feel a little claustrophobic.

Squeezed.

The wind picked up, blowing cloudlike mist into the upper branches, dimming the light that reached the forest floor even further. A troop of monkeys scampered down to the lower branches and chattered at him.

"Hello to you, too," he said, putting on the cracked helmet in case one of them pooped on him. A moment later, one of them did.

"Kind of rude," Luther said. "But a nice shot."

He took off his helmet and wiped it on the ground. The monkey's chattering sounded like laughter. As he scraped off the last smear, the chattering stopped. Luther looked up to see what was going on with the jokesters. They were scurrying away in silent panic. When he looked back down, he realized he wasn't alone. He was being watched.

"What the —"

Six brown eyes, three heavily tattooed faces, unsmiling, and dead serious. Three blowpipes pointed inches from his stubbled head. As he always did in dire situations, Luther tried to defuse the problem by flashing his trademark grin. It didn't work. The blowpipes remained in place, unwavering. Luther's grin turned into a grimace. He was three breaths away from being turned into a pincushion. He put his hands up in the air very, very slowly, hoping they knew what he meant. They didn't appear to. They continued to hold their breaths. Since the newcomers were frozen like statues, Luther had plenty of time to look at them, and he didn't like what he saw. They were stocky and short, not much more than four feet tall, but they were powerfully built and nimble looking. They were barefoot and naked aside from small flaps of leather over their privates, held up by strings around their waists. A pouch hung on each of the strings. Luther assumed the pouches were filled with more lethal darts. Hanging next to the pouches were wicked-looking clubs with two-foot handles, each topped by a ball the size of a large grapefruit. The tattoos on the men's faces, arms, and chests were jaguar spots.

Definitely a cat-and-mouse thing going on here. And I'm the mouse.

The men lowered their blowpipes. Luther let out a long sigh of relief until he saw that their teeth looked like they had been sharpened with files, which could not be a good thing. One of them tore the tracking tag off his neck and snapped it in two. The other two grabbed him and tied his wrists in front of him with an itchy vine rope. Luther thought about resisting, but it was already too late. He thought about screaming his head off like he had at Noah's Ark when Butch had grabbed him, but there wasn't much point in that, either. He was a long way from camp.

Maybe the monkeys will come back and rescue me.

He looked up at the canopy. Rain was dripping through the thick cover. The monkeys were nowhere to be seen.

Cowards.

The three jaguar men seemed to relax a little after they tied his hands, which made Luther more nervous. One of them touched the stubble on his head, said something to the others, and they all laughed. Luther was used to people laughing and making snide remarks about his hair, but he wasn't used to someone examining his head like a future trophy. He thought back to all the images of shrunken heads he had seen and took some solace in the fact that all the shriveled former humans had long hair. Luther's hair grew fast, but he figured he had a couple of weeks before they severed his head and filled it with hot sand to shrink it.

He held his hands out. "This vine might cause a rash."

They ignored the complaint.

"My parents are, like, billionaires, and I'm their only son. You really think they're going to let you shrink my head? They'll come after you big-time."

He wasn't exactly sure about this. He hadn't heard from his parents in days, and quite honestly they didn't know where he was. The last time he'd texted them, he had kind of forgotten to tell them he was heading down to the Amazon.

He decided to see what would happen if he just started walking toward camp. One of the jaguar men immediately whacked him across the legs with his blowpipe.

"Hey!" Luther shouted. "That hurt!"

His response got him a second whack on his shoulder.

"Why don't you untie me and give *me* a stick? See how you like it."

This elicited a third whack across his back.

"Ouch!"

The jaguar men pointed their blowpipes in the opposite direction of the camp.

"Okay, okay, but the only reason I'm going with you is because I'm curious to see where you live. Otherwise, I'd be heading back to the jaguar preserve. Going with you is my choice, not yours."

The jaguar men stared at him.

He started walking in the direction they were pointing. The rain was falling harder now, finding its way to the ground through the thick canopy. They wouldn't miss him back at camp until the next dino feed, which was still several hours away. They'd have to track him in the dark, which was going to be difficult, and the rain wasn't going to help.

Ten minutes into Luther's forced march, they passed a tree with a rope ladder dangling against the trunk. Luther kicked himself. If he hadn't dawdled along the trail, he might have been able to get to the tree before they grabbed him. They would never have been able to catch him on a zip line.

The jaguar men came to a stop a couple of hundred yards

past the tree and started talking among themselves. Luther couldn't understand a word they were saying, but he was glad to see they at least had language. He watched them carefully and listened intensely. Foreign languages were not his strong suit, but if he could pick up a few words, he might be able to communicate with them. His goal was to be able to say *Please don't kill me!* in their language by the time they got to wherever they were taking him.

One of the men stepped off the trail and started gently parting the thick bushes as if he were looking for something. The other two directed him to the right. He moved a few feet, parted some more bushes, then nodded. They prodded Luther off the trail.

The road less traveled, or in this case, the trail less traveled, hidden by a green tangle of vicious leaves.

He was certain that Doc and Laurel, Wolfe and Raul, Flanna, and even Jake were all good trackers, but they were gone. He wasn't sure whether Ana or Buck possessed any tracking skills, and he doubted Grace would know what to look for. He was going to have to give them some help. He decided to do this by tripping and breaking as many leaves and branches as he could on the way down. He knew he'd slice his hands up, but it couldn't be any worse than the hatchling bites he already had. Luther stumbled and fell forward with his arms outstretched. Unfortunately, the jaguar men anticipated the move and caught him before he touched a single leaf. He struggled to get away, knowing he would fail, but escape wasn't the point. Damage was the point. The jaguar men anticipated this as well. One of them clubbed him on the head. Luther's world went from green to black.

DAY FOUR

DEAD IN THE WATER

Ted slowed the *Rivlan* down just after midnight. Marty, Dylan, and Agent Crow were all strapped into their chairs behind him.

Marty looked at the monitors, which had been going in and out for the past hour and a half. It had gotten so bad that Ted had him pull the dragonspy off Yvonne and the *Anjo* to scan the boat traffic upriver instead.

"It's clear up ahead. Why are you slowing down?"

"Because we've arrived," Ted answered. "Almost, anyway. You can all unbuckle. We'll go up top for the final leg."

Marty was happy to get out of his chair at last. He landed the dragonspy outside the wheelhouse, slipped off the spyglasses, and was about to put the Gizmo in his pocket when Ted stopped him.

"We're not done with that. I want you to fly the bot back downriver and check on Yvonne and her crew. We need to keep an eye on her."

"Mind if I skip the spyglasses? They work great, but it's hard to walk and fly at the same time."

"Fine, but don't lose them."

Marty buttoned the glasses into his cargo pants.

They climbed up to the deck and were hit by a blast of hot, humid air, which was a shock after coming from the air-conditioned helm. It was raining and pitch-dark outside.

Ted pointed a floodlight at a narrow tributary emptying into the Amazon. "The jaguar camp is up there about a half a mile. I'm going to steer the *Rivlan* in the old-fashioned way, manually." He sent Dylan and Crow to the bow to keep an eye out for flotsam and jetsam, then climbed up to the wheelhouse and swung the *Rivlan* toward the opening.

Marty sat down on the gunwale and relaunched the dragonspy. He figured the only way to find the *Anjo* was to buzz all the boats heading upriver, ignoring the boats at anchor or tied up to shore. He was certain Yvonne was not sleeping. The boats were easy to pick out in the dark because they all used running lights and had people stationed at the bow looking out for things that might sink them and turn them into piranha chow. The bot was night-vision capable, but picking out details in the greenish hue wasn't easy. There were three people aboard the first boat. One in the pilothouse, one on the bow with a spotlight and a pike to push debris away, and a third in the stern lying on the deck sound asleep.

Definitely not whacked-out mercenaries. One boat down, a thousand to go.

Staring at the Gizmo screen and hopscotching the dragonspy from boat to boat made Marty forget he was heading up a narrow tributary. He was abruptly reminded when a huge branch whacked him on the side of the head. He shouted out for help and caught himself from going over the side by just four fingers. Crow grabbed him by the wrist a second before he was scraped off the side of the hull, and pulled him over the gunwale like a dead fish.

Crow looked down at him splayed out on the deck. "You need to be more careful."

"Duh *du jour*."

"What?"

"Yeah," Marty translated. He sat up, wiping tree slime off his face and arms.

"You better check for leeches," Crow said. "Bet you got a load of them."

Leeches were nothing new to Marty. He'd been covered with them before. He was more worried about the Gizmo. He had dropped it when he got smacked overboard, and he wasn't sure if it had fallen on deck or into the water.

Crow bent down. "You looking for this?" He picked up the Gizmo and looked at the screen. "What's that spy bug thing doing?"

"Dragonspy," Marty said, taking the Gizmo from him. It didn't seem the worse for wear. "It's in a hover. That's what it does when you take your hands off the controls. Stops it from crashing."

"You better stay in the center of the boat so *you* don't crash."

"Good safety tip," Marty said.

Crow walked back up to the bow. Marty got back to tracking killers. He was getting good at jumping the dragonspy from boat to boat and was making good time downriver. He skipped the slow boats, barges, and dugout canoes, concentrating on boats with motors moving fast. He was guiding the dragonspy around one of these when another boat zipped by, rocking the boat the dragonspy was on in its wake. The men aboard shook their fists and swore.

Marty caught the speeding boat about a mile upriver. He flew the dragonspy into the open door of the wheelhouse.

Gotcha!

Yvonne was standing next to the goon piloting the boat, scanning the river through a pair of night-vision binoculars.

"You sure you didn't miss them?" the goon mumbled. He had a nasty chewed cigar stuck in his mouth.

"I don't think so," Yvonne said.

"If I was them, I'd hide up one of the tributaries, wait for us to shoot by, then head back downriver."

"They are not going back downriver, Spike," Yvonne said, the binoculars still glued to her eyes. "They are heading directly to the jaguar preserve."

"Yeah? We've been running full bore since we saw them. How are they staying in front of us in that junker?"

"It's not a junker. They're faster than us."

"Hard to believe."

Yvonne unclipped her sat phone from her belt and held it out to him. "You want to call Blackwood and ask him about it? I'm sure he'd be delighted to hear from you."

"No thanks. It's your show. And your head if you're wrong. What's the preserve setup?"

"I don't know. "

"Doesn't matter. How hard can it be to take out a bunch of science geeks?"

Harder than you think, Marty thought. He looked at the corner of the Gizmo screen. The dragonspy had calculated the *Anjo*'s distance and speed. Yvonne would be at the jaguar preserve in a little over two hours.

Ted brought the *Rivlan* to a stop and stepped out of the wheelhouse wearing a headlamp. Dylan and Crow tied the *Rivlan* to the dock next to the helicopter.

"They'll be here in two hours," Marty announced.

"That quick," Ted said. "Guess they decided to come directly here."

"And kill us," Marty said. He told them about the conversation he had overheard.

"They're consistent anyway," Ted said.

"Where's our greeting party?" Dylan asked.

"I hope they're sleeping," Ted said. "Let's go wake them up."

Marty put on his headlamp and gave his spare to Crow.

They followed the path up to the camp. The only light came from the untended campfire in the center of the huts. It cast an eerie hue on the surrounding forest.

"What's that smell?" Crow asked, sniffing the air.

"Uh, that's —"

"We'll get to that in a minute," Ted said, cutting Marty off.

He'd been about to say *dinosaurs*.

Ted called out a hello. No one answered.

"Wait here," Crow said. "I'll check the huts out."

"Why you?" Ted asked.

Crow pulled a pistol out of his waistband. "Because I have this." He walked into the first hut.

"Let's take a look at the hatchlings to see if they're okay," Ted said. "Actually to see if they're still here."

They walked over to the building attached to the corral and

switched on the lights. The hatchlings were in the holding area sound asleep.

"They've been fed recently," Marty said.

"What makes you say that?" Ted asked.

"Because they have two modes," Marty answered. "Screaming and starving. Sleeping and farting."

Crow walked into the holding area. "The huts are empty. What are those?"

"Those are a couple of dinosaurs," Dylan answered.

"That's impossible. Where —"

"Mokélé-mbembé," Marty said. "From the Congo."

"So this is what Blackwood is really after," Crow said. "You didn't tell me about these on the *Rivlan*."

"Would you have believed me?" Ted asked.

"No," Crow said flatly, without taking his eyes off the snoring hatchlings.

"Blackwood is after everything," Ted said. "I know this is a lot to take in, but we have more pressing matters at the moment. No one in any of the huts?"

"Empty. No sign of a struggle."

"I'm not sure what's going on, but the fact that the hatchlings are still here is a good sign. If Blackwood or his people had been here, they wouldn't have left the hatchlings behind."

"Then where is everybody?" Marty asked.

"I have no idea. All I know is that it's time to go on the offensive. We can't help anyone if we get captured or killed. Our first priority is to protect ourselves. I want you and Dylan to stay here. Feed the hatchlings when they wake up. Crow and I will head downriver and see if we can stop Yvonne, or at least slow her down."

"I will?" Crow asked.

"Of course, you don't *have* to," Ted said. "This isn't your fight. But I could use your help."

Crow gave him a curt nod. "Seeing as Buck Johnson doesn't seem to be here at the moment, either, I might as well give you a hand. If for no other reason than to make sure you don't do anything illegal."

"Can't guarantee that," Ted said.

Crow smiled. "I have a broad definition of *illegal* when it comes to stopping bad people."

"Glad to hear it." Ted looked at Marty. "Do you have any spare tracking tags?"

"I have a couple in my pack."

"Perfect. While you're feeding the hatchlings, you might want to figure out how to get tracking tags on them."

"The tags aren't working," Marty pointed out.

"As soon as we get a break from people trying to kill us, I'll look into that and try to get them back online. If we aren't successful in stopping Yvonne, you're going to need to get out of here. If you need to run, you won't be able to take the hatchlings with you. You'll need to let them go so Blackwood doesn't get them."

"But they'll starve," Marty protested.

Ted shook his head. "They'll get hungry, and then they'll figure it out, just like every living organism on earth, including you and me. The rain forest is full of food."

As if to prove Ted's point, one of the hatchlings raised its head, took a vicious snap out of the air, then put its head back down, all without opening its eyes.

"Bad dream," Dylan said.

"Bad news for us if they don't want tags around their necks," Marty said. "How are we going to stay in touch with you?"

Ted looked at Crow. "That reminds me. . . . Is your sat phone working?"

Crow took it out and shook his head. "No signal."

"I'm not sure how he did it, but Blackwood has jammed all communications here. On the bright side, that means he can't communicate, either. Jamming signals is an all or nothing proposition, with the exception of the dragonspy, which he obviously doesn't know about. We'll use it to stay in touch."

"It'll be a one-way conversation," Marty said. The person flying the dragonspy could hear sounds and people within the dragonspy's range but couldn't talk to them. Marty held his Gizmo out for Ted.

"You keep it," Ted said. "You're a better bot pilot than I am, and I'm going to have my hands full with the *Rivlan*. We'll figure out a way to communicate when I'm back on board." He looked at his watch. "Time to go. Stay alert. We'll be back. Good luck."

"You know," Crow said. "I'm not that comfortable leaving a couple of kids by themselves in the jungle."

Ted smiled. "They're more resourceful than they look."

"Thanks a lot, Ted," Marty said.

"And they're faster than we are," Ted added. "If they have to run, we'd just slow them down."

Crow gave him a reluctant nod, threw one last glance at the hatchlings, then followed Ted down the dark trail back to the dock.

Marty watched them go, then turned to Dylan. "You want to get the meat buckets ready?" Marty asked. "I'll check out the huts to see if I can find something to attach the tracking tags."

Marty walked over to the closest hut. It was obvious that it was being used by Grace and Ana. There was a Moleskine journal on one of the hammocks, with a fountain pen stuck between its pages. On the other side of the hut, Ana's laptop sat on a crude desk made from a split log.

He knew better than to peek inside Grace's journal.

But this is an emergency!

It turned out it wasn't Grace's Moleskine. He could tell from the smell that it was one of Rose's journals. He flipped through the pages quickly, admiring the sketches and wondering why she had drawn them. All he knew was that the swollen journal had nothing to do with their current dilemma. He tossed it back on the hammock and hurried over to Ana's laptop. Her last journal entry was on the screen. She was frantic about the communications being down and everyone disappearing. She felt as if they were getting picked off one by one. Marty scanned the entry quickly until he reached the final paragraph.

> Now Luther is gone. . . . We don't know if he wandered away from camp or was taken. Buck and I are going to go out looking for him. Grace is going to stay in camp and feed the hatchlings, which have just woken up.

This meant that Ana and Buck had been gone for several hours, and Luther a lot longer than that.

Where's Grace?

He started to leave the hut, then remembered why he'd

come here in the first place. He rummaged through a cupboard and found a roll of twine.

Dylan had the buckets ready, and the hatchlings were snapping the air so wildly Marty thought their sharp teeth would shatter. Getting a string around their necks with the tracking tags was not going to be easy. He decided to wait until they were asleep to give it a shot.

As they fed the hungry hatchlings, Marty told Dylan about what he had learned from Ana's computer.

Snap!

"So we have ten people missing in the rain forest," Dylan said.

Snap!

"Dang, that was close!" Marty checked his fingers to make sure they were all there, then fished out another hunk of meat from the bucket. "I guess you're right. Ten missing in ac—"

"I'm not missing and you're feeding them all wrong."

Marty and Dylan whirled around. Grace was standing three feet behind them, looking as if she had been swimming in a swamp, swallowed by a gator, and spit back out. She was covered with leaves and slime from the top of her head to the bottoms of her boots.

"What happened to you?" Marty asked.

"I got lost. Found my way back here by the lights. And your loud voices. Ana and Buck aren't back?"

Marty shook his head.

"Luther?"

"No," Marty said, wiping the blood off his hands.

"Where's Ted?"

Marty told her about Yvonne.

"Slowing Yvonne down won't do us any good," Grace said. "He needs to kill her."

Hearing this from his normally pacifist cousin and former twin was a little shocking.

"That's not how Ted and Wolfe do things," Marty said. "Which is what separates them from Noah Blackwood. And what do you mean we're feeding the hatchlings wrong?"

Grace stepped forward, grabbed a couple of pieces of meat, and tossed them into the air.

Snap! Snap!

"Oh," Marty said.

"Wow," Dylan said.

"Buck came up with the technique."

"You mean Buckley Johnson?" Marty asked.

"I guess. Everyone here calls him Buck." Grace continued tossing meat, finishing up the feeding in less than two minutes. She opened the corral door and the hatchlings staggered outside full as ticks, then collapsed on the ground and fell asleep. "I'm going to change," she said.

"That would be good," Marty said. "Then we can figure out what we're going to do." He turned to Dylan and showed him the roll of twine. "Time to lasso a couple of sleeping dinosaurs."

Getting the tags on the hatchlings turned out to be no big deal. The worst part was being so close to them as they digested their food. By the time they finished, Grace had reappeared looking more like herself and less like a swamp monster.

"What are you doing?"

"Tagging dinosaurs," Dylan said.

Grace shook her head. "I knew it would happen."

"What?" Dylan asked.

"I knew if you hung around Marty and Luther, they'd corrupt you. You'd start sounding just like them. It's a disease. Incurable."

Dylan grinned and climbed over the fence. "Tracking tags," he said.

"Why?"

"In case we have to let them go," Marty answered, joining Dylan.

"We're not letting them go!" Grace protested.

"I said *in case*." Marty walked over to the water bucket and washed the gore off his hands. "Tell us what's been going on here."

When Grace finished filling them in, they all gathered around the Gizmo. Yvonne was still in the wheelhouse next to G.I. Joe, barreling up the Amazon in the *Anjo*.

"She doesn't seem to be slowing down," Dylan said.

Marty looked at the GPS. The *Anjo* was an hour away. He flew the dragonspy out of the *Anjo*'s wheelhouse to look for the *Rivlan*. He found it about a mile upriver.

"What are they doing?" Grace asked.

The *Rivlan* was slowly chugging across the river from right to left. Ted and Crow were standing at the stern looking at something behind them. "I don't know," Marty said. "But if they don't hurry up, Yvonne will be on them. She's only a few minutes away."

They continued their odd course all the way to the left bank. Ted jumped off the boat to shore. Even with night vision they couldn't tell what he was doing. Marty flew the dragonspy higher to get a bird's-eye view.

Yvonne's boat was tearing up the middle of the river. When it got parallel to the *Rivlan*, there was a loud, grinding explosion.

Yvonne's boat went airborne for about twenty-five yards, then slammed back onto the water like a rock.

"They pulled a bunch of flotsam and jetsam into Yvonne's path," Marty said.

Yvonne's boat started to spin out of control back downriver, past where the *Rivlan* was tied to shore. They could see figures running around the deck desperately trying to get the boat under control. Marty flew the dragonspy back to the deck of the *Rivlan*, slowing it to a hover within an inch of Ted's face. Ted smiled into the lens and gave them a thumbs-up.

"Guess that'll take care of Yvonne," Dylan said.

Grace shook her head. "No, it won't," she said. "She doesn't give up."

Crow came into view. He was pointing to something off-screen. Marty flew the dragonspy up into the air so he could see what it was.

"Uh-oh," Marty said.

Dylan looked at Grace. "You were right."

The *Anjo* had recovered and was heading back upriver, not nearly as fast as before, but steadily. It was already past where the *Rivlan* was tied up along shore. Marty flew the dragonspy into the *Anjo* wheelhouse. Yvonne and the other guy were in the same position. Yvonne was holding a bloody towel to her forehead. The guy at the wheel was holding his left arm across his chest like it had been injured.

"Wounded, but undeterred," Grace said.

"Eyes straight ahead," Dylan said. "Looks like they don't know the stuff they banged into was pulled into their path intentionally."

"It's going to be hard for the *Rivlan* to get in front without Yvonne noticing," Grace said.

Marty took the dragonspy three hundred feet above the river. "It's going to be impossible. They can't pass them on the river and the forest is too thick to use the hover mode to get around them."

He flew back to the *Rivlan*. Ted and Crow were below deck in the control room. Ted had opened a hatch in the floor and was fiddling with some electronics.

Ted looked up at the hovering dragonspy. "Can you hear me?"

Marty turned up the volume as far it could go, then flew the dragonspy up and down as if he were nodding yes.

"Listen carefully," Ted said. "The *Rivlan* is dead in the water. We aren't going anywhere. There's something wrong with the fuel cells. It could take me several hours to fix, and to be honest I might not be able to fix it at all. You need to run. You need to hide. If Ana and Buck and Grace are back, take them with you. Let the hatchlings go. We'll round them up later. And I've been thinking about the Gizmos and the tracking tags. If you've already put the tags on the hatchlings, take them off. Take your tracking tags off, too. Destroy them. I think Blackwood has gotten his hands on a Gizmo. That's the only way he could have found a back door into our system and shut it down. Once he has his people in place down here, he's going to turn the system back on, and when he does, he'll know exactly where you are. Keep the dragonspy close to your location. I'll figure out a way to hack into it with my Gizmo to find you. Do you have all that?"

Marty glanced at Grace and Dylan. They looked as worried as he felt. He flew the dragonspy up and down.

Yes.

BLINK

Waking up the hatchlings was like trying to wake the dead. Dylan and Marty pushed and cajoled them while Grace gathered supplies from the huts.

"They're like slugs with long necks," Marty said, leaning his entire body against one of them.

"At least they aren't trying to snap our heads off," Dylan said, pushing on the other.

Marty circled around his hatchling and pulled on its massive tail. He was rewarded with a blast of gas that sent him staggering backward. For a moment he thought he was going to faint. When his head cleared, he grabbed the knob on the end of the hatchling's tail and held his breath. He was about to give it another jerk when he noticed something blinking. At first he thought the noxious gas had messed up his vision, but then he leaned in closer. There was a flashing green light just beneath the surface of the hatchling's mottled skin.

"I think I just discovered how Noah Blackwood knows where the hatchlings are."

Dylan joined him and looked down at the flashing light, then went over and checked his hatchling. "This one has one, too."

Grace walked up to the corral, shouldering two heavy backpacks. "What are you doing? We have to go."

"We can't go until we wake them up enough to walk. And if we don't get rid of this . . ." He pointed to the flashing light. ". . . Yvonne will find them in about ten seconds."

"Subcutaneous tracking tags!"

"Sub-what?" Marty said.

Grace dumped the packs and climbed over the fence.

"Yvonne must have put them in when they were at the Ark." Grace reached into her pocket and pulled out a knife, as Marty gaped. This was definitely not the same kind and gentle Grace he'd known his entire life. His cousin did not carry a knife in her pocket. She expertly flipped the blade open with her thumb.

"Uh . . . ," Marty said. "What are you going to do?"

"Dino surgery."

Before he could object, Grace made a shallow cut where the light was flashing. The hatchling turned its head and bared its sharp teeth at her.

"So that's the trick," Marty said. "To wake them up, all you have to do is stab them."

Grace squeezed the bloody tracker out and dropped it into his hand. It was about the size of a thumbtack.

"Thanks." Marty stuffed it into his front pocket.

The patient got to its feet sluggishly. Marty, Grace, and Dylan backed away. It was one thing to feed a hatchling over a barrier, and another to be standing within its enclosure right next to it. The hatchling was taller than all of them, and it did not look happy.

"You better get the other tag out quickly," Dylan said. "I don't like the look in his eyes."

Marty didn't, either. The dino looked ticked off at being woken up and stabbed. Grace hurried around the back of Number Two and got to work.

Snap!

Marty grabbed Grace by her shirt collar and yanked her out of the way just in time.

"Thanks," Grace said. "I made the incision, but I didn't get the bug."

The dinosaurs had whipped around and were facing them with their heads bobbing on their long necks.

"Maybe it will fall out on its own," Marty said.

"And maybe it won't," Grace said.

"Distract them," Dylan said. "I'll try to get behind this one and get it out."

"Are you sure?" Marty asked.

Dylan didn't answer. He was on the move, following the fence. Marty and Grace started jumping up and down and waving their arms to get the hatchlings' attention. Dylan positioned himself directly behind them and started to crawl on his hands and knees.

Number One swiveled its head.

"Busted!" Marty shouted. "Get out of there!"

But it was too late. Number Two swung its tail, sending Dylan sprawling into the fence. Both dinos started moving toward him. Marty dashed in and grabbed Number Two's tail. It let out a terrible scream.

"Run!" Marty shouted, still holding on to the tail. "Get out of here! Open the gate!"

Grace ran over and yanked Dylan to his feet. They stumbled over to the gate, swung it open, and ran through. Marty let go of the tail. The two dinos turned on him. He ran.

Snap! Snap! Snap! Snap!

He dove headfirst over the fence, not sure if he'd been bitten or not. He rolled, got to his feet, and ran into the forest. He didn't look back until he had taken refuge behind a large tree. The dinosaurs had found the gate and were dashing through the opening. Grace and Dylan were hiding behind the building. The hatchlings slowed down when they reached the center of the camp. They sniffed the fire pit, then made some odd guttural sounds that Marty hadn't heard before. He stepped out from behind the tree. Grace and Dylan came out from behind the building and joined him.

"Are you okay?" Grace asked.

"I think so," Marty said. "A few scrapes and bruises on the front, but what I'm worried about is my butt. I think they might have snapped a chunk out of it." He turned around.

"Got your back pocket and a piece of your tee," Dylan said. "It looks like you've lost a lot of blood."

"Hilarious." Marty turned back around.

"Did you get the other tracker?" Grace asked.

Marty opened his hand, revealing a flashing tracker. "It popped out when they swung around to kill me. I caught it on the fly as I was diving over the fence. You should have seen it. It was beautiful."

"I'm sure," Grace said. "Crush them both and let's get out of here."

"Not so fast," Marty said. "I think we should keep them intact until we figure out the best use for them. At the very least, we should see which way the hatchlings go and head in the opposite direction with the trackers in order to get Yvonne off their trail."

"Looks like they're going that way," Dylan said, pointing.

The hatchlings were moving quickly toward the edge of camp. They had their heads down as if they were on the scent of something.

"They're headed for the main trail," Grace said. "Do you think they'll be okay?"

Marty felt where his pocket had been. "I think they'll be fine. Where's the main trail go?"

"To Flanna's web."

"Her web?"

Grace nodded. "Zip lines. I haven't been up there, but Ana told me she has miles of line strung throughout the canopy with observation platforms, shelters, and provisions."

Marty began to reconsider his decision to head in the opposite direction from the hatchlings.

"I'm not sure how far down the trail you have to go to get up," Grace continued. "I'm pretty sure that's where Luther was heading when he disappeared."

Marty was pretty sure, too. Luther had never seen a tree he didn't want to climb.

"Luther was a monkey in a former life," Marty said. "Can you get up top going the opposite direction?"

"I think so," Grace said. "But I think it's farther down the trail on that side."

"But the web is all connected?"

"That's what Ana said."

"Then that's where we'll go." He looked at the Gizmo. "They're forty minutes out. I hope the way up isn't too far down the trail."

He also hoped Ted would get the *Rivlan* working, and that Luther and the others were all okay, and that Wolfe was close to finding his parents.

TRIPS

Luther was not okay. He had been sliced, poked, bitten, and stung, and he was exhausted and hungry. Especially hungry. He'd hoped that when it got dark his captors would stop and fry up a monkey or a parrot or something. But they had kept moving, seemingly unaffected by the dark or their growling bellies. During the day, with his hands tied, it had been difficult enough to protect himself from getting whacked by thorns and sharp leaves. Now that it was dark, it was impossible.

Death by a thousand cuts, he thought again. *Tenderizing me before they throw me into the communal pot.*

Luther's only respite had a been terrifying ride in a dugout canoe across a river. When they finally reached the opposite shore, he'd thought they would push him down a short path to their village and the walking torture would be over. But it wasn't over. They continued walking, and walking, and walking, or in Luther's case, stumbling. His tired feet seemed to be finding every exposed root and rodent hole in the rain forest.

I'm not walking forward, I'm falling forward.

They picked him up for the millionth time and shoved him on, only for him to fall down again three steps later. But this time he jerked away from them.

"Enough! I'm tired! I'm thirsty! I'm done!"

The silhouettes of a club and two blowpipes appeared instantly.

"Go ahead and kill me," Luther declared. "Eat me right here. I don't care. I'm not taking another step until you give me a drink of water and untie my hands."

This is it, he thought resignedly.

He hoped they would use the darts instead of the club. But they did neither. The blowpipes and club were lowered. They talked among themselves for a second, then one of them stepped up to him and said, "Okay."

"You speak English?" Luther shouted.

"A little. You hurt our ears."

"Sorry."

"If I untie, you no run."

"Run where? I don't know where I am."

The man started to untie the knot, but was having a hard time of it.

"There's a knife in my pack," Luther said. "There's also a headlamp."

The man opened the pack, found the knife, cut the vine shackles, then handed him his headlamp.

Luther rubbed his wrists. His hands were numb. When he got some feeling back into them, he slipped the headlamp over his forehead and turned it on.

One of the other men handed him a plant.

"What's this for?"

"Water."

It was a bromeliad of some kind with stiff prickly leaves, but there was water trapped in it. Luther put his head back and emptied the contents into his parched mouth. It was great until something solid hit the back of his throat and he started gagging. It took him several seconds to dislodge whatever it was and spit it out on the ground. It was a tiny colorful frog. It hopped away. The three nearly naked kidnappers found this hilariously funny. Two of them were rolling on the ground laughing. The third had his hands on his knees trying to catch his breath. At first Luther was mad, but after thinking about it for a minute, he had to admit that gagging on a frog was pretty funny.

"Look before you drink," the knee man said.

"Poisonous?" Luther asked.

Knee man shook his head. Luther wasn't sure he believed him.

"There's bottled water in my pack. How about giving me one?"

Knee man handed him a bottle of water. Luther couldn't get it open quickly enough. He drank it straight down. By the time he finished, the other two men were back on their feet looking like they hadn't laughed in ten years.

Luther handed the empty water bottle to knee man, and it occurred to him that knee man, at least, was not *uncontacted*.

"What's your name?" he asked.

"I am called Ziti."

"You're named after my favorite Italian dish," Luther said.

"No understand."

"Not important. Why did you kidnap me? Where are you taking me?"

"We go now," Ziti said.

"I guess that means you're not going to answer me."

"Yes," Ziti said.

"You mean no."

"Not understand."

"Story of my life. At least tell me how far we're going."

"Not far."

"Thanks."

Ziti took the lead. The other two followed behind Luther. He was pretty sure now that he wasn't on the dinner menu and that his head was going to remain on his neck and stay the regular size. But this still didn't explain why they had grabbed him.

They trudged along for another hour, then came to a stop. The men talked among themselves for a minute, then one of them took off running.

"What's going on?"

"Almost there," Ziti said. "Must warn so they no kill."

Luther took this to mean that wherever they were going had armed sentries, and they had sent the third man ahead to tell them not to turn them into pincushions.

"How about that other bottle of water in my pack?" Luther wasn't particularly thirsty. He was using the water to keep the conversation going. He figured if he could keep Ziti talking, he'd be less likely to turn Luther into ziti.

Ziti gave him the bottle. Luther took a sip. "Where did you learn to speak English?"

"From my creator," Ziti answered.

Ziti's English was not as good as Luther had first thought. He'd read there were a lot of missionary groups working in the Amazon basin. By *creator*, Ziti probably meant a missionary or a preacher.

"So you went to a missionary school?"

Ziti shook his head. "What happened to hair?"

Luther had completely forgotten about his shaved head. He ran his hand across his head and felt a mat of fuzz growing back in.

"I cut it off. It's growing back in. But back to your English and the guy who taught it to you."

"My creator," Ziti said.

"Right. That guy. Where did you —"

The runner returned and said something to Ziti.

"We go now. Quiet. People sleep."

They started off again. It wasn't long before Luther saw firelight flickering through the trees in the distance. They wove their way toward the light, passing several stone-faced sentries armed with blowpipes and clubs. Luther nodded and smiled at all of them as they walked by. His greeting was not returned.

They stepped out of the trees into a small clearing. There were three crude structures made out of branches and leaves. Two of them were long and had open walls. Inside the long huts Luther could make out people sleeping in hammocks. Even if he hadn't seen them, he would have known the structures were bunkhouses because several of the people hanging inside were snoring. All the cuts on the bunkhouses looked fresh, which either meant that this was a temporary camp or they hadn't been here very long. In between the bunkhouses was a small, round hut with brush sides and a door made out of woven sticks, which was flanked by two grim guards with clubs. It was pretty clear where Luther was going to be spending the rest of the night, and he wasn't looking forward to it.

There were several small cooking fires around the edges of the camp and one large fire in the center. The cooking fires were smoking more than they were burning. No doubt to keep the millions of buzzing insects away.

Ziti walked over to a large tree near the central fire and hung Luther's backpack on a broken branch. Luther was about to make a plea for not being thrown into the fire and cooked when he saw something hanging next to his pack that stopped him in his tracks. It was a leg, or part of a leg. On the end was a size fifteen hiking boot. Luther knew only one person with a boot that size.

Wolfe.

Apparently, Ziti didn't notice Luther's surprise . . . or else he didn't care. He pushed Luther over to the round hut. One of the guards pulled the stick door open while the other guard stood close by with his club raised.

"In," Ziti said.

Luther stepped inside. Wolfe was sitting on the ground leaning against the far wall, about six feet away from the door. He squinted as Luther's headlamp shined in his eyes.

"Sorry." Luther flipped the lens up toward the ceiling.

"Luther?"

"Yeah."

"Who's with you?"

"Nobody." Luther sat down across from Wolfe, happy to get off his sore feet, and explained what had happened.

When he finished, Wolfe thought a minute, then said, "Let me get this straight. Doc and Laurel are missing in action. Jake and Flanna are out looking for them. Presumably, Grace, Ana, and Buck are out looking for you. You and I are here. And

Ted, Marty, Dylan, and the FBI guy are headed upriver to an empty camp." He looked at his watch, his face reddening. "If they aren't already there."

Luther had never seen Wolfe get really mad, but it looked like he was about to. The temperature inside the hut seemed to have instantly risen about ten degrees. Normally, when Luther saw an adult begin to go ballistic, he took the nearest exit. In this case, there wasn't one.

"What about Raul?" Luther said, trying to lighten things up.

"He led me to the guys that kidnapped me," Wolfe said.

"Oh."

"You didn't see him out there?"

Luther shook his head.

"What about my leg?"

"It's hanging on a tree," Luther said. "The boot's still on it."

Wolfe glared at him.

"Kind of a weird conversation we're having," Luther said.

Wolfe continued to glare, then his features softened and broke into a grin. A second later he started laughing loud enough to wake the entire camp. Luther joined him. He couldn't help himself. The door whipped open and the two guards looked in. They were not laughing. One of them raised his club. The other put his blowpipe to his lips and pointed it at Wolfe.

Wolfe stared them down. "Give it your best shot, sport."

Luther wasn't sure that was the best thing to say, even if they didn't understand him. The guy with the blowpipe took in a deep breath.

"Go ahead," Wolfe taunted. "Exhale."

Luther was closest to the pipe and was ready to knock it away, knowing he'd probably get clubbed in the process, when Raul and Ziti pushed past the two guards.

"You must be quiet," Raul said.

"I don't have to do anything," Wolfe said defiantly.

"They will kill you," Raul said.

Wolfe shrugged. "So be it."

Luther hoped Raul and Wolfe were both bluffing.

"I'll make a deal with you," Wolfe said.

"No deals," Raul said. "You are prisoner."

"There's always a deal," Wolfe said. "You bring me my leg, some water, and some food. In exchange, I'll be quiet until sunrise. If you don't, I'll shout my head off, and Luther and I will take this hut apart stick by stick."

We will? Luther thought.

"They will kill you both," Raul said.

"Bring it on!" Wolfe roared.

Huh? Luther didn't like how this was going.

Raul looked at Luther with pleading eyes, as if he wanted him to say or do something to calm Wolfe down before they were slaughtered.

"We want our backpacks, too," Luther said, surprising himself. His voice was a little high-pitched and not nearly as forceful as Wolfe's. Raul backed out of the hut and slammed the stick door.

"Nice one," Wolfe said.

"No biggy," Luther said. "We'll be dead in a few minutes anyway."

"I don't think so," Wolfe said.

Luther could hear voices outside the hut. "What do you think they're saying?"

"I have no idea."

"So Raul's a traitor."

"I think it's more complicated than that."

"What do you mean?"

"He may not have had a choice. They could have taken him out, or us, anytime they wanted. Did you notice how they moved through the woods on the way here?"

"Yeah, like snakes."

Wolfe smiled. "More like ghosts."

"That can see in the dark," Luther added.

"I noticed that, too. Strange. My point is, they didn't bring us all this way to kill us."

"What about shrinking our heads?"

"That would entail killing us first."

"Oh yeah," Luther said, a little embarrassed.

"I think they're waiting for something, or someone. Did they hurry you along here?"

"Yeah, except when I stopped and told them I needed water and choked on a frog."

"What?" Wolfe looked very confused.

"They have a good sense of humor."

"You're not making any sense," Wolfe said, looking even more confused and a little irritated.

"It's not important," Luther said. "You're right, the guys with me were in a big hurry. What's that have to do with anything?"

"It seems to me that they were on some kind of schedule. This was all planned."

Luther thought about this for a second, then shook his head. "They might have had a plan with you, but I don't think they did with me. There's no way they could have known I was going to take off by myself and do some exploring. I didn't know it myself until I did it."

"Why did you go off by yourself?"

"Probably wasn't the smartest move," Luther admitted. "But I didn't think I'd get kidnapped."

Wolfe stared at him silently. Luther thought it best to change the subject. "When I got here, I heard a bunch of people snoring in those sheds or whatever they are. How many do you think there are?"

"I've been watching them since I got here." Wolfe pulled himself over to where Luther was sitting, which was a little uncomfortable for Luther to watch. He parted some branches over Luther's right shoulder. "Take a look."

Luther twisted around and peeked out the opening. One of the guards was still near the door with a club and blowpipe in hand, which seemed ridiculous with Wolfe only able to crawl around. The others had moved to the fire pit at the center of camp and were talking quietly among themselves.

"You notice anything about them?" Wolfe asked quietly.

"There are seven of them standing around the fire," Luther said.

"I'm not asking what they're doing," Wolfe said, a little impatiently. "Describe them."

Luther was beginning to wonder if Wolfe had gone a little nuts during his short captivity. "Uh . . . they're all about four feet eight except for Raul. He's a couple of inches taller. And of course he's dressed in western clothes and the other guys are kind of naked."

"They're triplets," Wolfe said.

"What?"

"Two sets of triplets," Wolfe clarified.

Luther stared at the group around the fire, but they were too far away for him to tell if Wolfe was right. He hadn't paid much attention to the faces of the guys who had grabbed him. He'd been more interested their clubs and blowpipes.

"Are you sure?"

"Positive," Wolfe said. "There are at least a dozen people in camp. And they all appear to belong to sets of triplets."

"Except for Raul," Luther said.

Wolfe nodded.

"What are the chances of that?"

"Just about zero."

"Any girl triplets?"

Wolfe shook his head. "Not here. This is obviously a temporary camp. By the look of it, I don't think it's been here more than a few days. My guess is that they have a more permanent camp elsewhere. That must be where the women and children are."

Luther looked back through the opening. "They're coming this way."

Wolfe scooted to the other side of the hut. Luther continued looking through the opening. He wanted to see if Wolfe was right. He couldn't tell if the three guys in the lead were the same guys who had taken him, but they sure looked like triplets. Luther pulled himself away and sat down next to Wolfe.

"Are you really going to holler and tear this place apart if they don't give you your leg back?"

Wolfe nodded. "I want the packs and water, too. Are you with me?"

Luther didn't think he had much choice in the matter. If they killed Wolfe, they would probably kill him, too. "I'm with you," he said reluctantly.

The door opened. Raul stuck his head inside.

"They have gone through your packs and taken out anything that might harm them." He tossed the packs through the door. The next thing through was Wolfe's leg. Luther caught it before it hit the ground. Raul closed the door.

"Nice catch," Wolfe said. "Did you notice how Raul said *they*?"

Luther shook his head.

"It may mean he's not a hundred percent with them."

"I hope you're right," Luther said. "Now what?"

Wolfe began to strap on his prosthetic leg. "Now we wait."

THEY'RE COMING

"I think this is it," Grace said.

They had been on the jungle trail for about half an hour and were standing next to a huge tree with a rope ladder dangling down from the upper branches. Marty tipped his head back and looked up. The light from his headlamp disappeared into the canopy above; the top of the ladder remained invisible.

"We should go up one at a time," Grace said.

"You go up first," Marty said. "When you get up top, throw a line down. I'll tie our gear to it, and we'll haul it up after us."

"Dylan should go up first," Grace said. "He's stronger. He can start pulling the gear up right away."

"See you upstairs," Dylan said, and started up the ladder.

Marty pulled his Gizmo out and looked at the screen. Yvonne was still at the helm of the *Anjo*, moving upriver.

"They're ten miles out."

"What about Ted?" Grace asked.

Marty flew the dragonspy out of the wheelhouse and headed it downriver. He hoped to find the *Rivlan* barreling upriver at two hundred miles an hour. What he found instead was the boat dead in the water at the exact same spot where it had broken down.

"He's not going to be much help," Marty said, showing her the screen.

Crow was on his knees in front of a hatch holding a handful of tools. Ted poked his head up through the hatch. His face was covered in grease. He looked at the dragonspy, smiled, and looked at Crow. Marty turned the volume up.

"We've got company," Ted said, nodding at the dragonspy.

Crow turned his head and looked startled. "I didn't even hear it," he said. "That thing creeps me out."

Ted laughed, which made Marty think that things were going well and they'd be on their way soon. He was wrong.

"Major problems here," Ted said. "And I'm not sure I can fix them. We might have to hitch a ride upriver. I'm not sure how long that's going to take." He paused and looked at the dragonspy. "Can you hear me?"

Marty flew the dragonspy up and down.

Yes.

"Have you left camp?"

Yes.

"Is Yvonne at camp?"

No.

Marty wanted to say "Not yet" and give Ted her ETA, and the fact that he couldn't made him want to scream in frustration.

"Did you let the hatchlings go?"

Yes.

"I'll do the next three one at a time. Is Ana with you?"

No.

"Buckley Johnson?"

No.

"Grace?"

Yes.

"Thank God for that anyway. Did you take your tags off and destroy them?"

Yes.

"Are you all okay?"

Marty looked at Grace.

"We're alive," Grace said.

Yes.

"I guess all you can do is keep an eye on Yvonne and her thugs with the dragonspy. Just stay out of their sight. We'll regroup when I get there. I'm going to spend a little more time on the *Rivlan*. If I can't get it back on the river, I'll start working on our communications and we'll figure out a way to get to you. I better get back to it," Ted said. "And you need to keep on the move." He gave the dragonspy a big smile. "Stay safe."

He disappeared back into the hatch like a greasy rabbit.

Dylan dropped the line down.

"I'll tie our stuff off," Marty said. "See you up there."

Grace started up the ladder. Marty followed her after he got their packs secured. When he got to the top, he pulled the ladder up behind him. Dylan had untied their packs. Grace was helping him sort out the gear on the small wooden platform Flanna had put up.

Marty knew Grace had never been on a zip line, but she was good on a tightrope. He was certain she'd be fine on a zip, providing she didn't crack her skull open. He looked at Grace. "Did you bring helmets?"

Grace shook her head. "I forgot, but I have first aid supplies."

"That might come in handy when someone cracks their head open," Marty said, eyeing the supplies. "What time does it get light here?"

"About seven," Grace answered.

"That means we'll have a couple of hours of nocturnal zipping." He looked at Dylan. "Have you ever been on a zip line?"

Dylan shook his head. "How hard can it be?"

"It's not hard, except for the fact that you can break your neck if you make a mistake."

"What are you going to do with the tracking implants?" Grace asked.

Marty took them out of his pocket and held them in his palm. The tiny implants were still flashing. He had an idea about what he wanted to do with them, but he wasn't sure it would work.

"You guys go ahead," Marty said. "I'll be right behind you."

"I don't like the sound of that," Grace said. "I think we should stick together."

Marty had anticipated the objection. "You know, when you were on your swanky vacation with Noah Blackwood, we got along just fine without you bossing us around."

Grace folded her arms across her chest. "We wouldn't be in this mess if you hadn't tried to rescue me."

"We *did* rescue you," Marty said. "You just didn't know you needed rescuing. I need to check on Yvonne one more time, then fly the dragonspy back here so we can try to figure out where everyone is. You need to go ahead and pull up every ladder you can find so Yvonne and her trigger men can't get up here. Besides, we can only have one person on the zip line at a time, which means we're going to have to leapfrog our way through the canopy."

"All of that kind of makes sense," Dylan said.

Grace gave him the stink eye. Dylan returned the look with a smile. Grace blushed.

Marty watched them both. *That's interesting.*

"Okay," Grace said with reluctance.

Marty found this interesting as well. Grace usually didn't give in so easily. He got the harnesses ready, helped Dylan and Grace into them, then gave them a brief lesson on how to use a zip line without cracking their heads open like eggs.

"You need to go slow until you figure out what you're doing. There's a hand braking system on the harness. Pull yourself along until you figure out how to use the brakes. If you start freewheeling, you can end up going out of control. But don't panic, there's a bungee brake on the other end of the line that should slow you down so you don't smash into a tree. Keep your eyes open for what lies ahead. Flanna probably cleared this area at one time, but if she hasn't used the lines recently, it'll be overgrown again. You can actually watch plants growing here." He looked at Grace. "You better go first."

Grace hooked on to the line, tested the harness, then zipped off into the night. Dylan joined her a little too fast.

"Keep the brakes on!" Marty shouted after him.

"Duh *du* —"

"Ow!" Grace shouted. "That hurt!"

"Sorry."

Marty smiled. They'd work it out. Now *he* had something to work out. He took his Gizmo out and sat down on the platform. Yvonne's boat was already tied up at the jaguar preserve's dock. Yvonne was standing on the dock, holding a small antenna up in the air, obviously tracking the hatchlings. Marty turned up the dragonspy's volume.

"Well?" Spike asked.

"The hatchlings are definitely on the move, or at least they were. They've stopped. They're half a mile out."

"What's that mean?"

"Wolfe's people know we're coming. They're moving the hatchlings." She took her sat phone out and hit a button. "No signal."

"That's because Blackwood has jammed everything for a twenty-mile radius. We're operating dark. What do you want to do?"

Yvonne looked confused, and a little frightened, which brought a smile to Marty's face. It was clear that Blackwood hadn't given Yvonne detailed instructions prior to knocking out the communications. She didn't know what to do, but she made a quick recovery.

"The *Rivlan* isn't here, which means we passed it coming upriver, or else it's been here and has moved on. The helicopter is still here, which means Wolfe is either away from camp or incapacitated. If he knew we were coming, he would have loaded the hatchlings up and flown them out of here. Can you disable the helicopter?"

"Sure." Spike nodded at one of his men. "But that doesn't answer my question, does it? What do you want to do?"

"Our priorities have changed," Yvonne said. "We need to go after the hatchlings."

"I've heard you mention them before. What are they?"

"You'll find out soon enough."

"Whatever." Spike spit his slimy cigar into the water. "After we get these . . . uh . . . hatchlings. Then what?"

"Then we come back here and clean up."

Spike laughed. "You mean kill whoever is left over."

"That's why you're here, isn't it?"

Marty had heard enough. He hit the HOME button on the Gizmo.

The dragonspy arrived at the platform in less than a minute. He wasn't sure if what he had planned was going to work. The tracking implants were tiny, but so was the dragonspy. He turned off the bot's power and gave it a close examination. There were only two places he could attach the implants: on the underside where the legs were and on top between the wings.

He pulled out the first aid supplies Grace had cobbled together in camp and searched through them until he landed on a tube of surgical glue. He opened the tube, squeezed a tiny drop onto the first implant, and gently pressed it to the dragonspy's back. He swatted the real insects buzzing around his head as he waited for the glue to set.

Here goes nothing . . . or everything.

He activated the dragonspy and launched it. To his relief, it took off. He did a couple of loops around the platform. The bot was a little sluggish, but it was flying. He brought it in for a landing.

He attached the second implant. As he waited for the glue to set, he thought about his next move. He obviously needed to keep Yvonne away from the hatchlings. He also needed to keep her away from them. Discounting the Amazon River, the direction they were heading, and the direction he assumed the hatchlings were traveling, there was only one direction he could lead her, and that was south. He hoped there was something really horrible to the south.

Marty hit the LAUNCH button on the Gizmo, and his heart sank. The dragonspy's wings rattled on the wooden platform as if it had been swatted and was dying. He kicked himself for attaching the second implant. He might have been able to dupe Yvonne with just one implant.

But what were the chances of one of the implants going out the exact same moment she started to follow them?

He looked down at the vibrating dragonspy. There seemed to only be two choices, and neither was good. The glue had set. There was no way to get the implants off the bot now. The only way to disable the implants was to crush the dragonspy.

"No big deal," he said aloud. "Except it cost Ted and Wolfe a million bucks to build it."

His only other choice was to put the dragonspy in his pocket and head south himself. He walked over to the south side of the platform, hoping that Flanna had strung lines in that direction. She hadn't. Which meant he'd have to lead them astray on foot. Which brought him back to his first option.

Squish the bot.

He turned around and was about to take a million-dollar step when he noticed he could no longer hear its wings rattling. At first he thought the dragonspy had run out of juice trying to get off the ground. He shined his headlamp all over the platform, but the dragonspy was no longer there.

What the . . .

He stared at the Gizmo screen and saw the back of his own head bowed over the Gizmo. He looked up. The dragonspy was hovering about twenty feet above him, holding its own.

Must have needed time to get used to the new payload.

He flew the dragonspy in a couple of circles, maneuvering it through the dense branches and tangled vines. It was definitely slower now, but that could turn out to be an advantage. One of the things he'd been worried about was the dragonspy's speed. It seemed to have three flying modes. Hover, dead stop, and extremely fast. His plan had been to fly south a few minutes, stop, then fly on again, hoping this would fool Yvonne into thinking the hatchlings were moving at a realistic speed through the rain forest. Now he didn't have to worry about it. The sluggish dragonspy was now moving at the speed of two jogging baby dinosaurs.

He heard a whirring sound. A headlamp was zipping its way toward him. Grace made a perfect landing on the platform — difficult to do in the dark.

"What are you still doing here?"

"Hello to you, too," Marty said. "Where's Dylan?"

"He's about half a mile ahead, which is where you should be."

"I had to take care of some stuff. It took longer than I thought." He explained his plan.

"I hope you lead them off a cliff," Grace muttered.

Marty grinned. *Killer Grace.* "Me, too."

"Where are they?"

"I'm guessing they're about fifteen minutes away. I overheard Yvonne talking to one of Noah's thugs. They're tracking the implants. The hatchlings are the priority. Once they've captured them, they'll come back and kill everyone at their leisure."

"You definitely need to lead them off a cliff."

"I'll give it my best shot." Marty looked at his watch. "I'm glad you came back. We still have a little time. I'm going to start Mr. Dragonspy south. It might be a good idea to get rid of any obvious footprints beneath this tree. If they see prints, they'll know we're using the zips."

"I'm on it," Grace said, throwing the ladder over the edge of the platform.

While she climbed down, Marty put the dragonspy into infrared mode and started it south. It was a smart little bug. It would fly indefinitely in the direction he sent it, avoiding obstacles, until he gave it instructions to do something else. The infrared video was a little hard to interpret on the tiny screen. He put the spyglasses on, which weren't much better. It would be a lot easier when the sun came up. He looked over the edge of the platform. He could see Grace's headlamp bobbing around a hundred feet below. He watched her for a while, then scanned the forest beyond and saw a flash of light in the distance.

"Crap!"

Yvonne had made better time than he had expected.

If it is Yvonne.

He couldn't take a chance that it wasn't Yvonne. The light flashed again, then a second light appeared and vanished. It looked like the lights were heading their way. Grace was still bobbing around with her own headlamp, oblivious to the fact that there were people coming her way. He couldn't shout out a warning. He turned off his headlamp and hurried down the rope ladder.

Now all I have to do is get her to notice me without making her scream.

The only way to do to this was to make enough noise to get Grace's attention, but not enough to be heard by the group coming their way. She was about fifty feet away with her back to him. He coughed. She didn't turn around. He coughed louder. She still didn't turn around.

Is she deaf?

He stepped a few feet closer and tried another cough. This one worked. She whipped around and painted him with her headlamp beam.

"What are you doing down here?" she asked irritably. "I just got rid of our footprints."

"They're coming," he whispered, hoping she got the hint. She didn't.

"Who's —"

"Why does everything have to be a debate with you? Yvonne is here. Turn your headlamp off. Let's go."

Without another word, Grace started up the ladder. By the time she reached the top, Marty could not only see the headlamps, he knew how many there were.

Four.

They were only a hundred yards away when he started up the hundred-foot ladder. Halfway up, they were twenty yards away. He stopped climbing. He'd never make it to the top before they reached the tree. He hooked an arm around a rung and started to pull the slack up behind him. Yvonne and the others were now close enough that he could hear them talking.

"Did you hear that?" someone said.

"Yeah. A scraping sound. Better take out your tranquilizer gun."

"It isn't the hatchlings," Yvonne said. "They're a quarter mile away and making good time. If we want to catch up with them, we need to pick up our pace. Less talking, more walking."

"Yes, sir!"

The others laughed, but not Yvonne.

No sense of humor, Marty thought.

Two of them stopped directly below where he was dangling. They lit cigarettes.

Smoke break. Perfect.

Yvonne and the other two continued on. Marty grabbed a vine to steady himself. He didn't want his swaying to knock something loose from the tree and have it fall on their heads. He looked down on the two smokers. He hoped Grace was looking down on him, *and* the smokers, and was keeping her mouth shut. If the men looked up, it was all over for him. They'd probably shoot him out of the tree, and they wouldn't use a tranquilizer dart. After his bullet-riddled body hit the ground, they'd climb up and grab Grace. They'd find the Gizmo and figure out his dino chase scam. It wouldn't be long before Dylan got worried and came back looking for them, zipping right into their clutches. He prayed Dylan didn't pick this moment to come back. Zip lines made an unmistakable hum.

"Yeah, I hear you," one of the men said irritably. "Lighten up. We're right behind you."

Marty guessed that they were wearing earpieces because he hadn't heard the question. The second man said something about Yvonne that would have enraged her had she heard it. The first man topped the insult with one of his own, causing Marty to stifle a laugh.

That's all I need. Start laughing, then . . . Blam!

"What do you think these hatchlings are?"

"Probably another one of Blackwood's mutants. Bottom line, I don't care what they are. As long as he keeps putting coin in my piggy bank, I'll chase after anything he wants. Easiest scratch I ever made."

The men flicked their cigarettes into the rain forest, then headed south. Marty waited until their headlamps disappeared before clambering up to the platform to Grace.

She helped him over the edge. "That was close," she said.

"Tell me about it."

"I heard them talking, but I couldn't understand what they were saying."

"They were making fun of Yvonne and talking about how much money Noah was paying them." Marty checked the dragonspy on the Gizmo. It was making steady progress in a southerly direction. "We better catch up with Dylan. He's probably going nuts with worry."

Grace looked down at the Gizmo. "Why catch up with him?" she asked.

"Huh?"

"The reason we came up here was to get away from Yvonne and lead her away from the hatchlings. Thanks to you, mission accomplished."

Marty wouldn't have admitted this to anyone, especially Grace, but he was pretty happy with the compliment.

"What's to stop us from going back to camp?" Grace asked.

Marty stared at her a moment, a little confused, until he realized what she was getting at. The answer was, nothing was stopping them from going back to camp to see if anyone had made it back. If no one was at camp, they could head in any direction they wanted, as long as it was away from Yvonne.

"We need to get Dylan," Marty said.

As if on cue, they heard the zip line humming. Dylan hopped onto the platform.

"Where have you been?" Dylan asked.

"About time you showed up," Marty said.

"Me?"

"How do you like zipping?"

"It'd be awesome if I could see where I was going and there weren't people trying to kill me."

"We're heading back to camp," Grace said.

"What about Yvonne?"

"We'll explain on the way," Grace said.

MODEL PRISONERS

"Nobody home," Marty said.

They had just arrived back at the jaguar camp, which was exactly as they had left it. Empty. While Grace and Dylan searched the huts in the early morning light, Marty pulled out the Gizmo and checked on the dragonspy. The spyglasses were back in his pocket because he still couldn't walk and watch at the same time. The dragonspy was making steady progress to the south, but there was no way of telling how far ahead of Yvonne it was. He flew the bot above the canopy to get the lay of the land. It was velvety green for as far as he could see.

Not a cliff in sight. But there's probably something else just as bad. All I have to do is find it.

He dropped the dragonspy beneath the canopy again and put it into a hover. He didn't want to get too far ahead of Yvonne and her crew, or they might get suspicious.

Grace and Dylan joined him.

"I think we should stick around camp," Grace said. "Someone is bound to show up."

"Yeah," Marty said. "Like another platoon of Noah's thugs. I think we need to keep moving. We need to find out what happened to everyone."

Grace looked at Dylan. "What do you think?"

"As much I would like to climb into a hammock and sleep for twenty-four hours, I agree with Marty. We need to get out of here and keep moving until we find someone who isn't trying to kill us."

"What if Ted shows up?" Grace asked.

"I don't think he's going to get the *Rivlan* fixed," Marty said, although he hoped he was wrong. "He has an inflatable Zodiac on board, but it will take them hours to get this far upriver."

"What about the ultralight?" Grace asked.

"He could fly here," Marty admitted. "But I don't think we should wait around to find out if he does. He told us to keep moving."

"So, we're on our own," Grace said.

Marty shrugged. "What else is new? Let's get out of here."

"We're not getting out of here," Ted said. "At least not on the *Rivlan*."

"The Zodiac?" Crow asked.

"Unless you can fly."

"What do you mean?"

Ted slapped one of the crates on deck. "Ultralight. It has pontoons."

"You have more than one?"

"I'm afraid not. We've seriously underestimated Blackwood. He knew where we were going. He's hacked into our communications system and taken it down. He's been ahead of us every step of the way. He has someone working for him on the inside on Cryptos and out here as well."

"Who?"

"I don't know. Maybe your friend, Buck."

"He's not my friend," Crow insisted. "But Buck's not the type. I doubt he's the guy."

"Regardless of who it is, the only way Blackwood could have shut us down is to have someone on both ends. Al's working on the problem on Cryptos. I need to get to camp and work on it on this side. We're toast if we don't get the comms back up."

Crow nodded. "You need help with the plane?"

Ted shook his head. "You better start your way upriver in the Zodiac. You'll be lucky to get to camp before dark."

Luther thought he heard someone say the word *daylight*, but he wasn't sure. Then he thought he felt someone, or something, shaking him and shouting, "Luther! Luther! Are you okay?"

Luther opened one eye. He had no idea where he was. He wasn't surprised. He never knew where he was when he woke, which always made waking interesting. It felt like his ear and cheek were lying in the dirt.

That's interesting.

A huge, black-bearded guy was squatting over him, slapping his face.

That's interesting, too. And a little scary.

He sat up.

The big guy with the beard was Travis Wolfe.

What's he doing here? Where is here?

Luther looked around. They were in a hut made out of sticks and logs. The hut was maybe ten by ten feet and about five feet tall. Gray morning light was leaking through the chinks onto the dirt floor. His mind fog started to lift, and the events of the previous day came back to him.

"Are you okay?" Wolfe repeated.

"Yeah, I'm good. Takes me a while to wake up."

"I thought you were dead."

"Deep sleeper is all."

"It's kind of disturbing."

Luther grinned. "So I've been told." He looked at Wolfe's pant legs. There was a scuffed boot sticking out from each cuff. "Time to escape?"

"Time to do something." Wolfe moved over to the crude door and peered through a crack.

Luther joined him. Three jaguar men were standing around a smoking fire pit thirty feet away. Three others were standing a few feet outside the door. Now that he saw them in the light, it was clear that Wolfe was right. The men were identical triplets.

"I think we can take them," Luther whispered.

"What about the other twelve or thirteen guys?" Wolfe asked.

"Probably not one of my better ideas," Luther admitted.

"We'll just play it by ear. See what they have in mind before making a move. It's best to let them think we're cooperating, being passive."

"Model prisoners," Luther said.

"Exactly." Wolfe opened his backpack and took out his smashed Gizmo.

"Is it working?"

Wolfe shook his head. "But the weird thing is that they left it in the pack. While you were sleeping, or whatever you call what you do when you close your eyes, I went through both of our packs. They removed everything that we could use as a weapon, but they left the Gizmo and your cell phone. I don't know how tech savvy these triplets are, but Raul knows enough to take our communications devices away. He's been at the jaguar preserve for months."

"So he knows they don't work," Luther said.

"Right. But he also seems to think they aren't going to come back on."

"Are you saying he knocked out the devices?"

Wolfe shook his head. "A hacker took them out. A very good hacker. Raul and the Trips aren't acting independently. They're working for someone else."

"Noah Blackwood," Luther said.

"Who else? And if they're working for him, it means he's been operating down here for years. Sylvia and Timothy must have figured this out."

"And Blackwood had them —"

"Shot down," Wolfe said. "I saw the wreckage. It wasn't an accident."

"You think they're still alive?"

"We're alive," Wolfe said. "They could have killed us anytime they wanted to. They could have taken us out without our ever seeing them. If these are the same guys who took Sylvia and Timothy away from the crash site, there's a chance the two of them are still alive. At the very least, the Trips know what happened to them. We need to find out what they know."

Luther peered out the crack again. The Trips around the fire were joined by another set of Trips.

"Have you noticed how they always hang out in threes?" Luther asked.

Wolfe nodded. "Good eye. We might be able to use it to our advantage."

They continued to observe. Five minutes later, another set of Trips joined the fire pit crew. A couple of minutes after that, Raul appeared and started talking to them. When he finished, he headed toward the hut.

"Take anything out of your pack that you think we might need, in case they take the packs away. Conceal it as best you can."

Luther grabbed a small LED flashlight, his worthless smartphone, a small notepad, and a pencil. There wasn't anything else worth grabbing. He had just stuffed the phone down his pants when the door burst open.

An angry-looking Raul stood just outside the door. "Outside now!" he shouted.

Luther looked at Wolfe. "What did we do wrong?"

"Good question. Let me go first. Take your pack."

Luther was happy to let him lead the way since Raul was flanked on either side by two sets of Trips brandishing blowpipes, bows, and spears. They looked like an indigenous firing squad. Wolfe had to almost double over to get through the small door. Luther had to duck, too, but not nearly as far. He straightened up outside, blinked at the bright morning light, and nearly fled back into the hut in terror. Standing to the side of the squad, smiling, was Butch McCall. He looked a little worse for wear. He had a black eye, his nose was smashed, and his jaw was swollen. Butch's smile broadened when Luther met his eyes.

Luther swallowed his fear, knowing that guys like Butch fed on fear. He wasn't about to serve Butch breakfast. He returned Butch's smile.

"Hey, Butch, looks like you got the crap beat out of you. How many were there?"

Butch frowned.

Luther's smile broadened. "Let me guess. One skinny geek dude by the name of Ted?"

Butch pulled a pistol out from a holster behind his back and pointed it at Luther's head.

Luther frowned. Butch's smile returned. He flipped the safety off and pulled the hammer back.

"There's no need for that," Wolfe said, stepping in front of Luther.

Luther tried to move back into the open, but his body ignored his mind's noble command.

Looks like I'm going to feed Butch breakfast after all.

"Luther's just a kid. He doesn't know what he's saying."

Butch tightened his finger on the trigger. Luther knew exactly what he had been saying, and wished he hadn't said it, even though it was true. His dad had told him a thousand times that his mouth was going to get him killed. Now it looked like it was going to get Wolfe killed, too.

"Stand down, Butch," Wolfe said. "You've got us."

Butch released the pressure, slightly, but kept the gun in his hand. "We've got everybody," he said. "Or we'll have everybody before the day's out, including the hatchlings. Game over, Travis. You lose."

"Fine," Wolfe said. "Now what?"

"Step out from behind him, Luther."

Luther emerged to stand next to Wolfe, hoping that Butch didn't notice he was trembling.

"If it was up to me, I'd drop both of you right where you

stand," Butch said. "But your ex-father-in-law has other plans, at least for you, Wolfe. I suspect you're going to wish I had killed you right here." He looked at Luther. "Your little friend wasn't part of the equation, but he might be useful."

"How?" Wolfe asked.

"We're running behind schedule. I need to take you someplace."

"Where?"

"That's exactly what I'm talking about," Butch said. "You're delaying things by asking questions that you know I'm not going to answer. When we start walking, you'll drag your feet, hoping that by slowing things down something will change and you'll figure out a way to save yourself. That's not going to happen. This outcome was set in stone the day you took Rose away from Noah Blackwood. Now it's the endgame, and I want to get it over with." He looked back at Luther. "You want to keep the kid alive, you move fast without questions, without delay. If I think you're screwing around with me, I'll shoot him in the head. Deal?"

Wolfe hesitated, but only for a second. "Fine," he said.

Luther hoped Wolfe was agreeing to the former part of the deal, not the shooting in the head part.

Butch lowered his gun, but didn't holster it. He gave Luther a cold stare. "Goes for you, too," he said. "You step out of line, you're dead." He took two pairs of plastic flex-cuffs out of his pocket and tossed them to Raul. "Drop your packs and put your hands out."

Raul walked over and cinched their wrists. When he finished, he turned to Butch and said, "I go now."

Butch shook his head.

"We had deal."

"The deal is we can't leave you alive," Butch said.

He nodded at a set of Trips. Before Raul could take a single step, he was surrounded. Butch stepped into the circle, raised his pistol, and shot him in the temple. Raul fell to the ground, his sightless eyes staring up into the canopy.

Luther's knees buckled. He dropped to the ground and threw up. When he finished, he looked up at Wolfe. The big man had gone pale. His fists were clenched. He glared at Butch with raw hatred.

"Not a word, Wolfe," Butch said. "Or your puking friend joins Raul. Don't know why you're upset. Raul set you up. Of course, he had some extra incentive. He was told that he and everyone at the preserve would be killed if he didn't help us out. Guess he didn't read the fine print that he and everyone else were going to be killed anyway. The goal was to separate you and take you one by one. Worked out pretty good."

Wolfe reached down and helped Luther to his feet. Luther couldn't look at Raul. His legs were still wobbly.

Butch said something to the Trips in their own language. They divided themselves with military precision, six in front of them, six in back. Butch took up the rear and shouted another command.

They moved off into the rain forest.

DUNG HEAPS

The hardest thing about following the hatchlings was avoiding the steaming piles of dung they were depositing about every thirty feet. Marty, Grace, and Dylan could have followed their path blindfolded.

Marty paused at yet another stinking mound lit by a shaft of morning sunlight.

"Stick your finger in it," Dylan suggested. "Maybe we can tell how far ahead they are by the temperature."

"Be my guest," Marty said.

Dylan squatted down as if he were going to do it, but instead he changed the subject. "I bet this pile weighs five pounds. If this keeps up, the hatchlings will weigh nothing by the time we catch up to them. We'll be able to put them in our pockets."

"Maybe we should keep moving instead of talking about dinosaur bowel movements," Grace said. "Everyone we know is missing, and there are people trying to kill us."

"What else is new?" Marty said. "Doesn't mean we can't enjoy ourselves while we run for our lives." But he understood perfectly what she was getting at. He was still sick with worry over his parents. And now with everyone else missing, it was all he could do to put one foot in front of the other and not collapse from the horror of it all. The only thing that was keeping him going was pretending that none of it was a big deal.

They moved on to the next deposit, which was considerably smaller than the previous pile.

"Smaller and smaller," Dylan said. "They'll be on empty soon. I'm guessing they've dropped twenty pounds since we let them go."

The hatchlings had pretty much stayed on the trail, stopping once in a while to tear into some foliage, or dig at something in the ground, or drop a load.

Marty squatted down to take a closer look at one of their digging spots. It was muddier along this section of trail, and the tracks were clearer.

"Luther!" he shouted, pointing at a tennis shoe print.

Grace and Dylan joined him.

"We've been so preoccupied with the hatchling spoor, we haven't been looking for human footprints," Grace said.

"You're right," Marty said. "Hang on." He jogged back along the trail to the previous scratching. It took him a while to find it, but sure enough, he found a partial tennis shoe print.

He backtracked to the next spot and found what he thought was another partial, but he couldn't be sure because the print had been almost completely obliterated by the hatchling's claws. He jogged back to Grace and Dylan and told them what he had found.

Dylan walked over to some of the bushes along the trail that had obviously been attacked by the hatchlings. He got down on his knees and looked at the ground.

"Here!"

Marty and Grace joined him, staring down at two perfectly

formed tennis shoe prints in the soft ground beneath the bushes.

"It's almost as if they're marking every place Luther's been," Grace said.

"I think you're right!" Marty said excitedly. "Remember when we let them go? They were sniffing the ground like a couple of bloodhounds on the scent of an escaped convict."

"And the sound they made," Grace said. "I'd never heard it before. They're imprinted on him. Luther is their surrogate mother. They must be trying to find him."

"Looks more like they're hunting him down," Dylan said.

"Either way," Marty said, "they're leading us to him."

They hurried along at a more determined pace, stopping at the place where the hatchlings had jumped off the trail.

"What are the chances of Luther leaving a perfectly good trail in favor of cutting through the jungle?" Grace asked.

"Zero," Marty said. "Unless he was being chased, or someone grabbed him and took him off the trail."

Ten paces into the tangle, they found Luther's tennis shoe prints, hatchling prints, and a couple other footprints, which had to belong to Ana and Buck, and . . .

"Uh-oh," Marty said.

Mixed in with the shoe prints were several sets of bare footprints smaller than Luther's and Ana's.

"Someone grabbed them?" Dylan asked.

"Let's find out." Marty led the way into the brightening rain forest.

THE COMPOUND

Raul's brutal murder looped through Luther's brain like a scene in a horror movie. He'd never seen a man killed before. He'd never seen a dead person. He never wanted to see one again.

He walked quietly, directly behind Wolfe, who, true to his word, was moving down the trail at a pretty good clip without any delaying tactics. A half dozen Trips led the way, with Butch and the rest taking up the rear. Every once in a while, Luther got a spidery feeling on the back of his neck that made him think Butch was going to put a bullet in his head just for the fun of it. Luther told himself not to look back at Butch, but he couldn't help himself. Each time he looked, Butch was just trudging along, his bruised and bearded face dripping with sweat, his eyes as cold and deadly as glacial ice. But no gun. He had tucked it away in its holster.

What stopped Luther from thinking about Raul was their arrival at a twelve-foot heavy-gauge chain-link fence topped by rolls of razor wire. The shock of seeing a fence in the middle of nowhere even stopped Wolfe.

"Keep moving!" Butch bellowed. "And don't brush up against it unless you want to be barbecued."

He didn't have to tell them. They could see a fried monkey and a cooked parrot clinging to the mesh. Along the top of the fence, every thirty feet or so, were video cameras that swiveled as they passed. In between the cameras were small satellite dishes pointed up at the canopy.

Luther wanted to shout "What is this?" But he didn't because Butch would probably answer by shooting him in the back of the head. His only choice was to follow Wolfe's silent lead, acting like it was as common to discover a seemingly endless electrified fence in the middle of a rain forest as it would be to find biting insects.

They passed five more dead monkeys, several scorched birds, a toasted three-toed sloth, and some kind of dead deer that had made the mistake of munching a leaf too close to the mesh. After about a mile, they came to a stop in front of a small gate, barely distinguishable from the rest of the fence, with a small red light flashing above it. Butch punched in a number on a keypad attached to the gate. There was an audible click, a green light came on, and the gate swung open.

"Don't touch the frame as you enter," Butch said, as if he didn't care whether they touched the frame or not.

They filed through, and the gate swung closed behind them. Butch punched in a number on a second keypad on the inside of the gate and the light turned from green to red. Once inside, the Trips visibly relaxed after they passed through the gate, breaking ranks and chattering in their strange language. It was clear that they felt safe now. Even Butch seemed more relaxed and almost cheerful.

"Done deal now, Wolfe. Endgame. No escape."

Wolfe said nothing.

"You can talk now," Butch said. "I'm sure you have a lot of questions. I'm happy to answer them. I'll consider it a condemned man's last request."

Wolfe continued walking without a word. Luther had a million questions, first among them: *Where are we, and what's going to happen to us?* But he didn't get to ask them because Wolfe broke his silence.

"What is this place?"

Butch laughed, sounding more like hyena snorting than an actual human.

"The original Ark."

"World War Two," Wolfe said.

"Good guess."

"Cryptos Island had a similar fence around it when Ted and I started things up there. We took it down."

"Maybe you should have left it up to keep out unwanted visitors."

"Maybe," Wolfe said casually.

Luther was surprised at the tone of the conversation. Wolfe was acting like Butch was giving him a tour of a resort property, totally ignoring the fact that their wrists were tied, the tour guide had a gun, and his friends had clubs, spears, and blowpipes.

"You've done some upgrades with the cameras and sat dishes."

"Gotta keep up with technology," Butch said. "You know that better than anybody. Of course, when the technology fails, you're kind of screwed. That's when a good old-fashioned electric fence comes in handy."

"And an infinite number of people to keep the fence in good repair," Wolfe said.

"You got that right. You wouldn't believe the number of man-hours it takes to keep the fence up and the juice flowing through it."

Luther suddenly realized what Wolfe was doing. *He's taking advantage of Butch's good mood and milking him for information like a contented cow.*

"German made?" Wolfe asked.

"Certainly not Brazilian or U.S.," Butch said.

"Nazis?"

"They paid for it and helped build it, but they're long gone now."

"What does Noah do here?"

Butch snorted again. "A better question would be, what *doesn't* Noah do here?"

"Okay, then," Wolfe said. "How long has Noah been operating down here?"

"His entire life," Butch said. "Noah Blackwood was born here. So was Rose."

This caused a hitch in Wolfe's stride, which caused Luther to plow into his back, which caused Butch to pull his pistol and the Trips to raise their spears, blowpipes, and bows. Luther put his cuffed hands over his face and waited for the end.

"No need for that," Wolfe said.

Luther peeked out between his fingers and found himself looking down the barrel of Butch's gun. Four or five seconds passed; no one moved or breathed. It felt like four or five hours to Luther. Then Butch gave an almost imperceptible shake of the head, and the Trips slowly lowered their weapons.

Butch glared at Luther. "Lucky," he said. He shifted his gaze to Wolfe. "Stop again and you're both dead. Walk."

Butch went silent. The cow had gotten cranky, which ended the tour, at least the narrative part of it, leaving Luther and Wolfe to fill in the blanks themselves by looking around as they walked.

The compound was gigantic. Luther strained to see the fence line through the tangle to get an idea of the layout, but it seemed to have disappeared. The trail led them to a narrow, muddy road covered with wheel ruts, which meant there were vehicles inside the compound.

That means there has to be a road leading here, which means civilization can't be more than a gas tank away. Or maybe not . . .

He'd seen satellite photos of the jaguar preserve and the surrounding area, and there hadn't been any roads. The nearest town was a hundred miles downriver, and the only way to reach it was by boat, floatplane, or helicopter.

But if they didn't drive, how did they get the vehicles here? Who takes care of the vehicles?

He couldn't imagine any of the Trips crawling under a four-by-four to change the oil.

Where do they get their gas? Their food?

The answer to his last question lay around the next bend in the road. They came upon a huge clearing planted with fruit trees, vegetable gardens, and fields of grain and corn. There were at least a dozen people tending the gardens. The workers couldn't miss them walking down the rutted road, but oddly, not one of them even glanced in their direction. The other odd thing was the sunlight. Now that they had emerged from under the canopy, it was as if the whole area ahead of them lay under a shadow, but there was nothing close to the road or the clearing to cast a shadow that big.

Luther looked up. Two hundred feet above him, stretching as far as he could see, was some kind of barrier, but it didn't look like it was made out of fabric. It shimmered, and seemed to undulate, or move, like a weird force field. This might explain why the area didn't show up on satellite or GPS. Blackwood had invented some kind of new technology.

Or else he swiped it from the Nazis. Luther shook his head. *Don't be stupid! There weren't satellites during World War Two, or computers, or iAnything back then. Though I wouldn't be surprised if it turned out that Blackwood was a member of the Hitler Youth. . . .* Luther shook his head again. *Hitler was long gone by the time Blackwood was born, but there were Nazis running all over South America after the war, weren't there? Didn't a bunch of them go into hiding down here to escape prosecution?* Luther wished he'd paid more attention during history class at OOPS. *If Blackwood could make this compound disappear off the face of the earth, knocking out our satellite and cell signals was probably a cinch. Noah is more tech savvy than we thought. Wolfe and Ted underestimated him. We all underestimated him.*

The road ended at a lake that was maybe half a mile across. On its banks was a small village populated by men, women, and children. Unlike the field workers, they were very interested in the new arrivals. They were all armed with spears, crude knives, bows, and fierce threatening expressions, including the little kids, who had the fiercest expressions of all. The villagers formed two lines down to the lake. Butch pushed Wolfe and Luther down the aisle between them. Luther wasn't sure what creeped him out more . . . the fact that the villagers all appeared to be triplets, or that they didn't utter a sound as he and Wolfe passed by.

Luther looked up. The shimmering sky shield stretched all the way across the lake, casting a dusky light over the water. Ahead of them, a small dock with a couple of boats tied to it jutted into the lake. At the lake's center was an island housing a large concrete building surrounded by rain forest.

Butch pointed to one of the boats. "Get in."

Luther climbed in behind Wolfe and sat down on the bench seat near the bow.

"We'll be fine," Wolfe said under his breath.

For the life of him, Luther couldn't think why Wolfe would say this. They were being held hostage by Butch McCall inside a former Nazi compound that no one knew existed.

The motor started up and the boat puttered slowly toward the island.

"Don't look at me," Wolfe said. "Nod if you can hear me."

Luther gave him a slight nod.

"The motor is louder where Butch is. This might be our only chance to talk, but I'm going to do the talking. Don't say anything."

Luther gave him another nod.

"Butch would have already killed us if Noah wanted us dead. We're okay on that front for now, but it's important you don't do anything to antagonize him."

Luther nodded, but he wasn't convinced. Raul hadn't antagonized Butch, and look where it had gotten him.

"Everyone is looking for us," Wolfe continued. "They're not going to stop until they find us. Eventually, they're going to stumble across this compound."

Luther had to bite his lower lip to stop himself from saying "Like we just stumbled across it seventy years after it was built?

Butch led us here!" Wolfe was treating him like a little kid, which is what adults always did when they were scared out of their wits. Noah Blackwood was not a step ahead of them, he was a hundred miles ahead of them. It was almost as if he had lured the entire Cryptos crew down here. What better place to get rid of them than at a place that didn't exist?

"What I'm saying is that we need to cooperate," Wolfe whispered. "Or at least appear to cooperate. That's our only —"

The boat rocked to one side as a large head burst out of the water with a mouth full of what looked like a thousand sharp teeth and twenty feet of armored body behind it. The creature's jaws snapped closed with a harsh sound as loud as a firecracker. Butch swerved the boat so they didn't collide with it.

"Nessie!" Luther shouted. He couldn't help himself. He looked back at Butch, expecting to be shot, but Butch had his hand on the tiller and an actual smile on his face.

"Not quite," he shouted above the noise of the engine. "Giant alligator. You think you're the only ones who have cryptids? Noah Blackwood *invented* cryptids. The only reason these monsters are still here and not at one of the Arks is that Noah hasn't figured out how to get the behemoths out of here."

"There's more than one?" Luther asked.

"The lake's full of them."

Luther turned back, but the giant gator was gone. He looked at Wolfe, who was scanning the lake.

"Interesting," he whispered.

"You think?" Luther whispered back.

Butch maneuvered the boat alongside the island's dock.

"Out." He waved his pistol at them. "And no funny stuff."

Luther didn't know about Wolfe, but he wasn't in a funny mood, and with their hands tied on a remote island patrolled by a lake full of monsters, what could they do?

Butch tied up the boat and hustled them along the dock and up a short set of stairs to a dirt path. The path led up a hill through thick rain forest and ended at a cement two-story building that looked like it could withstand a nuclear blast. Its sides were covered in creepers and vines, giving it the appearance of an ancient ruin. A humming sound emanated from somewhere inside, loud enough to make it feel like the ground was vibrating. They stopped in front of a foreboding steel door. It was twenty feet square and looked to Luther like the kind of door you only passed through once, because you never came out again. A pair of cameras above the door frame whirred in their direction and scoped them like sights on a rifle. He wondered if Noah Blackwood was staring at them from the safety of his Seattle Ark, and gloating.

Butch punched in a code and the door slid open like a giant elevator, revealing a long, dimly lit, concrete hallway. It looked like a World War Two version of Noah's underground warren at the Seattle Ark. The humming had gotten louder. Luther figured it was coming from their power plant.

But where do they get the fuel to power it?

"Keep your eyes open," Wolfe whispered. "Memorize everything. Try —"

"Shut up!"

Butch pushed them inside. The door slid closed behind them.

BOT HOP

Marty stopped and pulled his Gizmo out.

"What are you doing?" Grace asked.

"Checking my email," Marty snapped. "What do you think I'm doing?"

Grace was surprised at her cousin's outburst. Marty was sarcastic and smart-alecky, but never snappish.

"What's the matter?"

"Let me think . . . Everyone we know is either dead or missing, including my parents and my best friend. We're relying on a pair of dinosaurs to lead us to Luther, and trying to outsmart a platoon of killers using a bot, which I can't fly back to check on them because then *they* would know that they aren't following a couple of dinosaurs. Oh . . . And Ted is broken down on the Amazon River with a retired FBI agent, who's probably fishing because there's nothing else for him to do."

"Is that all," Grace said, smiling.

He gave her an angry glare, and for a second she thought it was going to stick, but it morphed into a lopsided grin.

"Yeah," he said. "So things aren't too bad."

The optimistic Marty was back. "That's what I was thinking," Grace said.

He sat down and turned the Gizmo on. Grace joined him on one side. Dylan sandwiched him on the other. The little screen came to life. The dragonspy was perched on a branch about twenty feet above the ground, looking down. Something moved below it. Marty zoomed in.

"Three-toed sloth," he said.

Its long moss-colored hair and slow-motion movement made it almost invisible.

"What's it doing?" Grace asked. "I thought they were arboreal."

"That means tree-dwelling," Marty informed Dylan.

"I know what *arboreal* means!" Dylan said.

Marty grinned and looked back at Grace. "Potty break," he said. "They come down once a week to poop."

"Wow," Dylan said. "That's constipated."

"No kidding," Mary said. "Especially when you consider that all they eat is vegetable matter."

"Speaking of which," Dylan said, "we haven't seen any dino poop in miles. They're running on empty."

Marty continued stare at the sloth. "They carry their babies on their backs. When the baby gets older, they give their territory to them and find a new one for themselves. I'd guess this takes a while, because they're slowest mammal on earth. But the weird thing is, they can swim. They use those long-clawed arms to stroke across —"

"Can we get back the people trying to kill us?" Grace interrupted.

"Oh yeah, those guys," Marty said. "The problem is that I don't exactly know where they are. I think they're somewhere behind the dragonspy. But if I fly the bot back to them for a peek, they'll think the hatchlings are within catching distance."

"So?" Grace asked.

"So . . ." He thought for a minute. "So, I guess you have a point. Even if they figure out that the tracking tags aren't in the hatchlings anymore, they'll have no idea how we're moving the tags around. They don't know about the dragonspy. It'll blow their minds." Marty looked at Dylan. "What do you think?"

Dylan shrugged. "Your plan to lead them off a cliff probably isn't going to work. Might as well try to drive them crazy. If nothing else, it will be fun to watch."

"First I have to find them," Marty said. "And we won't be able to watch them for long. We need to keep looking for Luther and the others."

He gave the three-toed sloth its privacy.

Yvonne wasn't sure how much longer she could hold up. She felt as though the rain forest was slowly melting her. She was covered in scratches and insect bites. Salty sweat stung her open wounds, and she was certain that some of the nicks were going septic. But this was not the worst of her problems. Her legs felt like they were rooted to the ground, and every step she took was an agony of cramped muscle tissue. She began to think that Noah Blackwood had sent her to the rain forest to be walked to death.

The three men with her were also covered in sweat, bitten, and scratched, but it seemed to have no effect on them. They moved through the painful tangle, laughing and joking with one another as if they were spending a casual day at a park.

"You sure your telemetry gear is working?" Spike asked.

"Yes," she said with effort.

"Then I take it your hatchlings are birds."

"They're not birds."

"It would be helpful if you told us what they are so we know what to look for."

Yvonne stopped walking, not sure she had the breath to move and speak at the same time.

"We're following their signal, not their trail," she said slowly. "Obviously, they've taken a different path from ours. The last time I looked, we were gaining on them." She took her tracking antenna out, grateful for a chance to stand still. She held the antenna over her head and looked down at the small screen. The hatchlings were on the move again. She was disappointed until she realized that they were moving toward them. "Look!"

The men gathered around her. The hatchlings were less than a mile away, moving rapidly in their direction.

"Spread out," Spike ordered. "We'll set up a picket line."

"Tranquilizer guns," Yvonne said. "Aim for big muscles so you don't damage vital organs. You harm a hatchling, you're dead."

And I'm dead, too, she thought grimly as she took up a position behind a fallen tree.

"What about the people with them?" Spike asked into her earpiece.

Yvonne had never set up an ambush in her life. *What am I doing here? I'm an animal trainer, not a soldier.*

"Take them out," she heard herself say. "But the priority is the hatchlings. We can clean up later."

Her firm response brought a smile to her face.

Perhaps I am a soldier.

She looked at her tracking screen. The hatchlings were moving toward their position in an odd zigzagging pattern, and they were moving fast.

Too fast for anyone to keep up with them. What are they doing?

The zigzagging continued for ten minutes as the hatchlings drew closer and closer, then they suddenly stopped.

"They're here," Yvonne whispered, straining to see them through the thick foliage. "Does anyone see them?"

She got back four negatives.

Impossible.

According to the tracking device, the hatchlings were twenty feet away from her.

"There's our favorite twisted animal trainer," Marty said, zooming in on Yvonne's sweaty head.

She was hiding behind a downed tree with a rifle in one hand and some kind of tracking device in the other. Her red face was covered with nasty-looking welts. Her normally perfectly coiffed hair looked like a pile of rotting moss. She was desperately scanning the rain forest for dinosaurs.

"Looks like she's been simmering in a slow cooker all night," Dylan said.

Marty left her and found her partners. They, too, were scanning the forest but didn't look nearly as wrung out as Yvonne.

"Time to turn up the heat," he said.

He flew the dragonspy away from them and landed it on a branch.

Yvonne and the mercenaries were on their feet immediately, cautiously moving toward the landing spot.

"I don't need a cliff," Marty said happily. "I can exhaust them to death."

"The soldiers don't look very tired," Grace pointed out.

Marty zoomed in on Spike. Grace was right. He looked as if he could trudge through the rain forest for a century like some kind of tropical cyborg. The others didn't look quite as lively as Spike, but they were in a lot better shape than Yvonne.

Marty flew the dragonspy ahead a couple hundred yards, happy in the knowledge that he could keep doing this until they either gave up or dropped dead.

"It's almost like having a leash tied to them and pulling them through the jungle."

"Something's coming our way," Dylan said.

Marty looked up from the screen. It sounded like a herd of elephants.

He jumped up. "Hide!"

He dove into a pile of leaf litter and burrowed into the rotted slime like a mole, hoping it would conceal him and that nothing in the pile would bite him. He heard a squealing noise and raised his slime-covered head to see what it was.

Three animals the size of small pigs trotted by not ten feet from him. They were covered in brown fur, and by the look of their eyes, they were terrified.

Capybaras, the largest rodents in the world. But they aren't big enough to make . . .

The hatchlings descended on the large rats from two directions with incredible speed and violence. The trio of rodents were tossed into the air and dead before they hit the ground. The hatchlings tore them apart and gulped the bloody flesh down in seconds. Marty stayed exactly where he was to avoid becoming part of the feeding frenzy. Ted had been confident the hatchlings could make it on their own in the forest.

I guess he was right.

Marty felt sorry for the rain forest animals, then thought about Luther and wondered if . . .

His stomach lurched. The hatchlings had clearly been tracking him.

What made them come back? Did they catch up to him and . . .

He squeezed his eyes closed, trying to rid his mind of the image of Luther being torn limb from limb and devoured. The eyes closed thing didn't work. He felt bile creep up his throat. He opened his eyes and saw something that horrified him even more. Grace had come out of hiding and was standing ten feet away from the vicious dinosaurs with her hands out like she wanted to pet them.

"No!"

He popped out of the leaf slime like a jack-in-the-box. The hatchlings jumped at the sudden appearance of the leaf slime monster and turned on him.

"What are you doing?" Grace shrieked.

"Saving your life!" Marty shouted back. "Run! I'll distract them."

The hatchlings eyed him warily.

Dylan emerged from his hiding place. "I wouldn't run," he said. "It's one of those predator/prey things. They're hardwired to chase things."

"Who do you think you are?" Marty said. "Noah Blackwood? Run! Both of you!"

They had inadvertently surrounded the hatchlings. The dinosaurs were whipping their bloody heads around as if they were deciding who to kill first.

"Don't be ridiculous," Grace said. To prove her point, she touched one of the hatchling's heads.

Marty was absolutely certain her hand would be snapped off at the wrist and swallowed, starting a feeding frenzy that would kill them all. But instead, the hatchling lowered its head, closed its eyes, and leaned in closer to her, making a hissing sound that kind of sounded like a cat's purr.

"You're a dino whisperer!" Dylan said.

"You're lucky you're not a big juicy rodent," Marty said. "I think the only reason those little monsters didn't attack you is that they're full from eating Luther."

"You're the one who looks like a monster. You're covered in rotting mulch."

"Then I'm a mulcher, not a monster."

Dylan laughed.

"Don't encourage him," Grace said. The second hatchling leaned in for a head scratch. "See?" She used both hands to scratch, one for each vicious head. "They're not man-eaters."

Marty thought about reminding her that Mokélé-mbembé had killed her mother and bitten off her father's leg, but he didn't want to upset her. He was amazed at his self-control.

"Why are you smiling?" Grace asked.

Marty hadn't realized that he was smiling. "Forget it," he said, and pulled out the Gizmo. It was time to check on their friends and lead them farther afield. His smile turned into a frown as the video came onto the screen.

"Bad news."

Grace and Dylan gathered around, as did the two hatchlings. One of them hacked up a clot of foul-smelling slobber onto the screen.

"Gross!" Grace said.

Dylan retched.

Marty wiped the Gizmo on his pant leg, then showed them the screen.

"Busted," Dylan said.

Marty nodded. "Looks that way."

Yvonne and the goons were staring directly at the dragonspy. One of them raised his shotgun. Marty flew the dragonspy away.

"Missed," he said. "They probably realized it's not a real dragonfly."

"Now what?" Grace asked.

"I guess they'll head back to camp to see if there's anyone there to kill. Our only option is to follow them with the dragonspy."

"They'll know we're keeping an eye on them," Dylan said.

"So what," Marty said. "If I fly the dragonspy back to us, they'll know where we are. I can't take the tracking tags off without destroying the dragonspy. I stuck them on with superglue."

Marty looked at the hatchlings. They were scratching around on the ground for capybara scraps. Marty was pretty certain there wasn't a toenail left.

If capybaras even have toenails.

"Looks like our bloodhounds have lost interest in finding Luther," he said.

Mindful of what a shotgun blast would do to the dragonspy, Marty flew the bot back toward Yvonne and her gang of thugs. They were on the move again. The men led. Yvonne lagged behind with her head down and feet dragging as if the next step might be her last.

"She looks wrung out," Dylan said.

"Couldn't happen to a nicer person," Marty said.

"I wouldn't count her out," Grace said. "Yvonne runs on ambition and hatred. She has enough of both to keep her on her feet for decades. What do you want to do?"

"We can't go back to camp, because that's where they're probably headed," Marty said. "Now that they know we have the dragonspy, they'll be looking for the green lights. I guess we should follow the hatchlings. They were tracking something, and I don't think it was giant rats. Unless you think Luther is a giant rat."

"Maybe a naked mole rat," Grace said.

"He does kind of look like one with his head shaved," Marty agreed. "But before we take off, I need to figure out what to do with the dragonspy."

"Why don't you do what Luther did," Grace suggested.

"Huh?"

"Aboard the *Coelacanth*," Grace answered. "Just before I took off in the helicopter with Noah, Luther flew a dragonspy into my shirt pocket."

Marty remembered. It had actually been a smart thing to do, but Grace had not taken advantage of it. The signal had died within days. He stared at her.

"What?" Grace asked.

"Where —"

"Oh my God!" Grace grabbed her pack and started opening

pockets. "I'm such an idiot. I'm so sorry. I completely forgot . . ." She pulled the dragonspy out and held it in her palm.

It looked like a dead insect, but Marty knew better. It wasn't dead. All it needed was some sun juice.

His face broke into a smile. "This changes everything."

"I should have —"

"Forget it," Marty said, gently taking the bot from her. "All that matters is that we have it now." He took off his baseball cap and attached the dragonspy to the brim. With the thick canopy overhead it would take a while to fully charge, but the dragonspy didn't need that much energy to get into the air.

Grace's backpack gave him an idea for the first dragonspy. He looked at the Gizmo screen and zoomed in on Yvonne's backpack. On the side of the pack was deep pocket without a flap or a zipper. Wisely, Yvonne hadn't used it. Without a closure, the pocket was worthless.

But it makes a perfect dragonspy hideout.

He flew the dragonspy to the pocket and made it crawl inside. The video turned black.

"That's going to drive them nuts," he said. "Their GPS will tell them the bot is right on top of them, but they won't be able to see it."

"Unless Yvonne checks the pocket," Grace said.

"Exactly, but who cares? They can't fly it without a Gizmo that's linked to it, and I have the only one." Marty checked the dragonspy on his cap; it was just beginning to move slightly.

The hatchlings had found the trail again and were sniffing the ground, making the same odd sounds they had made back at camp. After a short pause they moved off in the direction the capybaras had come from.

"I think they're back on the scent," Dylan said.

Marty pocketed the Gizmo and put his cap on. "They're probably after more rat snacks, but we might as well follow them. We don't have anyplace else to go."

They took off after the sniffing hatchlings.

Thirty feet down the trail, the dragonspy on Marty's cap moved one of its four wings, but he didn't see it.

INSIDE

As Butch pushed Luther and Wolfe down the wide corridor, Luther couldn't get over the similarities between the Ark and Noah's secret bunker. The bunker was clearly older than the Ark, made out of cement with none of the high-end finishes. There were doors on either side of the corridor, but instead of being numbered, they were named, presumably in German, which Luther could not decipher. The corridor here was darker than the Ark, a little musty smelling, filling Luther with a sense of foreboding. The only sound was the clicking of Butch's boots. He stopped in front of an elevator door, punched in a code, which Luther strained to see, but couldn't because Butch was careful to block both of their views. The door slid open with an eerie screech. Inside was a freight elevator big enough to hold a small school bus.

Creepy. Definitely not the Ark.

They stepped inside. Butch punched the button for 1, which surprised Luther because he thought they were on the first floor. The elevator started down with a stomach-dropping lurch. They continued past Floor 2 and came to a bumpy stop.

Four levels, Luther thought. *Two on top, two below. We're under the lake.*

The doors creaked open. The first level was darker, danker, and mustier than the level they'd entered on, but what disturbed Luther more was that it looked like it hadn't been used in years, maybe decades.

"What is this?" Wolfe asked.

"Shut up," Butch said, and pushed them down the damp corridor past several rusty doors. He stopped in front of a door with yet another keypad. "End of the line."

Luther didn't like the sound of that. He looked at Wolfe, hoping he had some kind of plan to get them out of this mess. It didn't look that way, unless staring at Butch with dull hatred was going to stop him.

"This isn't necessary, Butch," Wolfe said.

Again Butch managed to punch in the code without their being able to see it. He'd obviously done this many times before.

"I'll decide what's necessary and what isn't."

He swung the door open. It was dark inside. Wolfe started forward.

"Not you," Butch said, waving him off with his pistol.

Wolfe shot him a dirty look. "Why?"

Butch smiled. "Because I said." He pointed the gun at Luther's head. "I can kill him right here if you like. Up to you."

"That's okay," Luther said. "I kind of like dark scary rooms. I'll be fine."

"Good choice," Butch said. "And just so you know, the vents are welded shut."

Luther nodded, but he was disappointed to hear it. That was how he had escaped from the Ark after his last unfortunate encounter with Butch.

He held his hands up. "What about the cuffs?"

"I'm sure you'll figure out a way to get them off," Butch said, and shoved Luther into the dark room. The door slammed closed behind him. He heard the latch close and the lock click into place. As he waited for his eyes to adjust to the dark, he thought back to the last time he'd been in this situation, only a couple of days ago.

At least there's no chupacabra trying to kill . . .

The thought took his breath away. Back at the Ark they had played a dirty trick on Yvonne, fooling her into thinking she was trapped in a room with the chupacabra. She completely deserved it, but that was beside the point. Yvonne, Butch, and Blackwood probably didn't think their trick was very funny.

Where's the chupacabra now? Did they bring it to Brazil with them? Is it in the room with me?

He tried to listen, remembering the horrible sound of its razor-sharp claws clicking on stainless steel. He couldn't hear anything except for his heart beating in his chest. Marty said the chupacabra's eyes were fire orange. He didn't see any flames in the dark.

Of course, Marty was shining a light in the chupacabra's ugly face at the time, and I'm in a pitch-black room, and my eyes don't seem to be adjusting, which means there isn't any light leaking in, even under the door. The room is completely sealed. That can't be good.

Luther thought he heard something. It wasn't a skitter or a click. It sounded more like a rustling. He flattened himself against the wall and held his breath. The sound came again.

Definitely a rustling sound, maybe twenty feet away.

He wasn't alone, but what was in here with him? A genetically engineered killing machine? Or a rat?

Please be a rat.

He began feeling the wall for a light switch.

Light or dark, I don't stand a chance against that chupacabra, but at least I'll see it coming. I wish I had my headlamp. He remembered that he had his cell phone stuffed down his pants. He was certain there wouldn't be a signal, but it would work fine as a flashlight. All he had do was figure out how get it with his wrists cuffed.

"Is someone there?"

Luther nearly jumped out of his pants.

"Yeah, someone's here," Luther said, relieved beyond belief. The chupacabra couldn't talk.

"Luther?"

Luther didn't recognize the voice.

"It's Buck. Are you okay?"

"Hang on a minute." Luther managed to extract his phone, turn it on, and shine it at the wall. "I'm trying to find a light. . . . Ah, here it is." He hit the switch. A single light came on. There were several fixtures hanging from the high ceiling, but only one of them seemed to have a working bulb.

Buck was sitting in the center of the huge room holding his head. Ana was lying about ten feet away from him. Not moving.

Luther hurried over to her. Buck was already at her side feeling for a pulse.

"Is she —"

"She's alive," Buck said. "Unconscious, but alive."

Buck had dried blood on the back of his head.

"What happened?" Luther asked.

"We tried to make a break for it, and I guess we got clubbed in the head. I'm still a little uncertain about how it went down. Three indigenous guys grabbed us while we were out looking for you."

"Triplets?"

"What?"

"Never mind. What happened?"

"They were taking us somewhere and Ana went for one of the guy's spears. It didn't work out." Buck looked around the room as if he were seeing it clearly for the first time. "Where are we?"

"Some kind of bunker, built by the Nazis."

"What are you talking about?"

Luther quickly filled him in.

When he finished, Buck said, "You sure you didn't get bonked on the head, too?"

"I'm fine."

Ana started to stir.

Luther glanced around and noticed several cardboard boxes stacked along the walls. He checked them out while Buck tended to Ana. The boxes were filled with bottled water and MREs — Meals Ready to Eat. They weren't going to starve to death or die of thirst. The concrete room was about twenty feet square with an old toilet and sink in one corner and nothing else. The ceiling was fifteen feet high. He counted five vents. They wouldn't be able to reach them even if they weren't welded shut like Butch said. He didn't see any cameras, but he was certain they were there. On top of one of the boxes of water was a box cutter.

You'll figure it out, Butch had said. He grabbed the cutter and a bottle of water, and walked back over to Buck.

"Good find," Buck said. He took the cutter and sliced through Luther's flex-cuffs. Luther did the same for him and for Ana, who was sitting up now, shielding her eyes against the dim light.

"Want me to turn the lights off?" Luther asked. "Or I should say the *light* off? There's only one working."

"No, leave it on," Ana said. "And you're a lot of trouble."

"I just went for a walk," Luther said.

"Open the bottle and hand it over," Ana said grumpily. "What else did you find?"

"Gasoline, propane, food," Luther said. "Enough food to last for months."

"That can't be good," Ana said, taking a drink.

Buck looked up at the ceiling.

"Air vents," Luther said. "Too high to reach. Butch told me they were welded shut."

Buck pointed at the door Luther had been pushed through. "We know where that goes, but what about the other doors?"

Luther looked. He hadn't noticed them, but there were metal doors on three of the walls. "I'm sure they're locked." He tested one.

It opened.

Butch pushed Wolfe back into the elevator and stabbed the button for the top floor. Wolfe expected the door to open into another corridor, but it didn't. He stepped out into what appeared to be a tropical park. It was filled with plants and trees. Colorful parrots flew between branches. Butterflies danced around the flowers. Monkeys chattered down at them from the trees. The park was covered with a fine mesh that was nearly invisible in the shadowy canopy.

Butch waved his gun at him. "Follow the path."

The path was made out of cement and was clear of foliage. He knew by the way the rain forest grew that it probably took a small army of gardeners to keep the path clear. There were cages along the path, some big, some small, with every kind of rain forest animal imaginable . . . jaguar, ocelot, tapir, capybara, anaconda. . . . An animal he'd never seen before rushed out of its holding area, jumped on the chain link, and started snarling at them. It was wearing a radio harness with one of Ted Bronson's cameras attached to it.

"Shocking, isn't it?" Butch said.

The animal was about the size of a coyote. It had long, curved canine teeth, protruding spines running down its back, brown-black fur, and three lethal-looking claws on each of its front feet. Wolfe had thought the boys had been exaggerating when they had described it to him. Looking at the chupacabra now as it tried to get at them through the mesh, he realized they had actually downplayed the ferocity of Noah's beast. It was truly frightening. Butch let him look at it, obviously enjoying his reaction.

"We call him Nine," Butch said. "You should have seen the first eight. Now, those were aggressive buggers. Uncontrollable."

"You can control this one?"

Butch pointed his gun at the slavering mutant. "I can control everything with this."

"He doesn't appear to like you," Wolfe said.

"Doesn't matter," Butch said.

The cage next to the chupacabra was empty, no doubt as a buffer between the chupacabra and the animal in the third cage, so that they didn't tear each other to pieces through the mesh. The animal in the third cage looked like a cross between a grizzly bear and a lion, and acted like one, bashing itself against the mesh and roaring.

"You sure that cage is secure?" Wolfe asked.

Butch laughed. "You scared, Travis?"

Wolfe didn't answer. He glanced back at the chupacabra. It

was now lying on top of a log, completely calm, watching them with intelligent golden eyes. In a way, Wolfe found this more frightening than when it was in attack mode. There was raw intelligence behind those eyes.

Wolfe looked back at the animal in the third cage. "What do you call this?"

"Bearcat."

"Mutants," Wolfe said.

Butch shrugged. "Whatever."

They heard someone in front of them yell out a stream of curses that would make a truck driver blush. Wolfe recognized the voice.

Impossible, he thought.

Wolfe had been surprised to see Butch in the middle of the rain forest. It was almost as if Butch had left the States before they did, which meant Blackwood still had spies on Cryptos Island. Someone had told Blackwood and Butch where they were going.

But how did Blackwood get here so quickly?

"Sounds like the old man is upset," Butch said, smiling. "Bad timing on your part. You know how he is when things don't go his way."

Wolfe knew exactly how Noah Blackwood was when things didn't go his way. It wasn't pleasant. He'd known Blackwood since he was a teenager. Wolfe's father had been a friend of Noah's until their acrimonious falling out.

"How'd you get down here so fast?" Wolfe asked Butch.

"Because I know what you're going to do before you know you're going to do it."

"How did Noah get down here so fast?" Wolfe clarified.

"He was with me," Butch answered.

"How long have you and Noah been down here?"

"A few days. Surprised?"

"Not really," Wolfe said, but he was surprised. Very surprised.

Blackwood's cursing died down and the birds and monkeys started chattering again.

"Move it!" Butch pushed him up the path.

They didn't have far to go. The path ended at a luxurious swimming pool surrounded by lush jungle foliage dotted with beautifully colored, and no doubt rare, orchids. Noah Blackwood was sitting in a comfortable chair, sipping an ice-cold drink. In his other hand he held a small electronic tablet. He was smiling, completely composed. He didn't look like a man who had thrown a tantrum two minutes before. He looked like a man completely enjoying himself, as if he were on vacation in a tropical paradise.

"It's good to see you, Travis."

Wolfe stared at him. Noah didn't have a hair out of place, or a trickle of sweat on his starched khaki safari suit. It was spotless.

"Please sit down."

Wolfe remained standing. Noah nodded. Butch slammed his fist into Wolfe's stomach and pushed him into the chair across from Noah.

"That's better," Noah said calmly.

Wolfe remained bent over, trying to catch his breath and not throw up. It took several seconds before he could sit up. Butch stood directly behind him.

"Let Luther go," Wolfe said. "This is our fight, not his."

Noah laughed. "The fight is over, Travis. You've lost. Unfortunately for Luther, he was on the wrong side. All your friends were on the wrong side."

"You won't get —" Wolfe stopped himself. Telling Noah he wouldn't get away with it sounded trite even to him, and he knew Noah probably would get away with it. He'd gotten away with *it* his whole life.

"Yes?" Noah asked.

"What is this place?"

"Ah . . . It's a research center. It's been here since before World War Two. But it's much more than that. It's where I was born. It's where Rose was born."

"So Butch told me," Wolfe said.

Noah's eyes narrowed and his face flushed in anger. Wolfe wished he could see Butch's face. He suspected that Butch was no longer smiling. He realized he needed to let it play out the way Noah envisioned it. He needed to keep the conversation going, because when the conversation ended, it would all be over.

"I didn't believe him," Wolfe said. "Rose shared very little about her childhood, but she certainly would have told me that she was born in the middle of the Amazonian rain forest, if it was true."

"I anticipated as much," Noah said, the flush fading from his face. "I would wager that Rose never showed you any photographs of herself when she was a baby." He picked up a file from the side table. "The reason she didn't share her baby pictures with you is that she didn't know any existed — at least not these."

Noah laid several color photos out on the table. The baby had a shock of black hair and the most beautiful blue eyes Wolfe had ever seen. It was unmistakably Rose Blackwood. There were photos of her with Noah cradling her exactly where he was sitting right now, photos of her in the village at the edge of the lake being nursed by one of the Trips, photos of her being pushed in a carriage along the corridor Wolfe had walked moments before.

It was a full minute before Wolfe could speak. He stared down at the photos and thought his heart might break.

"Did she know she was born here?"

"I think she had her suspicions," Noah said. "I took her to the States when she was fourteen months old. I never brought her back down here, although I would have, had you not taken her from me and killed her."

"I didn't kill her," Wolfe said.

"Letting her die in the Congo amounts to the same thing," Noah said, his face reddening again.

Wolfe had no defense. In a way, Noah was right. If he hadn't taken her to the Congo to find Mokélé-mbembé, she would still be alive. But she was the one who had insisted they go on the expedition. One of her justifications was to get as far away from her father as she could. He'd argued that Cryptos Island was close and secure. She'd insisted that if Noah knew where she was, he would find a way to get her back. She wanted to disappear, and she had. Forever.

"What about her mother?"

"We'll get to that eventually," Noah said. "We'll get to *everything* eventually." He looked at his expensive watch. "Right now I have business to tend to." He gave Butch a nod.

"Want me to put him down with the others?" Butch asked.

"What others?" Wolfe asked.

"No," Noah said, ignoring Wolfe's question. "I think we have an opening between Nine and the bearcat. Put him there."

DOORS

Beyond the door was another dark room.

Luther used his cell phone to find the light switch and flipped it on. The room was the same size as the one Butch had put him in, and here, too, cardboard boxes, wooden crates, and old equipment were stacked along the wall. The only obvious difference was that the ceiling lights in the second room had four working bulbs instead of one. There was a steel door leading to the corridor. Locked. And another door on the far wall. Luther walked over and tried it. In opened into yet another dark room.

He turned and looked at Ana and Buck, who were rummaging through the boxes along the wall. "Why would they leave these interior doors unlocked? I mean, when Butch, or whoever, comes down here to check on us, how's he going to find us?"

"Cameras," Ana said. "They must have them."

"Or else no one is going to come down and check on us," Buck said. He pointed at the boxes. "More MREs. Medical supplies. Bottled water. Blankets. Someone has already been through the med supplies, and the MREs have been picked through, too. They come in several versions. Most of the breakfast boxes are empty."

"What does that mean?"

"It means that someone is partial to breakfast, and I doubt it's Butch or Blackwood. We could live down here for years, maybe decades. And we're not alone."

Luther was trying to wrap his mind around what Buck was saying when he heard a screeching sound. He peered into the third dark room and saw a square of light on the far wall as the door opened, and the silhouette of one — no, two — people coming through the doorway.

"We've got company."

One of them flicked on the light. It was Flanna Brenna and Jake Lansa.

"Did you notice they didn't go to sleep after their last . . . uh . . . meal?" Grace asked.

"You mean slaughter," Marty said. "Yeah, I noticed."

They had been following the hatchlings through the jungle for miles at a grueling pace without a break. The hatchlings' sleep pattern was not the only thing that had changed. Their behavior had, too. They were ranging ahead about a half a mile, then frolicking back to the exhausted trio, circling them a couple of times, then taking off again like unleashed puppies. They had just completed another circling maneuver and taken off again, crashing through the forest.

"They're making enough noise to wake the dead," Dylan said.

"Do you think the dragonspy is charged yet?" Grace asked.

In their numbing slog through the stifling rain forest, Marty had completely forgotten about the second bot. He quickly grabbed his cap off his head and breathed a sigh of relief when he saw the dragonspy had not been scraped off by a bush or a branch. He stroked the folded silvery wings and felt it tremble at his touch.

"I think it's good to go," he said, slipping the Gizmo out of his pocket.

"Which way are you going to send it?" Grace asked.

Marty checked the dragonspy in Yvonne's pack. "They're about a mile from camp, not moving very fast."

"The dragonspy must be *bugging* them," Dylan said.

Marty laughed.

Grace rolled her eyes. "You guys have been spending *way* too much time together. How's the battery holding up?" she asked.

"I was just about to look," Marty said. *But I really should have checked on that a while ago,* he thought. *What is wrong with me? If I don't start paying attention, I'm going to get us all killed!* "There's just enough juice left to crawl out of Yvonne's pack, and maybe, maybe, fly up into a tree."

"What if they see it?" Dylan asked.

Marty shrugged. "If it dies in the pack, they're going to find it anyway."

"Providing *they* don't die before they find it," Grace added.

"Not much chance of that," Marty said. "Since they're the ones on the hunt, and headed to an abandoned camp. And what's the deal with your newfound violence? I'm not complaining, but it's kind of a new look for you."

Grace flushed with embarrassment. "I guess I'm just mad. Frustrated. I want this all to stop."

"Welcome to the club," Marty said, then got back to the dying dragonspy in Yvonne's pack. He had to concentrate. Crawling it was much harder than flying it. And flying it wasn't easy. He maneuvered the bot around until he saw a sliver of light at the top of the pocket, then started up. At the top of the pocket, he swiveled the bot's head back and forth. "It looks like Yvonne is taking up the rear. I don't see anyone behind her."

"Maybe they ditched her," Dylan said.

"Fingers crossed," Graced said.

Marty glanced at the bot's battery indicator. It was just about at zero. He opted for the *drop and see what happens* approach because he didn't think there was enough juice to get it into the air. As soon as dragonspy hit the ground, he turned it so he could see Yvonne walking away. The problem was that Yvonne was not walking away. She had stopped and was looking down at the dragonspy angrily as if she was about to step on it.

She turned her head and shouted, "Hey! Spike!"

A second later, Spike appeared next to her, peering down at the dragonspy. "Those your hatchling trackers flashing?"

Yvonne nodded. "They must have cut them out of the base of their tails."

Spike squatted down for a closer look. "Then attached them to this little drone thing. Then led us off their trail. Then followed us around with it to drive us nuts." He laughed. "Pretty smart. Brilliant really."

"Fly it away, Marty!" Grace shouted.

He did. The little shot of sunlight was just enough get the dragonspy into the air quickly. Unfortunately, Spike was quicker. He grabbed it out of the air like a frog snapping up an insect and treated them to an extreme close-up of his and Yvonne's faces as they examined the dragonspy.

"I think those are tiny cameras," Yvonne said.

"Think they're watching us?"

"Presumably," Yvonne said.

"Think they can hear us?"

"I doubt it. What should we do with it?"

"I'm keeping it," Spike said. "Bet it's worth money to someone."

"Smarter than he looks," Marty said.

"Not really," Grace said. "If Al Ikes and the CIA find out, they'll hunt him to the ends of the earth."

"Then let's hope he keeps it," Dylan said.

Spike did keep it. He buttoned it in his shirt pocket. The Gizmo went dark and the voices became so muffled they could no longer hear what they were saying.

"At least we'll be able to keep track of them," Marty said, showing them the battery indicator. It was about an eighth full. "The bot should last a while piggybacking on Spike." He switched to the second dragonspy. "No point wasting this little guy to keep an eye on them. We'll fly it ahead and find the hatchlings."

It didn't take long. The hatchlings were halfway across a raging river, swimming like a pair of dolphins.

CHICKEN

"All the doors between the rooms are unlocked," Flanna explained as she and Jake led Luther, Ana, and Buck through one room after another. "But the doors to the corridor are locked up tight."

"Where are Doc and Laurel?" Luther asked.

"They're in the main room. Not surprisingly, Doc resisted when they were captured. He's a little banged up, but he'll survive."

"And Laurel?"

"She's fine and as sharp as a tack. She already trying to put together a lexicon of our kidnappers' language."

"The Trips," Luther said.

"The what? Oh, triplets. The Trips. I get it. Bizarre, isn't it? Laurel thinks she's heard enough of their language to communicate with them. A set of Trips was waiting for us behind a waterfall we used to cross a river. Somehow, they knew we'd be there."

"Did you see Butch McCall?" Luther asked.

"Who's he?" Jake asked.

Luther explained how he and Wolfe were captured.

"Raul's dead?" Flanna said, shocked.

"Yeah. Butch shot him and left him in the forest. He force-marched us here, shoved me into a room, then took Wolfe somewhere else."

"Any idea where?" Jake asked.

Luther shook his head.

"He could be in another room like you were," Flanna said. "We'll continue searching after we get you to the main room. If he's down here, we'll find him."

"Are there cameras?" Luther asked.

"Presumably," Flanna said. "Probably behind the grates in the ceiling, which are too high to reach. Our jailers have the ability to lock off any of the rooms remotely whenever they want. Apparently, that's how they get supplies down here. They isolate us in whichever room we're in, dump the supplies, then unlock the doors so we can get to the supplies."

"The perfect prison," Buck said. "No direct contact. No chance of us overwhelming them."

"Buried alive," Luther said.

"In a big coffin," Ana added.

Flanna opened a door to yet another room. It was the same size as the others, but that's where the similarity ended. It was like a gigantic concrete loft with sofas, chairs, tables, and beds. In the right-hand corner was a fully equipped kitchen. Laurel was sitting at the kitchen table, so totally absorbed in her work that she didn't look up. A man Luther assumed was Doc was sleeping on a sofa, his head wrapped in bandages. Standing in front of the oven were another man and woman. Luther had only met them a few times in his life, but he ran to them anyway.

"You're alive!" he shouted.

"Luther?" Sylvia O'Hara asked, her eyes squinting in doubt.

"I cut my hair," Luther said, throwing his arms around her. She was a lot thinner than he remembered.

Timothy dried his hands on a towel and gave Luther a pat on the back. "Grace? Marty?"

"Marty was on Ted's boat with Dylan Hickock and Agent Crow, who I guess you don't know. They must have reached the jaguar preserve by now. The last time I saw Grace she was back at camp." He looked at Buck and Ana for help.

"We sent her back to feed the hatchlings when we went out looking for Luther," Buck said.

Luther felt his ears burning. His little walk had caused a lot of trouble.

Ana hugged Sylvia and Timothy with tears in her eyes. "We'd just about given up hope."

"O'Haras are hard to kill," Timothy said. "I wish our reunion was under happier circumstances. This tomb is the last place we wanted to see you, or anyone else."

"It's Blackwood's?" Ana asked.

"Who else?" Timothy said tightly. "But we didn't know that for sure until Doc and Laurel showed up and told us. We haven't seen a living soul since we were locked in here."

"But Blackwood is at the Seattle Ark."

"No, he's not," Laurel said, looking up from her work. "He brought us down here personally and locked us in a room with a little help from his little triplet friends."

Luther looked at Sylvia. "So you know about the hatchlings and everything."

"Probably not everything, but we'll have plenty of time for you to fill us in."

"An eternity," Timothy added. "No one's going anywhere. We've been trying to escape for months."

"We'll continue the loop," Flanna said. "We didn't get very far. Wolfe might be in another room."

"I'll head in the opposite direction," Buck offered. "Meet you in the middle. It will save time, and that way we won't miss them if they're walking in the same direction you're moving."

"I'll go with Buck," Ana said.

"I'll go with —" Luther began, then smelled, and saw, the chicken sizzling on the frying pan.

Buck smiled. "We have this covered. Just save some food for us."

"Okay," Luther said. "Where did you get the chicken?"

"From the chicken coop," Sylvia said. "When we first got here, they gave us eggs. Timothy built an incubator and we hatched them. Saved some for laying, some for eating."

"And as soon as they figured out what we were doing, the fresh eggs stopped," Timothy said. "Which means they're watching us."

"If you don't mind . . . ," Sylvia said, looking at Buck. "When you pass by the chicken room, can you throw some scratch to the chickens and water the garden?"

"You have a garden down here?" Buck asked.

"Full spectrum grow lights, and dirt, provided by our keepers," Timothy said.

"The vegetables are kind of pitiful with the compost we've managed to produce," Sylvia added. "But they're a welcome break from those stale MREs. What we need is fertilizer."

"Do you have carrots?" Buck asked.

Jake laughed. "You and your carrots."

"I'm afraid we don't," Sylvia said.

"We're going to have to do something about that," Buck said.

"I hope we don't get stuck down here long enough to grow carrots," Ana said. "Let's get going."

Luther watched the two teams walk through their respective doors, then turned his attention back to the sizzling chicken.

"I wish Marty was here to do the cooking," he said.

Sylvia shook her head. "I don't. There's no way out of here. Believe me, we've tried. Wherever Marty and Grace are, there's a chance that they're safe. I don't want my kids anywhere near this place."

Luther didn't want to be the one to tell her that her "kids" had learned the truth after she and her husband had disappeared — that Grace was not in fact Marty's twin sister, as they'd both grown up believing, but his cousin.

"What's that faraway look for?" Sylvia asked. "What are you thinking?"

"Uh . . ." Luther hesitated. "I was wondering if I could have a drumstick when the chicken's finished cooking?"

"Sure," Timothy said, smiling. "But I get the other one."

"Deal," Luther said. This was going to be interesting.

TOO FAR

"It's not safe," Grace said.

"It's a little late for us to be worrying about safety issues now," Marty said.

They were standing at the edge of a roaring river as logs the size of small ships tumbled past in the boiling current. The hatchlings were cavorting back and forth on the opposite shore a hundred yards away. They looked like a couple of puppies stranded on the wrong side of a busy highway.

"We'll be killed," Grace said.

Marty pointed at the footprints along the muddy bank. There were dozens of them, including sneaker prints that had to be Luther's. "Looks like Luther made it to the other side. The prints end at the water."

"Well, he didn't swim," Dylan said. The first day he'd met Luther, he had to save him from drowning.

"Nobody could swim across that," Grace said.

"They didn't swim," Marty said, pointing to the opposite shore. Pulled up onto the bank were several dugout canoes.

"It couldn't have been easy to cross in those, either," Dylan said.

"But possible," Marty said. "Let's see if they left us a dugout on this side."

They searched the river for a quarter of a mile in each direction and found nothing. By the time they made it back to their original spot, the hatchlings had moved on. Marty caught up to them with the dragonspy. They were running through the jungle, sniffing the ground once in a while.

"They're obviously still on the trail," Marty said. He dumped his pack on the ground and took off his T-shirt.

"What are you doing?" Grace asked.

"Going for a swim. Between us, I think we have enough rope to stretch across. I'll paddle across, tie the rope to a tree, and you two can pull yourselves over."

"No," Grace said.

"What? We're just going to give up?"

"No."

"You can't have it both ways, Grace."

"I realize that," Grace said. "I'll take the rope across."

"No offense, but you're not much of a swimmer."

"I'm not going to swim."

"You can't throw a rope a hundred yards."

"But I can take it over the top," Grace said.

Marty looked up at the tree branches hanging over the river. Most of them were touching, but the ends were pretty thin. "I'm not sure they'd hold your weight."

"What are you two talking about?" Dylan shouted. "Grace isn't a monkey. She can't possibly climb up there and get to the other side without falling and killing herself."

Marty continued to peer up into the canopy. "I wouldn't be

so sure. Grace is smaller and lighter than we are, she has almost perfect balance, she isn't afraid of heights, and before all this happened, she was headed to the circus to become a high-wire artist."

"And I'm standing right here," Grace said sharply.

"Sorry," Marty said. He hated it when adults talked about him while he was right in front of them.

"And I wasn't heading to the circus," Grace continued. "Laurel taught me how to walk a high wire to get me over my fears."

"Do you think you can get across without falling to your death?" Marty asked.

"Pretty sure," Grace said. "But I'll need your help playing the rope out so it doesn't get tangled in the branches. When I get to the other side, I'll tie it off, and you and Dylan can come across like it's a zip line."

"You're making it sound a lot easier than it's going to be," Dylan said.

"We always do that," Marty said. "We'll cut the rope on the other side so Yvonne and her gorillas can't use it to get across."

"But then we won't have a way to get back," Dylan pointed out.

"We can use the dugouts."

Grace led the way, with Dylan following and Marty taking up the rear. She had picked the biggest tree she could find closest to the water. It was covered with lianas — vines that could be used as foot- and handholds — but even then the climb wasn't easy. After about fifty feet, Marty was gasping for air, inhaling insects, and choking. Dylan, whose butt was about two feet from Marty's face, seemed to be having the same problem. Grace, on the other hand, was a hundred feet in front them, moving up the tree as quickly if she was crawling on level ground.

Marty caught up with Dylan, who had paused to clear his throat. "I think you're wrong about her not being a monkey."

It took Dylan a couple more good hacks before he could respond. "I think she's stirring up the insects, and we're climbing through her bug cloud. I think I swallowed a flying beetle."

"I found a good place to cross!" Grace shouted down at them. "Hurry up!"

Ten minutes later, they arrived at Grace's perch, out of breath, covered with bites and scratches. Marty looked at his cousin. She was sweating, but that was about it. He shook his head in wonderment.

"What?" Grace asked.

"You," Marty said. "The same thing happened when we were in the Congo. No bug bites. No scratches. It's like you have insect repellent in your veins instead of blood, and some kind of invisible anti-scratch barrier on your skin."

"What's your point?"

"Jealousy, I guess."

"Give me the rope."

Grace tied the rope around her waist. Marty tied the other end around a stout branch. From where they were straddling the branches, they couldn't see more than five feet through the hazy green. Marty took his Gizmo out of his pocket. The hatchlings were still cavorting through the jungle, and still on the scent. They didn't look like they were going to turn around anytime soon.

“I guess they don’t want to cross back over the river,” Dylan said.

“I wouldn’t, either,” Marty said, taking the spyglasses out and slipping them on. “I’ll keep an eye on your progress with these.” He flew the dragonspy back to the tree, and Grace started across a branch toward the river . . . on her feet.

“Wait a second!” Marty shouted.

Grace turned her head. “This takes concentration, Marty.”

“It would take a lot less concentration if you did it on your hands and knees.”

“The branch is a lot thicker than the wire I’m used to walking on.”

“It’s also slippery with dew and moss, and it’s swaying in the wind.”

Grace ignored him. She put her arms out to her sides for balance and disappeared behind the foliage with the rope stringing out behind her like a monkey’s tail.

“Can you see her?” Dylan asked as he played the rope out.

“I can see her,” Marty said, but wished he couldn’t. . . .

Grace was above the raging river, trying not to think about the tumbling flotsam and jetsam a hundred and fifty feet below, or the ache in her arms from her rapid climb up the tree.

If I fall, I’ll drown or be crushed.

She paused, closed her eyes, and remembered what Laurel had told her about the high wire. *Look at the wire in front of you. Don’t look down at your feet. Don’t think about the steps. Look beyond your fear at the goal.*

It had been weeks since Grace had been on a high wire, and she’d never tried to walk on a swaying branch. Marty had a point about crawling along the branch instead of walking on top of it, but what he didn't understand was that to keep your balance, you had to be light on your feet, and that was impossible on your hands and knees. Grace could feel the limb vibrating more the farther she stepped out on it.

Don't look down at your feet. Don't think about the steps. Look beyond your fear at the goal. . . .

Her goal was a stout limb growing from a tree directly opposite the one she was on. When she'd started out, that limb had appeared parallel to the one she was on, but now it looked about three feet higher. Her weight was causing the limb she was standing on to arc downward. She paused to catch her breath. The dragonspy was in a hover two feet above her head.

"I might have to come back," she said to the dragonspy. "I should have picked a higher branch." She wasn't sure that Marty would understand, but then the dragonspy took off to the end of the limb, buzzed around the limb she was trying to reach, and flew back to her.

"See what I mean?"

The dragonspy moved up and down.

"I'll just go a few more feet."

The dragonspy moved side to side.

"I'll be fine, Marty," Grace said. "Just a few more steps and I'll be able to tell if I can get to the limb."

Again, the dragonspy moved side to side, a little more frantically.

"Out of my way," Grace said. "Before I swat you."

The dragonspy hovered about an inch from her nose, as if it was trying to block her.

"Get out of the way. You'll make me fall. I have to focus."

She took a step, then another, then — *CRACK!* The branch gave way and Grace fell, but only about four feet. The rope had gotten tangled around the limb. It had saved her life but had knocked the wind out of her. The dragonspy was in a hover just above where she was dangling. She felt vaguely confused and wondered if she had broken her back. She tried to say something, but found she didn't have enough air to speak yet.

And what would I say anyway? Help? I'm okay? Or worse . . . You were right, Marty.

She grabbed the rope and righted herself, which took some of the pressure off her back and made it so she could breathe more easily. She heard something above her and looked up. Marty was scooting along the broken branch like he was straddling a horse. His quick appearance could only mean that he had left the trunk the moment she'd ignored his warning. Marty stopped about twenty feet from the end and looked down at her, then at the tangled rope. He appeared surprised and relieved at the same time.

"Lucky," he said. "I'm happy to see you."

"You saw the branch was compromised," Grace said.

"If you mean the branch was rotted, yeah. Of course you totally ignored me."

"It wasn't you, it was the dragonspy, and I had no idea what you — it — was trying to tell me. How about pulling me up?"

Marty took a closer look at the rope and the branch. "Easier said than done. If I pull on the rope, it's going to come loose and you're going to fall. If I scoot closer to you, the branch will break and we'll both fall. Any chance you can pull yourself up?"

Grace wasn't sure. She regretted scrambling up the tree like a monkey ahead of Marty and Dylan because now her arms were worn out. "Guess I don't have much choice."

Marty shook his head. "Afraid not. On the bright side, I can anchor the rope from here. If you fall, you won't fall very far."

"That's reassuring."

Grace started up the rope, feeling a little self-conscious with Marty looking on. If he was at the end of the rope, he'd be up it like a spider, despite having climbed the tree a few minutes before. After what seemed like an eternity, she finally reached the top and with great effort managed to straddle the branch. Marty was grinning.

"That wasn't funny," Grace said, still out of breath.

"That's not why I'm smiling. We haven't sat this way since we were kindergartners. It reminds me of the teeter-totter we used to play on. Remember?"

She did. Only Marty would think of something like that a hundred and fifty feet above the rain forest floor. "What I remember is that you always tried to bump me off."

"Yeah," Marty said. "But you always hung on."

Grace smiled back at him. "What now?"

"We scoot back to Dylan, but before you do, you need to unhook yourself from the rope."

"Why? We'll need it. All I need to do is find a branch that's higher than the one I'm trying to get to. That was my mistake."

"That, and picking a rotten branch," Marty said. "Which isn't your fault. Every branch on this tree could be rotten at the end. It could take us hours, maybe days, to find the right branch, and we don't have the time. Luther and the others are somewhere up ahead, and they're in trouble. We need to get across this river right now, and I have a good idea how to do it quickly, but it would take too long to explain."

"And I probably wouldn't like the explanation," Grace said.

"There's that, too," Marty said.

Reluctantly, Grace untied the rope from around her waist and joined Marty back at the trunk.

"That was scary," Dylan said as they scooted up. The rope was wrapped around the tree trunk, and he was holding the slack in his hand. In his other hand he held the Gizmo. He looked at Marty. "What do you have in mind?"

"I thought of it when Grace was climbing back up," Marty answered as he rummaged through his pack. "Perfect. I have everything I need. Give Grace the Gizmo."

Dylan handed it to her. The dragonspy was still hovering over the broken branch with a view of the raging river below.

"You still haven't told us what you're doing," Grace said.

Marty put his backpack on. "I'll explain when I get out there."

He scooted down the branch before she could grab him or voice further objections.

"What do you think he's going to do?" Dylan asked.

"Something insanely stupid," Grace answered.

"At least he's consistent." Dylan looked over her shoulder at the Gizmo screen. "Do you know how to fly it?"

Grace shook her head. A few minutes later, Marty appeared on the screen. He looked up and waved.

"Can you hear me?" he shouted.

It was almost deafening over the Gizmo's speaker.

"We can hear you!" Grace exclaimed. "You don't have to shout!"

Marty gave them a grin and took off his pack. He was sitting on the very end of the branch. He took something out of his pack and hunched over.

"Can you tell what he's doing?" Grace asked.

"No," Dylan said. "But whatever it is, it's making me nervous."

"Me, too," Grace said.

Marty finished and looked back up at the camera. "Dylan, give me a shout when you have that rope anchored around your waist."

"Done!" Dylan shouted.

"Great," Marty said over the speaker. "What I need you to do is to let about three or four feet of rope out every time I shout out the word *now*. Got that?"

"Yes!"

"It's kind of like a cross between Tarzan and Spider-Man," Marty said, and fell off the branch backward.

Grace was too stunned to scream. She watched in horror as her cousin fell fifty feet. Then the rope went taut and he bounced upward.

"Bungee jump!" Dylan said. "Why didn't he just tell us?"

"Because he knew I'd try to stop him," Grace said.

"Now!" Marty shouted.

Dylan let out three feet of slack, then tightened his hands.

Marty, hanging upside down, started to swing across the river, arching his body to increase his momentum. As he reached the apex of his swing, he shouted again. Dylan let out few more feet of rope.

"Perfect!" Marty shouted.

"He's going to smash into a tree and kill himself," Grace said.

"Or catch a branch on the other side and get us across the river."

"Now!"

Dylan let out a few more feet of rope. Marty was swinging dangerously close to the trees on both sides of the river.

"Unless he goes too far," Dylan said.

"Marty *always* goes too far," Grace said.

But not this time. Marty caught a limb that stretched down from a huge tree on the other side of the river and came to a sudden stop.

"Give him more line," Grace said, but Dylan had seen the catch and was already feeding out more rope.

They watched as Marty pulled himself up onto the limb. He managed to straddle it, looked up at the dragonspy, and let out Tarzan yell, startling a flock of colorful parrots that knocked him off his perch. Marty caught himself by one hand and heaved his body up again.

"Too far," Grace said.

BENEATH

Luther paced the room as he ate his drumstick, which wasn't bad. The room wasn't bad, either, for a prison. The O'Haras had obviously spent a lot of time making it as comfortable as possible. Luther poked his head into a little room in the corner, cobbled together with wooden crates. Inside was a toilet, a small sink, and a showerhead sticking out of the wall.

Sylvia came up behind him. "I hope you like cold showers."

Luther, in fact, liked long, hot showers, but at least there *was* a shower. "You built this?"

"Timothy did."

"Lucky you found plumbing supplies down here."

"Not luck," Sylvia said. "Observation."

"What do you mean?" Luther asked, continuing his tour of the room.

"It took us a couple of weeks to recover from our injuries."

"The helicopter accident," Luther said.

"It was no accident. It was a surface-to-air missile. Whoever shot us down, I don't think they planned on survivors. But when Timothy and I lived, they changed their plans and had us brought here."

"By the Trips?"

Sylvia smiled. "Is that what you call them? As best as I can remember, there were three sets of them. They had to carry us on litters. We couldn't walk."

"No Butch McCall, or Noah Blackwood?"

"Just the Trips, as you say. We had no idea who they were. At first, we thought they were rescuing us. Timothy and I were both in a pretty bad way after the crash, in and out of consciousness and delirious. Neither one of us has much of a recollection of how we got here."

"They just dumped you down here?" Luther asked with disgust. "No one came to help you?"

"Not in this particular room, but yes, they dumped us. And you all are the first people we've seen since we were brought here. They put us in a room with MREs, water, medical supplies, and a couple of mattresses. They took our watches and phones, and without a window, it was hard to know how long we spent in that first room. I'd say five or six days. Tim was the first to recover and go exploring. He liked this room better than the one we were in, so we set up here."

"Because of the bathroom," Luther said.

Sylvia shook her head. "The bathroom, such as it is, wasn't here when we moved in. Most of the rooms down here have toilets. I'm not sure why. But the sink and showerhead parts showed up in another room a few days after we moved in here, along with some plumbing supplies."

Luther looked up at the ceiling. "So they *are* watching. They brought the plumbing stuff down here because they thought you might need it."

"I think it's more complicated than that. Perhaps more

sinister. They put the plumbing supplies down here to see what we would do with them. Just like the eggs."

"Which you could have eaten," Luther said.

"But we chose not to. Two days later, supplies to make a crude incubator showed up. The day before the chicks hatched, we found a stack of chicken feed in one of the rooms. Earlier today, we found six mattresses." She pointed to where she and Timothy had stacked them along the wall. "We knew you were coming. They're not just watching us. I think they're studying us. And now they're studying you."

"That ought to be interesting for them," Luther said, and was about to say something else when he caught a movement along the far wall. He hadn't noticed them before, but there were three large circular holes cut into the cement wall about five feet up from the floor.

He hurried over to them. "What are these?"

"Portholes," Sylvia said. "It turns out we're underwater, and this is the only room that has them, which is why Tim picked it as our home base. A bit of light comes through, so we can keep track of the days."

Luther stood on his toes and looked through one of the portholes. A large gaping jaw filled with jagged teeth rushed at him. He jumped backward.

Sylvia laughed. "Startling, isn't it?"

"Another giant alligator! We saw one from the boat on the way to the island."

"An island. Yes, Flanna mentioned that as well. All this time we had no idea that this structure we're in is actually connected to land. And those creatures, we think they're a cross between an alligator and a caiman," Sylvia said. "Or maybe an entirely new species. The one you just saw was small compared to some of the others. They're watching us, too."

"Creepy."

Luther was about reach up for another look when the four explorers returned from their rounds.

Buck was carrying a bunch of carrots. "Ask and you shall receive," he said. "There were a couple of packets of carrot seeds as well."

Laurel looked up from her lexicon. "But no Wolfe."

Buck shook his head. "Not a sign of him."

Luther walked over to where she was working. "They speak English," he said. "Well, at least one of them did. A guy named Ziti."

"The ones that took us didn't speak English," she said. "Or if they did, they didn't let on. Their language is strange. A cross between German, Portuguese, and an indigenous dialect I'm not at all familiar with."

Luther looked at her scribblings to be polite, then walked back to the portholes for another look at the giant gators.

Wolfe sat dead center on the sleeping bench at the back of the cage, ensuring that neither the bearcat nor the chupacabra could reach him through the wire mesh on either side. The bearcat had tired of trying to maul him and was now asleep in the far corner of its cage. The chupacabra hadn't moved and continued to watch him with reddish golden eyes that rarely blinked. A surveillance camera watched him as well, shielded from harm, high above on the other side of the mesh. The door Butch had pushed him through was locked tight. On the ground was a stainless steel bucket filled with water and a pile of stinking meat crawling with maggots. It had looked relatively fresh when Butch had dumped it in with a laugh, saying in terrible French, "Bon appétit."

Wolfe supposed that after a few days, his hunger would reduce his revulsion for the food.

Noah will get a kick out of watching me eat this, which is probably why he's kept me alive and put me in his twisted menagerie. It's either that or he'll open the door between the cages and let in the chupacabra, or the bearcat, or maybe both. May the best mutant win.

Wolfe knew that with Noah, it was all about control and manipulation through fear, which is why Wolfe was sitting on the bench calmly, as if being locked in a cage between two genetic mutants was an everyday occurrence. The only way to fight Noah Blackwood was to do the unexpected.

As long as I'm alive, there's hope.

Agent Steven Crow cut the engine of his Zodiac before gliding down the tributary leading to the jaguar preserve. He decided it would be better to come onto the camp quietly, unannounced. He wasn't exactly sure why. It was just a bad feeling he had, and over the years he'd learned to pay close attention to those feelings. About half the time the feelings amounted to nothing, and he felt like a fool, but the other half had kept him alive.

He was exhausted after bumping up the river for several hours in an inflatable that was a far cry from Ted Bronson's *Rivlan*.

And what about this Ted Bronson? he thought as he slowly paddled through the opening. *And the mysterious Travis Wolfe in the stolen helicopter? And running into Dylan Hickock in the middle of the Amazon just as I'm about to catch up with Buck Johnson?*

Perhaps his bad feelings weren't entirely due to exhaustion. If he hadn't talked to Al Ikes, he would have never gone along with this.

He looked at the sky. It was getting dark, and it would be pitch-black by the time he reached camp, which suited him just fine. With luck he'd be able to stake things out and see what was going on before moving in.

It was dark by the time he reached the dock, but not too dark to see that he was the last one to the party. Tied up to the dock were two boats, the *Anjo* — Yvonne's — and another, which he assumed belonged to Dr. Lansa. Next to the boats were the hijacked helicopter and Ted's ultralight. Ted had buzzed him in it hours earlier as he'd slowly made his own way upriver in the Zodiac.

Crow grabbed his pack, stepped onto the wooden dock, and listened. There was plenty of noise coming from the rain forest, but none of it was human. He could see a dim, flickering light up the trail leading to the camp, which had to mean that it was occupied, or had been occupied recently. He decided to go halfway up the trail, then cut off into the trees and find a good observation site, but he didn't get the chance. A man stepped out from behind a tree and jammed the barrel of a short automatic rifle into his chest.

"Welcome. Put your hands on your head."

Crow did as he was told. The man was wearing jungle fatigues and was clearly one of Yvonne's men.

"Let's see if you can get to camp without me shooting you in the back of the head." The man shoved him forward.

Crow walked toward the dim light of the camp. When they arrived, the man hit him in the back of the legs and Crow dropped to his knees. Yvonne and two other men were sitting on camp chairs near a smoky fire, swatting insects.

"Who are you?" Yvonne asked dully, as if she really didn't care.

"Steven Crow. Federal Bureau of Investigation."

The men laughed.

"Wallet." Crow said, his hands still on his head. "Right shirt pocket."

The man behind him pulled it out, glanced at it, then tossed it to Yvonne. She held it up in the dim firelight, then passed it on.

"Look," Crow said. "I understand you being cautious, but now that you know who I am, I suggest you let me up and put the gun down."

This was greeted by another round of laughter from the men and an icy stare from Yvonne. "What's your connection here?"

"I'm after a fugitive whom I believe to be here."

"Who?"

"Buckley Johnson."

"What did he do?"

"He hijacked an airplane."

"Good for him," the man to Yvonne's right said.

Yvonne leaned forward with her elbows on her knees. "Where's Ted Bronson?"

"I thought he was here." There was no point in denying it. They had seen his tiny airplane tied to the dock.

"Where's Marty and the other kid?"

"They're on Ted's boat."

Yvonne stared at him. If he'd had any doubt about who the bad guys were, it was gone now. The look on her face sent chills up his spine.

"Wrong answer," she said. "Their footprints are all over camp." She nodded at the man to her right.

The man stood up. "One more question." He stepped over to Crow, took something out of his shirt pocket, and thrust it into Crow's face. It was blinking. "You know what this is?"

"I'm not an entomologist," Crow said. "I'm an FBI agent."

The man pulled his pistol from its holster. "Deceased FBI agent. We just stopped here to rest before we track the kids down. Bad timing on your part. We're outta here. Can't take you with us. Can't leave you here." He cocked the pistol.

Crow wasn't exactly sure what happened next. There was a sudden movement to his right. He heard the man behind him yell. The man with the pistol fired. A split second later, the pistol flew out of his hand. Crow scrambled for the weapon. The camp exploded with gunshots. Crow felt a searing pain in his left calf. He didn't let it stop him. He grabbed the pistol and rolled over, holding it in two hands. Yvonne was about to finish him off. He got her first — a head shot. Then he shot the man next to her. He looked for the other two men. They were lying near the fire. It looked like their necks were broken.

Ted Bronson was sitting between them.

"You hit?" Ted asked.

"Leg," Crow answered.

"Me, too. And my arm. Didn't work out exactly as I had hoped, but I guess any gunfight you can walk away from, or in our case crawl away from, is okay."

"You were here the whole time?"

Ted nodded. "Got here just before they came out of the woods. Couldn't very well leave and let you walk into this mess alone. A few minutes later, and I think you would have missed them."

Crow looked at the man who had pulled the pistol on him. "Bad timing," he said.

"At least we don't have to worry about them coming up behind us now, or going after the others." Ted looked off into the trees. "Wherever they are."

"Pretty fancy martial arts," Crow said.

"Yeah, but it's not the best defense against guns." He picked up something on the ground and held it up. "And they squashed my bot."

"Now what?" Crow asked.

"Looks like you and I are out of commission. All we can do is patch each other up and wait."

"What about communications?"

"Still jammed. I'll see if I can get them working after we stop bleeding."

DAY FIVE

BOOTS AND BARE FEET

Marty felt someone shaking his shoulder. At least he hoped it was *someone* and not *something*. His eyes snapped open. It was Grace.

They had made it to an abandoned campsite a little after midnight and discussed continuing on for less than a minute before they'd all fallen into an exhausted sleep without even removing their backpacks.

Marty blinked the sleep out of his eyes, looking past Grace at the canopy above. It was getting light out.

"What?" he asked.

"Luther was definitely here," Grace said.

"We knew that last night."

After Marty, Grace, and Dylan had crossed the river, the hatchlings had resumed their forging-ahead-then-circling-back routine. The dinosaurs had spent a considerable amount of time in the camp sniffing around, which could only mean that Luther had passed through there earlier.

"Wolfe was here, too."

Marty sat up. "What did you find?"

"A corpse."

"Excuse me?"

"Raul."

"Who's —"

"He's the guide who led Wolfe into the rain forest."

Marty didn't relish the idea of looking at a corpse first thing in the morning, or ever, for that matter. He stood up and took off his backpack, wondering how he had actually slept with it on.

"Let's go take a look," he said.

Grace shook her head. "I've seen enough."

"What's going on?" Dylan asked sleepily. With his backpack still strapped on, he looked like an upside-down turtle.

"I think we should have reminded each other to take our packs off before going to sleep," Marty said.

"I left mine on intentionally in case we had to make a run for it," Dylan said. "What were you two talking about?"

"Grace found a dead guy."

"Where?" Dylan jumped to his feet and sloughed off his pack.

Grace pointed. "Over by that shelter."

Marty followed Dylan over to the crude shelter, then wished he hadn't.

"Jeez," Dylan said, covering his nose and turning away.

Marty forced himself to look. Heat, humidity, insects, and a few animals had been at the unfortunate Raul, but the manner of his death was still obvious. There was a perfect hole in his right temple. On the ground, five feet away from the body, was a brass bullet casing glittering in a shaft of morning sunlight.

"Shot," Marty said. "Murdered."

There were footprints all around the body, which Marty was happy to examine so he didn't have to look at Raul. He pointed at one.

"That has to be at least a size fifteen," he said.

"Wolfe?"

"Unless Bigfoot is wearing boots, yeah. And here are Luther's prints."

"What about this one?" Dylan asked, pointing.

"Not as big as Wolfe's, and the sole has a different pattern."

Grace had joined them. "Butch McCall?"

"I guess if Yvonne is here, he could be here, too," Marty admitted.

"We need to bury Raul," Grace said.

"Easier said than done, considering we don't have a shovel," Marty said. "But let me check on the trail behind us first. If Yvonne is coming up on us, we're going to have to leave him where he lies."

"We'll start while you check," Dylan said, scratching at the ground with a large stick.

Marty left them to their digging and launched the dragonspy. He was pretty sure that Yvonne and her gang weren't hot on their trail. She would have had to get across the river just like they had, and he doubted she was going to play Tarzan, which meant she and her crew would have to cross somewhere else and backtrack to pick up the trail on the other side. Marty flew the bot along the trail in the direction of the river. As it had been last night, the trail was easy to follow because whoever had nabbed Luther and Wolfe was no longer trying to hide their tracks.

There was no sign of anyone else on the trail. When Marty reached the river, he flew the dragonspy downstream for several miles expecting to find Yvonne and the men looking for a crossing, or better yet drowned, but they weren't there.

Maybe they did drown and got swept away. He smiled to himself. *I'm beginning to think like Grace.*

"Hey!" Dylan shouted. "We're almost done."

Marty looked over at them. Grace and Dylan were covered in wet mulch. He wasn't surprised. No matter where you dug in the rain forest, the water table was only a few inches beneath the surface.

"That's probably as deep as you can go. I'll help you move him in a minute. We'll have to cover him with sticks and logs."

He didn't mention that he didn't think covering Raul up, or even burying him, would stop the animals from getting to him. The burial was more for them than it was for Raul. It was the decent thing to do.

CAGED

As the sun rose, Travis Wolfe was sitting calmly on the bench in the back of his cage, just as he had been sitting the night before when the sun had set. It looked as if he hadn't moved during the night, but nothing could be further from the truth. He had spent the entire night getting to know his mutant neighbors.

For the first part of the night, the bearcat had spent his time pacing back and forth in a rage, napping, and reaching his long sharp claws through the wire mesh trying to shred Wolfe to pieces. Fortunately, the mesh only allowed a couple of feet of leg and claw into Wolfe's personal space. All Wolfe had to do to avoid being mauled was lean to his right, but not too far, because the chupacabra, or Nine, was on the other side waiting for him to make a mistake.

Unlike the bearcat, Nine never left his bench, or napped. He simply stared at Wolfe with his intelligent reddish-yellow eyes, as if he were contemplating how he was going to prepare him for breakfast.

Wolfe felt sorry for both animals. As the results of genetic experimentation, neither one of them belonged on earth, or anywhere else in the universe. But of the two, he felt sorrier for

Nine. The chupacabra seemed to be completely aware of the fact that he was different somehow.

Wolfe had no doubt that before Noah finally murdered him, he would be given a demonstration of Nine's capabilities, and Noah's ability to control the beast. He might even use Nine to execute him.

Wolfe had been around animals his entire life, in captivity and in the wild. In many ways he was more comfortable around animals than he was around people. He would have preferred not to be stuck in a cage of his own between two mutants, but overnight he had decided to work with the situation.

First, he'd started talking to the bearcat in a soothing tone. It hadn't worked right away, of course, but after a while the bearcat's attacks had become less intense, and Wolfe had begun phase two.

Wolfe was thirsty and hungry. His wrists were still shackled by flex cuffs, but at least they were bound in front of him instead of behind his back, which would have made things difficult.

There was nothing he could do about the hunger unless he wanted to eat the rotting meat Butch had dumped into the cage. But he could slake his thirst. He had jumped off his perch, gotten onto his knees in front of the water bowl, and had scooped water into his mouth with his hands. He'd felt better after drinking. He had looked down at the rancid meat, covered with flies. The bearcat had watched him closely.

When Butch had pushed him into the cage the day before, Wolfe had noticed that the bearcat had no meat in his cage. He figured the animal must have gulped his meal down in two bites. Nine hadn't even sniffed his meat. It still lay in a flyblown pile like Wolfe's.

Wolfe had looked at the bearcat. "You want some meat?"

The bearcat had snarled.

"I'll take that as a polite yes."

Wolfe had tossed a small ball of tainted meat through the mesh. Two hours later, the bearcat was catching the meat balls in the air. Wolfe didn't think they were friends yet, but they had made progress.

An hour after sunrise, he heard someone whistling. A second later, Butch McCall was standing in front of his cage.

"Good morning, Travis. Did you sleep good?"

Wolfe didn't take the bait.

"Dr. Blackwood would like you to join him for breakfa —" Butch looked down at the empty food tray. "Oh, I see you've already eaten. Was that to your liking?"

Wolfe just looked at him. The big idiot was having so much fun, he hadn't noticed that the bearcat wasn't trying to get at Wolfe through the mesh.

"Doesn't matter if you're full," Butch continued. "You still have to go to breakfast." He punched in a number on the keypad. The door clicked open.

Wolfe jumped off the bench.

Butch stepped back from the door and drew his pistol.

Wolfe smiled. "I appreciate that, Butch."

"Appreciate what?"

"The compliment." Wolfe nodded at the gun. "And the respect. Here I am handcuffed after spending the night locked in a cage, and you think you need a gun to control me."

Butch frowned. "Move it."

Butch walked Wolfe down the path to the pool, where they found Noah Blackwood sitting at a beautifully set table, cracking open a soft-boiled egg with a silver knife. He was dressed in his signature starched safari suit with every white hair on his head and face perfectly in place. Butch sat Wolfe down in the chair opposite Noah. The table was set for one.

Noah looked at his gold watch. "Fifteen minutes, Butch," he said.

Butch hesitated, then turned and walked back down the path.

Noah scooped out half of the soft-boiled egg with a silver spoon, popped it into his mouth, then dabbed the yellow yoke off his beard with a white cloth napkin. Apparently, Wolfe had been invited to watch Noah eat breakfast, not to partake.

"I'm sorry we have to continue our conversation in these short snippets of time," Noah said. "But I'm so extraordinarily busy right now. On the bright side, the time it's taking me to explain things is prolonging your life."

Noah forked the other half of the soft-boiled egg into his mouth, then started cracking the second egg. There were four eggs all together, along with a stack of toast, a plate of bacon, coffee, juice, butter, and assorted crystal containers of jam and jelly. Wolfe wondered how Noah managed to keep himself fit eating like this.

"Are you hungry?" Noah asked.

Wolfe nodded.

"Good," Noah said, and continued eating. "How old do you think I am?"

"Where's Luther?" Wolfe asked.

"We aren't going to get very far if you keep answering my questions with questions."

"According to you, it's to my advantage to prolong this conversation as much as I can."

Noah smiled. "Good point. I'll make a deal with you."

"What kind of deal?"

"I'll tell you where Luther is, and everyone else. In return, you'll have to choose which one of them dies first."

Wolfe kept his face expressionless. "What do you mean, 'everyone else'?"

"Sylvia and Timothy, for starters."

"You have them?" Wolfe said, trying to hide his relief.

"Yes. And they're fine, along with Laurel Lee, Robert Lansa, his son, Buckley Johnson, and Flanna Brenna."

"You shot Sylvia and Timothy's helicopter down," Wolfe said.

"Not personally, no, but it was done on my orders."

"Butch?"

Blackwood nodded. "They were lucky to have survived."

"Why did you do it?"

"Because they had heard a rumor about this compound and were getting too close."

Wolfe stared at him. It was all beginning to make sense now. Sylvia and Timothy would have followed this trail to the ends of the earth.

"What about Grace, Marty, and Dylan?" Wolfe asked.

"They remain at large," Noah said. "As do the hatchlings, Ted Bronson, and the man he picked up downriver. Who is he, by the way?"

Wolfe saw no sense in lying. "He's an FBI agent."

Noah laughed as if he didn't believe him.

Wolfe didn't care if he believed him or not. "What do you mean by 'at large'?"

"I shut down all communications as a security precaution once we had most of you in hand. The kids and Bronson might have been captured by now and could be on their way here. Or they could be dead."

"You'd have your own granddaughter murdered?"

"Technically, she is not my granddaughter," Noah said.

"I don't understand."

"I've told you everything I'm going to tell you about your friends," Noah said, raising his voice. "We're back to my original question. How old do you think I am?"

Wolfe had no idea why Noah was asking this, and thought about diverting the conversation again, but he didn't. He knew when to push Noah's buttons, and how, but now was not the time.

"I'd say you're sixty."

Blackwood flashed him a dazzling smile. "You'd be off by twenty years. I'm eighty years old. I was born here in 1934, two years after my parents arrived."

Wolfe stared at him. Even with plastic surgery, there was no way Noah was eighty.

"My real name is Heinrich Kurtz," Noah continued. "My parents were geneticists. They were good friends with Adolf Hitler. One of the first things he did when he came to power was to send my parents here and fund their research. They and their team of scientists arrived on a freighter filled with equipment and gold bullion."

"Why here?" Wolfe asked.

"Like I said, they knew Hitler well. They knew things were going to go sideways in Germany. They didn't want their research to get caught up in their old friend Adolf's madness. They needed isolation and a population of people that no one cared about to experiment on. They ended up finding a population of people that no one even knew about."

"The Trips," Wolfe said, feeling sick to his stomach. If Blackwood had offered him an egg, he didn't think he'd have been able to keep it down.

"Is that what you call them?" Noah asked with a smile. "Marvelous!"

"So your parents were Nazis," Wolfe said, which wiped the smile off Noah's face.

"Technically, yes, but they weren't practicing Nazis. Hitler waged his war and forgot all about the Kurtzes and our research project."

"And you waged war on the indigenous population down here," Wolfe said.

"Harsh," Noah said. "And predictably narrow-minded. The Trips, as you call them, are much better off now than they would have been if we had left them alone. But I'm not going to get into a debate about this. That's not why I have you up here."

Wolfe took a calming breath and reminded himself that this was Noah's show, not his. "Fine," he said.

"As to my age," Noah continued, "my mother discovered a longevity gene. The fountain of youth, if you will, or so she believed, and it turns out she was correct, at least in my case."

"What are you talking about?"

Noah fixed his blue eyes on him. "I'm a human clone."

Wolfe stared back at him. "That's impossible."

"I suspect I was the *first* human clone," Blackwood said. "The second clone is a man you know. Or at least a man you've seen. We call him Mr. Zwilling."

"I don't know anyone named Zwilling."

"Oh, but you do," Noah said. "Do you speak German?"

"No."

"*Zwilling* is the German word for 'twin.'"

"So that's how you often seem to be in two places at once. You have a doppelgänger," Wolfe said.

"That's not exactly accurate. A doppelgänger is usually defined as a sinister double. Mr. Zwilling is anything but sinister. And I don't *have* a double. I *made* a double when I was twenty years old."

Wolfe wanted to get up and walk back to his cage. He was sick of looking at Noah, sick of listening to him. But his curiosity compelled him to stay. "Mr. Zwilling is at the Seattle Ark," Wolfe said.

"He's always at one of my Arks. He hasn't been down here in years. He's such a pro at handling the media."

"He's sixty and you're eighty, but he looks just like you. How does that work?"

"You always were bright," Noah said. "Mr. Zwilling doesn't have the longevity gene. We tried to give it to him, but it didn't take. I'm not sure why. But he's been very useful none the less. Not surprisingly, he loves animals just as much as I do."

Wolfe had to will himself not to roll his eyes. Blackwood didn't love animals; he collected them.

"Zwilling and I honed our skills with wildlife right here at the compound," Noah said. "But I digress. I was talking to you about cloning. I made a second clone, whom you also know. Or knew."

Wolfe's empty stomach heaved. He shook his head. "No. No. No."

"Rose," Noah said.

Wolfe rested his head on his cuffed hands. Rose had rarely talked about her childhood, but when she had, it had always been about the mother she'd never known. She had asked

Noah, her *father*, a thousand times who her mother was. He'd always refused to talk about it. Now Wolfe knew why.

"Rose had the longevity gene," Noah said. "But you cut her long life short. In a way, when you killed her, you killed me."

"I didn't kill her, Noah. She was killed by Mokélé-mbembé."

"You stole her from me. Rose was my creation. You took her to the Congo. If you had left her at the Ark, she would still be alive. She'd be alive for many years to come."

There was no point in telling him that Rose had loathed him and couldn't wait to get beyond his smothering control. Noah had to know this already. Rose would have been completely horrified to learn that she was Noah Blackwood's clone. Unless she had known, and not told him.

"My mistake was making Rose leave here too soon," Noah continued. "I should have waited to take her to the Ark when she was older."

Wolfe did not want to hear any more about clones. It was too painful to even think about. "Why did you even build the Arks?" he asked. "You appear to have everything you need here."

"I had the compound and the gold, but gold is worthless unless you use it. Zwilling and I were good with animals. I needed genetic material to expand my work and complete the experiments begun by my parents. I needed to turn the gold into cash."

"Your parents are dead?"

"Decades ago. Everyone who came here is dead. The longevity gene can only be inserted at conception. My parents didn't get to see that their fountain of youth was real. In fact, none of the original researchers lived to see it." A melancholy look crossed Noah's face. "One problem with living for an indefinite period is that all your friends, family, and colleagues die before you."

"So you decided to make new friends and a new family by cloning yourself."

Noah gave him a sad smile. "I don't expect you to understand."

"What are you going to do with us?"

"I haven't decided yet. But I certainly can't let any of you go. You're here for the duration. But in your case, that will not be long."

"Dad!"

Wolfe turned around. He recognized the voice. He opened his mouth to speak, but nothing came out. It was Grace. It was Rose. But it was neither. The black haired, robin's-egg-blue-eyed doppelgänger was a girl of eight or nine. She ran ahead of Butch McCall, jumped into Noah's lap, threw her arms around his neck, and gave him a loud kiss on his cheek.

"Scratchy whiskers," she scolded.

Noah laughed.

She turned her attention to Wolfe. "Is this the bad man?"

"Yes," Noah answered. "His name is Travis Wolfe."

"Why are you trying to hurt my dad?"

Wolfe was having a hard time breathing. It was like going back in time and meeting Rose when she was a little girl, like seeing his own daughter, Grace, as she might have looked a few years earlier. Noah eyed him with a broad grin, obviously enjoying his horror.

"I'm not trying to hurt your dad," Wolfe managed to say.

"Well, if you do, you will have to deal with me," she said.

"Then we have no worries," Wolfe said. "What's your name?"

"Violet Blackwood."

She didn't seem to notice, or didn't care, that he was handcuffed or that his wrists were bleeding.

"I saw you sitting in the cage this morning between the bearcat and Nine," she said.

"I didn't see you," Wolfe said.

Violet looked at Blackwood.

"Go ahead," Blackwood said. "You can tell him."

"We have cameras," Violet said. "A lot of cameras. I watched you on a monitor. You barely moved."

She had just answered one of his questions. The cameras were not infrared. She'd missed the bearcat training session. It suddenly occurred to Wolfe that Violet was Blackwood's big reveal, and that their conversation would likely be over soon. He needed to find out as much as he could before he was put back in his cage.

"I noticed something strange in the sky over your compound as we were brought in," he said to Noah, trying not to stare at Violet. "Some kind of strange shimmering."

"I was wondering if you'd seen it," Noah said. "It's a cloaking array, which is another reason I had to venture out from the compound. As technology has advanced, I've had to find ways to conceal ourselves better. I've never been worried about aircraft. No one flies over this area at low levels. But I was concerned about satellites inadvertently discovering us. Hence the cloak. We can also detect aircraft with it. That's how we found your sister snooping around in the helicopter. In addition, I bought up all the land for miles around the compound as a buffer, including Dr. Lansa's jaguar preserve."

"He obviously didn't know that," Wolfe said.

"No. He thought the land and his research were being paid for by a wealthy benefactor. The man who funded his preserve actually works for me. I control everything and everyone down here."

"What about Marty and Grace?" Wolfe asked.

Butch's expression soured at the mention of their names. He looked at Blackwood. "Has Yvonne caught them?"

"I hope so, for her sake," Blackwood said. "After we finish up here, I want you take some men outside and find out what's going on. They should have been here by now."

"Don't worry," Butch said. "I'll round the others up. Comms still down?"

"Yes, and we'll stay dark until we have captured, or eliminated, the ones who are still at large."

"That makes it kind of hard," Butch said.

Noah's eyes narrowed. "It's up to you to make it work, Butch."

"No problem," Butch said.

Wolfe watched Violet during this exchange. She was paying close attention to what Noah and Butch were saying, and she obviously understood what they were talking about. But she appeared unfazed by their plan to kill people.

"I want to keep the ones below," Violet said.

"I thought you told me you were getting bored with them," Noah said.

"I was getting a little bored with Timothy and Sylvia, but now that they have company, things have gotten a lot more interesting. The old man was asking if there were carrots. You should have seen the look on his face when he found a bunch of carrots in one of the rooms. He nearly jumped for joy. I'm going to send some fertilizer down so he can grow his own carrots."

It's like a dollhouse for her, Wolfe thought. *But instead of dolls, she's playing with living, breathing human beings. She doesn't know any better.*

"They spent a good part of last night talking about how to escape," Violet continued. "I love it when they do that. So far they haven't come with up an idea that will work."

Wolfe realized that if Blackwood had gotten his hands on Grace when she was young, she would have been playing the same twisted game.

"That's because there is no escape from below," Noah said. "Are you sure you want to keep them around?"

"Please!" Violet threw her arms around Noah's neck again.

"Yes, yes, all right," Noah said, laughing, then fixed cold eyes on Wolfe. "What should we do with this man?"

Violet stared at him, unblinking, without an ounce of compassion or sympathy. "I don't care," she said.

"I guess the verdict is in, Travis," Noah said. "Sorry it didn't go your way. We'll carry out your sentence soon." He looked at Butch. "Put him back in his cage, then go out and get the others. I want this finished before the end of the day."

Butch jerked Wolfe to his feet and pushed him toward the path. Wolfe glanced back at Violet. She was watching him with ice-cold blue eyes. Blackwood's eyes.

The cages had been hosed out during Wolfe's absence. There was a pile of fresh meat in the feed dish inside his cage, and another in Nine's. The bearcat's meat was gone.

Butch punched in the code. Wolfe only managed to catch two numbers before Butch shoved him through the opening.

6-6 . . .

The steel door slammed closed behind him.

"Get you anything to make your short stay more comfortable?" Butch asked sarcastically.

If Wolfe thought that dropping on his knees and begging would persuade Butch to let the others go, he would have done it.

"I'm good," Wolfe said, smiling, resuming his position on the platform at the back of the cage. "Thanks for asking."

"I don't know when the old man is going to kill you, or how he's going to do it," Butch said. "But I guarantee when the time comes, you won't be so cheerful."

"You're probably right," Wolfe admitted. "But there's no point in going there until I get there."

"How about that Violet?" Butch asked slyly. "She's a real piece of work, isn't she? Makes Noah look like a saint. He got her right this time. I wouldn't be surprised if he let her kill you. I'd be disappointed, of course. I've been wanting to kill you for years."

"I've always wondered about that," Wolfe said. "Why didn't Noah just have me killed after Rose died? It's not like I have tight security. He could have pulled the trigger on me anytime he liked."

Butch shook his head in disgust. "He had this harebrained idea that you were the only person on earth who could find cryptids, when in fact you're just lucky. If he'd let me look for cryptids rather than follow you all over the world, I would have gotten him all the genetic material he ever needed a long time ago."

"That's debatable." Wolfe jumped off the bench and held out his shackled wrists. "Cut these things off and let me out of here. We can settle this right now. Just you and me."

"Tempting," Butch said. "But I think I'll pass." He started to walk away.

"You'd better start thinking about what's going to happen to you after I'm gone," Wolfe shouted after him. "Without me, Blackwood won't need you."

Butch hesitated, then continued walking.

Worth a shot, Wolfe thought, resuming his seat on the bench. He looked at his neighbors. Nine stared at him like he wanted to eat him. The bearcat stared at him like he wanted to be fed.

"One or the other, or maybe both, of you are going to get your way," Wolfe said.

Nine shifted his fiery eyes to the path leading to their cages. The bearcat turned his vicious hybrid head in the same direction. Someone was coming down the path, although Wolfe couldn't hear or see anyone. His years in the field had taught him to pay close attention to the animals around him.

Nature's sentries. They see and hear things we can't.

A few seconds later, Violet came around the corner, obviously in a hurry, staring straight down the path, looking neither left or right. As she passed his cage, she reached out with her left hand and shoved something through the mesh. It dropped into the water bucket before he could see what it was. He jumped off the bench, but by the time he got to the front of the cage, Violet was gone. He looked down at the bucket. Shining up at him through the water was a knife. Probably the same knife Noah had used to crack open his soft-boiled egg. It wasn't sharp. He would have preferred it if she had slipped him the lock code.

But it'll do.

He allowed himself a small smile. Apparently, Violet was not the clone Noah thought she was.

And she's a far better actress than Grace or Rose.

BOT SPOTTING

"What's up with them?" Dylan asked.

He was referring to the hatchlings. They had circled back two hours earlier, but instead of forging ahead again, they had stayed close. So close, in fact, it was hard not to trip over them as they made their way up the path.

"Maybe they're hungry and want us to feed them," Grace suggested.

"We're fresh out of raw, bloody meat," Dylan said.

"I don't think they're hungry," Marty said. "I think they're nervous. I think something up ahead might have scared them."

"Like what?" Grace asked.

"Whatever it is, it can't be good. Before this, they weren't afraid of anything. I think we should stop and send the dragonspy ahead to scope things out."

Marty had been flying the bot along their back trail to make sure Yvonne and her men weren't sneaking up on them. So far, he hadn't seen any sign of them, which was making him nervous. He couldn't imagine Yvonne would stop chasing them. Something must have happened to them.

But what?

He was tempted to fly the dragonspy all the way back to camp to pick up their trail, but that would take time. And now there was the problem of the nervous dinos. He took his pack off, sat down, and leaned against a moss-covered tree. Grace and Dylan joined him. The hatchlings rooted around the forest floor for grubs, but didn't stray far.

Weird.

He slipped the spyglasses on. He was getting used to them, but they still seemed to work better when he was stationary. It didn't take him long to figure out what had frightened the hatchlings. A hundred yards ahead, he spied the skeletal remains of a fried monkey hanging on what looked like a fence.

"Uh-oh."

"What?" Grace and Dylan asked simultaneously.

He zoomed in on the gristly primate and showed them on the Gizmo.

"Is that a human?" Grace shrieked.

"Way too small," Marty said. "I'd say it is, or was, a spider monkey. See how long the arms are?"

"What happened to it?" Dylan asked.

"The more important question is why is there a chain-link fence in a supposedly unexplored section of the rain forest?" Grace said.

"I'd say that we've arrived." Marty flew the dragonspy along the fence's perimeter, passing by a couple more dead monkeys, a three-toed sloth, several birds, and a rusty sign with large red letters and a swastika.

ELEKTRIFIZIERT!

"I take it that's not Portuguese," Marty said.

"German," Grace said. "But it might as well be Martian. I doubt any of the indigenous people out here can read in any language."

"Guess we know why the hatchlings are nervous," Dylan said. "They might have gotten shocked."

"It's lucky they weren't killed," Grace said. "What is this place? Can you get a closer look?"

Marty flew the dragonspy along the fence until it came to a gate. He drew back and found a road leading up to the gate from the inside. "Tire tracks," he said. "And there. Footprints." He zoomed in on the gate again and found a keypad, a camera, and a flashing red light. He looked at Grace. "Think you can pick that?"

Grace was an excellent lock pick. For years, Marty had been begging her to teach him, but she'd refused.

"It's a keypad," she said. "There's nothing to pick. We need the code."

"I guess we'll have to find another way inside. I'll fly the perimeter."

"Before you do that, let's see what's on the other side of the fence," Grace suggested.

Marty flew the dragonspy along the rutted road and came to a clearing where dozens of people were tending fields, orchards, gardens, and livestock.

"They all seem to be working in threes," Dylan pointed out. "Weird."

"I think it's weirder than that," Grace said. "Zoom in on one of the groups."

Marty zeroed in on a trio of women throwing feed to a huge flock of chickens.

"Whoa," Dylan said.

"Triplets," Grace said.

"Identical," Marty said. One of the women swatted at the dragonspy and nearly took it down. "And they're quick."

He flew the bot over to a group of kids who were maybe seven or eight years old, pulling weeds in the massive vegetable garden. Three girls in one row. Three boys in the next row over. All identical triplets. He flew over to the livestock pens. The cows, sheep, and goats were being tended by three groups of older men. There were some variations between the groups of triplets, but not much. Zooming from face to similar — really, identical — face was making Marty a little dizzy. He flew the dragonspy back to the road.

"What are you doing?" Grace asked.

"Getting back on track. A bunch of triplets. Bizarre, but who cares? We're here to find our friends, not to study anthropological anomalies."

"Did you just say 'anthropological anomalies'?"

"You're not the only one who knows how to use big words," Marty said, feeling unduly proud of himself.

He continued to fly the dragonspy down the road and came to a lake, a village, and a large group of indigenous men, all triplets. These ones were not carrying shovels, hoes, or pruning shears. They were wielding bows and arrows, blowpipes, clubs, and spears. Their bodies were covered in jaguar tattoos. Their teeth looked like they had been filed to sharp points. Towering over them was Butch McCall.

"Guess we're in the right place," Grace said.

Butch was leaning against a World War Two vintage truck, talking to the warriors. Except for his black eye, he looked like he had completely recovered from Ted Bronson's beating.

"And those guys aren't farmers," Dylan said.

"No kidding," Marty agreed.

"Get in closer so we can hear what they're saying," Grace said.

Marty shook his head. "I doubt they're speaking any language you know. And if I get too close, Butch will spot the bot."

"He doesn't know about the dragonspy."

"He kind of does," Marty said. "He saw it at the Ark, but didn't know what it was. If he sees it again down here, he'll figure it out."

To make certain Butch didn't see the bot, Marty flew even farther away.

"What's that?" Dylan pointed. "Some ancient ruin?" A two-story building choked with jungle vines sat on an island in the center of a lake.

"I'd say more like World War Two," Marty answered. "Unless the ancients knew how to mix and pour concrete."

"I know this place!" Grace said.

Oh boy, Marty thought. The last time Grace had claimed she knew a place was in the Congo. It turned out that she had actually been born there, and lived there until she was a toddler, but she couldn't have possibly lived on two continents at the same time.

"Umm," Marty said, wondering if the heat, humidity, and exhaustion had finally gotten to her.

"My mother's journals," Grace said.

"I read your mother's journals and there was noth —"

"You didn't read the journals you soaked in rhino pee," Grace said. "They were filled with sketches." She pointed at the Gizmo screen. "Sketches of this island, the building inside and out, the village along the shore, the people. I thought she was drawing Lake Télé, or how she wanted Lake Télé to look in the future. But she wasn't. She was sketching this place from memory. She came here."

"You didn't happen to see a code for the gate in the journal did you?"

Grace shook her head. "There weren't any sketches of the fence."

Marty looked at Butch looming like a giant over the triplets. He was obviously explaining something to them. Every once in a while they nodded their jaguar-spotted heads and lifted their weapons into the air.

"What do you want to do?" Dylan asked.

Marty had a plan, but he wasn't sure if Grace and Dylan would like it. He wasn't sure that *he* liked it.

"Someone must be monitoring the cameras above the gate and along the fence," he said. "We need to find that person and get them to open the gate so I can use the dragonspy to steal the code. Then one of us has to get inside without them knowing it."

"One of us?" Grace asked.

Marty explained his plan. They took it better than he expected.

Butch had to go over his instructions several times before he was certain the men understood what he needed. Noah's Warriors, as they were known within the compound, were smart and tough, but a little slow in understanding the subtleties of a mission. They had been carefully selected over generations to seek and destroy any target they were given. The word *capture* was a difficult concept for them the grasp. But he had to admit they had done a magnificent job the past couple of days by bringing everyone in alive for Violet to play with in the dungeon.

Violet, he thought with a shiver. She creeped him out worse than Nine did. He turned his attention back to a set of triplets who were asking him something about the hatchlings. Their singsong language was hard to follow with all three of them chirping at the same time. He waved the two warriors on the right to be silent and pointed at the man on the left to proceed. They wanted to know if they could kill the hatchlings if they got violent.

Butch shook his head vigorously and explained once again that Noah wanted the hatchlings and the people captured alive. He told them that they could use violence to protect themselves against the bad people, but under no circumstances were they to harm the hatchlings. He started to go over the rules of engagement again to make sure they understood, but midway through, Noah's Warriors turned their attention toward the lake over his shoulder. Butch whirled around. A boat was rushing across the water and headed their way. Noah Blackwood was at the helm, his white hair swept back like a lion's mane.

Noah always flew into the compound, landing on the helipad in back of the building on the island, and he rarely left to visit his people face-to-face. He preferred to check in on them through the dozens of closed-circuit cameras scattered around the compound. The only people allowed inside the monitoring room were Noah, Butch, and Violet, who virtually lived there.

She spent so many hours inside the dim room that half the time she was unaware that Noah had taken off and was no longer in Brazil. If his absences bothered her, she never mentioned it. When Noah landed, she'd run out to the helipad and throw her arms around him as if he'd just returned from a short joyride, even if he'd been away for weeks, or months.

Noah was known to the people inside the compound as the Creator. By the time he climbed out of the boat and onto the dock, at least a hundred people had gathered to get a glimpse of him, and more were on their way. Noah gave the adoring crowd a cursory smile and a wave, then nodded for Butch to come over.

"The hatchlings are right outside the south gate," Noah said. "Or at least they were there a couple of minutes ago."

"Why didn't you just —" Butch stopped himself, remembering that Noah had switched all the comms off. "Who's with them?"

"Grace and that Dylan kid. I didn't see Marty or anyone else. They were heading east along the perimeter. If you go through the south gate and send some warriors through the east gate, you'll be able to squeeze them."

Butch had already thought the same thing, but didn't mention it. It was always better to let Noah think he was the one making the plans. "I'll get right on it," he said, knowing that he wouldn't be able to get on anything until Noah got back on the boat and returned to the island. The warriors and workers were staring at Noah as if Zeus had just paid a visit from Mount Olympus.

Noah finally seemed to take notice of the growing crowd. "Oh," he said. "I'll go back to the island and monitor it from there."

"Okay," Butch said. "After I get the kids and the hatchlings corralled, I'm going to stay out until I run everyone down. We need to get this thing over with. What do you want me to do with Yvonne?"

"I don't want to see her again," Noah answered. "She's served her purpose." He gave the crowd another smile, a half-hearted wave, and returned to the boat.

Butch headed back to the truck and started it.

Marty had watched their entire conversation on the Gizmo screen, from outside the fence, fifty feet up a tree. When Noah had showed up in the boat, he'd almost flown the bot in closer to eavesdrop, but he didn't dare. He didn't like Butch, but he had a lot of respect for the man's observational skills.

Marty watched Noah Blackwood head across the lake toward the island, then turned the dragonspy back to the truck bouncing down the road, overflowing with tattooed triplets.

His plan, such as it was, was working.

Noah must have seen Grace, Dylan, and the hatchlings through the security cameras. And if he had to come out of his fortress to tell Butch, that meant his communications were out, too, or else he would have just called or radioed.

Having Dylan join Grace and the hatchlings along the fence was not part of Marty's original plan, but when he'd laid it out for them, Dylan had insisted on sticking with Grace.

Gallant, but risky.

Marty didn't think that Butch would hurt Grace, but he wasn't so sure about Dylan. He'd told Dylan about Butch trying to throw him overboard on the *Coelacanth*, but even that hadn't changed Dylan's mind. Grace had sided with Marty, but not very vigorously.

It's almost as if she —

As soon as he thought this, he knew it was true.

How about that? My cousin has a boyfriend.

He watched the truck bumping over the rutted road, surprised that the triplets were able to hang on. It slowed, then took an abrupt left, which did throw three of them to the ground, but they were on their feet in a second trying to catch up.

Where are they going?

Marty expected them to come directly toward him, not head cross-country through the jungle. Ten minutes later, Butch slammed on the brakes, launching another set of triplets, to uproarious laughter, including from the three who had been hurled into the trees. All the riders jumped off the truck. Half of them ran into a metal shed and came out carrying ropes and long sticks. Some of them climbed back into the truck, while others followed Butch down a narrow path. Before Marty knew what was going on, Butch had opened a second gate. The triplets ran through. Butch slammed the gate behind them and started back to the truck.

Marty swore. If he had been paying attention, he would have gotten the code.

Butch maneuvered the old truck around and headed back the way he had come, slowing down, but not stopping, so the triplets he had dumped could clamber back into the truck bed.

Marty crossed his fingers, praying Butch would take a left when he got to the main road, and not a right.

Left . . . left . . . left . . .

Butch took a left.

Marty uncrossed his fingers and flew the dragonspy ahead to get into position, hoping Butch didn't take another turn. It was the longest ten minutes of his life. He wanted to check on Grace and Dylan. He wanted to check on Butch. He wanted to check on the triplets trotting along the fence. But he kept the dragonspy exactly where it was. Finally, he heard the truck in the distance.

From where he sat, he couldn't see the gate himself. In fact, he couldn't see the fence at all through the green blur of leaves. His plan depended on his not being caught by Butch or the triplets. He was straddling a branch, a hundred yards from the gate, and even then he felt vulnerable. Butch McCall could see and sense things other people couldn't.

He heard the truck come to a stop, the engine shut down, a door open and close, and then footsteps.

He stared at the Gizmo and held his breath. On the screen was a perfectly focused image of a ten-digit keypad. If Butch stepped in front of the keypad the wrong way, or noticed the strange insect dangling on a hanging vine three feet from the gate, it was over. Grace, Dylan, and the hatchlings would be captured for nothing. And they *would* be captured. Of that there was no doubt. It was part of the plan.

A scarred and battered index finger appeared on the screen and punched four numbers.

6-6-2-4

Marty let his breath out and shook his head.

I should have known. 6-6-2-4. N-O-A-H.

Butch and the triplets filed through the opening. Marty flew the dragonspy twenty feet straight up and put it into a hover. Butch was examining the ground on the other side of the gate. The triplets were gathered around him, waiting for instructions. He sent a set of triplets back through the gate. They piled into the front seat of the truck, turned it around, and headed back in the direction they had come.

The tattooed jaguar guys know how to drive. Good to know.

Butch closed the gate and said something to the rest of the triplets. They began moving east along the fence line. But not Butch. He remained standing outside the gate, looking off into the forest as if something wasn't right. Marty knew there was no possible way that Butch could see him, but it still made him nervous.

Butch stood scanning the trees for at least a minute before heading after his men. The camera above the gate swiveled and followed him. This was what Marty had been waiting for. The cameras were not motion sensitive. They were being toggled manually by someone inside the compound. His only chance of getting inside unseen was to have the camera pointed away from the gate like it was now. But still he waited, following Butch along the fence until he was certain Butch wasn't doubling back.

Finally convinced that Butch had been fooled, Marty climbed down from his perch and carefully made his way over to the gate.

N-O-A-H

Click!

Marty was inside.

DEAD MONKEYS

"I'm still having a hard time understanding Marty's plan," Dylan said.

"You aren't the only one," Grace said, wondering how far they had walked, and how long the fence was. They hadn't even reached the first corner yet.

"So you don't get it, either," Dylan said.

Grace shook her head. "Not exactly. I'm used to Marty's plans, but what I never get used to is how open-ended they are."

Dylan pointed at yet another dead monkey clinging to the fence. "That's number fourteen."

Grace had lost count. "Here's what I think Marty's thinking. We're all going to be captured anyway, so why not take advantage of it by getting the code to the gate, which is likely the same code used on all the keypads inside, and get someone inside they don't know about?"

"I'm not sure we would have been captured anyway," Dylan said.

"Really? They captured everyone else. Why wouldn't they be able to capture us? And even if they didn't manage to grab us, where would we go? We're marooned in the middle of nowhere, with two baby dinosaurs, and all of our friends are on the other side of this fence."

Dylan pointed. "And there's dead monkey fifteen."

Luther was walking in circles. One room after another. There were seventeen rooms altogether. He'd lost track of how many laps he'd done. Sometimes he went clockwise, sometimes he went counterclockwise, depending on his mood. He'd found the cameras in all the rooms. All of them out of reach. He gave each of them a smile and a wave when he strolled by. He also checked every door he passed. When he found it locked, which it always was, he turned to the nearest camera and gave it a thumbs-up, like a happy security guard.

He walked into the chicken room, which, not surprisingly, smelled like chicken poop. Buck had been in the room for several hours planting carrots. Sometime during the night, or maybe the day — Luther had lost track of time — the invisible prison elves had dropped off several bags of fertilizer and a box of vegetable seed.

"You still doing loops?" Buck asked.

"You still planting veggies?" Luther asked.

"Yep."

"Think we'll be down here long enough to eat them?"

"Maybe. Sylvia and Timothy have been down here awhile. Did you find anything new?"

Luther shook his head.

"You know, your rounds might be ticking them off."

"I hope so," Luther whispered. "Eventually, they're going to screw up and open a door at the wrong time. I'm going to be there when they do."

"When I tell you that you need to stop making rounds, you need to stop making rounds."

"Huh?" It seemed like an odd thing for Buck to say. In fact, everyone had been acting a little oddly the past few hours, and Luther didn't think it was because they were prisoners. Something was up. "What do you mean?"

"No rounds when I tell you to stop," Buck repeated.

"Fine," Luther said.

"How's Doc?" Buck asked.

"Not too good," Luther said. "He's drifting in and out of consciousness. When he's awake, they have a hard time keeping him in bed. He has a terrible temper."

"He has a terrible concussion," Buck corrected, loudly enough for the chickens to hear in the far corner of the room. "If he doesn't get some medical help soon, he could die."

Doc did have a terrible concussion, but the consensus was that he would be okay if they could keep him down for a few days. Buck's theatrics were an attempt to get more medical supplies, which they would need if they were going to be down there for any length of time.

Luther turned to the nearest camera. "You hear that? We need help!"

Buck stared at him like he was crazy, which Luther was used to.

"What?" Luther said. "We know they're watching and listening. And we know they speak English, because the stuff shows up after we talk about it in English. Might as well open a dialogue with them, even if it's one-sided." He looked back at the camera. "And I'm still waiting to hear how Wolfe is doing. Let me know as soon as you can."

"While you're waiting to hear back, think you can get these eggs to the bunkhouse without breaking them?" Buck pointed at a small bucket. In the bottom were four eggs.

"Sure."

"And this." He handed him a feed sack.

"Chicken?"

"What else?"

"One chicken between eight people doesn't go far."

"Seven," Buck said. "I don't eat meat."

"That's right. I forgot."

Luther grabbed the bucket and sack, and headed to the bunkhouse. He found everyone pretty much in the same places they'd been when he left. Jake was looking through the portholes. Flanna was sitting next to Doc. Laurel was at the table working on her lexicon. Sylvia and Timothy were asleep. Of all of them, Sylvia and Timothy were the two Luther was most concerned about. They were putting up a good front, but he knew their injuries and long captivity had done a number on them. They were thin, pale, and weak. Marty and Grace were going to be shocked when they saw them.

If they ever see them again. If we ever get out of here.

Luther put the chicken and eggs in the kitchen, wishing Marty was there to make something delicious out of it. Whoever was going to cook, and it was usually Timothy, was going to have to get to it soon. Without refrigeration, meat didn't last long. He wandered over to the portholes where Jake was standing.

"Anything new?" Jake asked quietly.

"The tells are all in place," Luther answered.

The *tells* were small blocks of wood, cardboard, and wadded-up paper he and Jake had secretly placed in front of every corridor door. If someone opened a door, it would push the tell away from the door. They were trying to figure out if one door was being used more than another. What purpose this would serve, they didn't know, but they both felt sitting around doing nothing was not an option.

"Want me to do a round?"

"Nah," Luther said. "I'll go again. I'm not very good at sitting."

Jake grinned. "I noticed."

"How's your dad?"

"He hasn't had a blowup since your last round, so I guess that's good."

An alligator swam passed the porthole, which seemed to take forever.

Luther cupped his eyes and peered through the glass. "How big do you think these things are?"

"Twenty feet," Jake said. "Maybe bigger, which is impossible, but a couple of days ago I would have said that seeing dinosaurs was impossible."

"Dead monkey nineteen," Dylan said.

Grace pointed ahead. "And the end of the fence."

"Technically, it's the corner of the fence."

"Whatever."

They turned left. The hatchlings followed along, keeping Grace and Dylan between them and the fence.

"Dead monkey twent —"

A set of triplets stepped out from behind a tree, pointing blowpipes at their heads.

Grace put her hands up in the air. Dylan followed suit.

"No sudden moves," Dylan said.

"No kidding," Grace agreed. The triplets looked a lot more fierce in person than they did on the Gizmo.

A second set of triplets stepped out of the woods carrying sticks and ropes. Grace looked at the hatchlings. Their heads were whipping back and forth between the two groups, obviously agitated.

"So this is the plan?"

"We'll be fine," Grace said, not believing it for a second.

The men started to unfurl the ropes.

"No!" Grace said.

The men stopped and stared at her.

"The hatchlings will come with us peacefully. There's no need for ropes. You'll hurt them."

The men continued to stare. Grace repeated the same three sentences in the six languages she knew, but they didn't appear to understand any of them. They eyed the hatchlings and tied nooses on the end of their sticks. Grace ducked under the blowpipes and stood in front of the hatchlings.

"Are you crazy?" Dylan said.

"I don't think they'll hurt me."

"Exactly. They might just skip to the poison-dart-killing part." Dylan tried to step over to her. One of the men whacked him in the head with his pipe. "Ouch!" His face flushed, and his hands turned into fists.

"Don't," Grace said. "I have this under control."

Three more triplets ran up, followed by another set. There were now twelve jaguar men surrounding them.

"Really?" Dylan asked, holding his ear.

"If they had really meant you harm, they would have put a dart in your neck."

"That's comforting."

Butch walked up behind the triplets.

"Oh my God!" Grace said, feigning shock and surprise just as Marty had told her to. Butch had to be convinced that they didn't know he was anywhere near South America, or he'd know something was up.

Butch's smile broadened. "Happy to see me?"

"No."

"I'm crushed."

"How did you get down here? What is this place?"

"Shut up!" Butch said. "I'm sure your grandfather will explain everything if he isn't too ticked off to even look at you."

"Noah is here?" Grace asked, but this time she wasn't faking being shocked.

"He's been here for days. We flew in together." Butch looked at the hatchlings, who hadn't moved. "What were you trying to tell my guys when I walked up?"

"I was telling them that there's no need for the ropes. The hatchlings will follow us wherever we go. And where are we going?"

Instead of answering, Butch said something to his men. They started re-coiling their ropes.

"I asked where we're going," Grace repeated.

"You and your friend may not be going anywhere," Butch said, taking his pistol out and pointing it at Dylan.

"You going to shoot us like you did Raul?" Dylan asked with unflinching defiance.

Grace wasn't sure this was the best way to handle Butch, but she had to give him props for bravery.

"Maybe," Butch said with a shrug. "So you stumbled across my old friend Raul? That must have been a sight."

"It was horrible," Grace said. "Why did you shoot him?"

"Because he'd served his purpose. You might have noticed the jag tats?"

Grace nodded.

"Raul was born in the compound, but he decided it wasn't to his liking. We were pretty happy to see him show up at Lansa's jaguar preserve. We've been looking for him for a long time. He thought that by cooperating he could save everyone. As you saw, that didn't work out for him."

"Then why should we cooperate?" Grace asked.

"First, because you have no choice." Butch cocked his pistol. "Second, because I'll shoot Dylan right here, right now, if you don't. Where's Marty?"

"I don't know," Grace said.

"Wrong answer." Butch took a step toward Dylan.

"I'm telling the truth!" Grace shouted. "We got separated trying to get away from Yvonne. We followed the footprints here. We figured he'd do the same."

"Where's Yvonne?"

"I have no idea. The last time I saw her and her men was west of camp. We were able to get past them and come this way."

"Is she still tracking you?"

Grace nodded. "We think so."

"Then why isn't she here?"

Grace shook her head. "Maybe she's tracking Marty, and he's not coming this way. We lost him just outside camp. Why don't you radio her?"

Butch didn't answer. Instead he looked up through the canopy for a moment, then lowered his gun. "I'm sure you're lying through your teeth, like always, but for now I'll let Dylan live. It'll be dark soon. We need to get inside."

"Who else is in there?"

Butch ignored her and waved the triplets to the south.

"Aren't we going to the gate?" Dylan asked.

"There's more than one gate," Butch said. "And if I hear another word from you, I will shoot you in the head." He pointed out yet another electrocuted monkey. "Or maybe I'll just push you into the fence and watch you sizzle."

Dead monkey twenty-one, Grace thought. *I hope Marty knows what he's doing.*

SO FAR SO GOOD

Marty had no idea what he was doing, but he wasn't overly concerned. He was used to not knowing what he was doing. He'd swiped the code and gotten into the compound.

So far so good.

He was fifty feet up yet another tree with a good view of the gate. Earlier, he'd taken a chance by flying the dragonspy in close enough to listen to Grace and Dylan's capture outside the fence. He'd caught the *click* of Butch's pistol and his threat to sizzle Dylan.

I told Dylan not to go with Grace. Next time maybe he'll listen.

He watched as they started through the gate. A couple of sets of triplets led the way, followed by Grace and Dylan, then the hatchlings, who balked at the entrance. Grace had to go back and coax them into the compound. It took several minutes, but finally one of them shot through the opening like a cannonball, quickly followed by the other. Butch slammed the gate closed.

Grace pointed at the vintage truck. "There is no way the hatchlings are going to climb into the back of that willingly."

"Willingly, huh?" Butch said. "I could truss 'em up and toss 'em in the back if I want. The only *will* that matters inside here is *my* will."

"Oh," Grace said. "So this is *your* place?"

Butch frowned.

Marty smiled. Grace knew how to get under Butch's skin, but she needed to be careful. Butch might shoot her where she stood. She could no longer rely on Noah Blackwood's protection. Not after what she had done to him at the Seattle Ark.

"If we walk to wherever we're going, they'll probably just follow us," Dylan said, obviously trying to defuse the situation.

Butch hit him on the side of the head, knocking him to the ground. "I warned you to keep your mouth shut."

Grace ran over to Dylan.

"If either one of you says another word, I'll kill both of you," Butch said. "The hatchlings are trapped. They can't get out of here. I don't care where they go. We can round them up anytime we like. Now get in the truck!"

Grace and Dylan climbed into the cab, the triplets piled into the back, and Butch took off through the trees with the hatchlings running behind. The dinos lasted about a quarter of a mile before dropping back, then giving up completely to jump onto a small deer flushed into their path by the passing truck.

Marty left the hatchlings to their dinner and followed the truck to the lake, where everyone piled out. Butch pushed Grace and Dylan down the dock to one of the boats.

Inside or outside? Marty thought.

It was an important decision, and he wasn't sure which way to go. It was getting dark, and he was pretty sure he could slip the dragonspy through the door of the building without Butch seeing it. But then what? If the bot got stuck inside the building, he wouldn't be able to use it to clear his way to the lake. There were hundreds of people inside the compound, many of them now making their way to the village after their fieldwork. Sneaking around them without the dragonspy would be difficult, if not impossible. And he still had to get across the lake to the island. Sauntering down to the dock and stealing a boat wasn't going to work. The dock was in the center of the village, and there were at least a dozen people hanging around there. He'd have to circle the lake and find another way across.

He followed the boat with Grace and Dylan across to the island. When they got there, Butch prodded them up to a giant metal door with his pistol and punched in the code. The door slid open. He pushed them through.

In? Out? Everyone else is inside. My parents might be inside. One swipe and I'll have eyes inside.

Marty did not take the swipe. The giant door slid closed as if the concrete building was swallowing them.

Luther's legs were getting tired and his feet were beginning to blister. He sat down on an empty water bottle crate and pulled off his sneakers and socks.

"Whew!" he said, holding the socks at arm's length. "We need a washer and dryer down here! Or a box of socks! These are a little ripe. Toxic actually."

He examined his feet and discovered a nasty blister on his left big toe and another hot spot on his right heel. He decided to forego sneakers for the time being. The cool concrete felt good on his bare feet. Sitting down also felt good. He wondered how many miles he'd walked.

I bet it's a hundred miles!

"I could use a pedometer, too," he said. "It's a thing that measures how many steps you've taken. Got that?"

He'd been making requests like this for hours, not expecting, or getting, any answers, so he was pretty shocked when the corridor door burst open.

Wow, that was fast!

For a second, he actually thought a box of socks was going to come flying through the door. Instead, it was Dylan Hickock and Grace Wolfe.

"Company," Butch said, grinning and slamming the door closed before Luther could utter a word.

Luther ran over and tried the door, but of course it was locked. There wasn't much he could have done anyway with Butch on the other side. He turned and looked at Grace and Dylan. "How's it going?"

"How's do you think it's going?" Grace shouted, getting to her feet.

"Just being polite."

"Are you alone down here?"

Luther shook his head. "Laurel, Ana, Doc, Jake, Buck, and . . ." He hesitated. "Sylvia and Timothy."

Grace wasn't sure she had heard Luther correctly. Her knees got wobbly, and for a second she thought she might faint. A hand reached out to steady her. Dylan. "They're alive?"

Luther nodded.

She had given up hope long ago, but had said nothing to Marty, or Wolfe, or anyone else about it. Sylvia and Timothy had been her parents up until a few months ago. *Mom and Dad.*

"How are they?" Grace could barely get the words out of her mouth.

"Thin," Luther answered. "They could use some sun. A little weak. But good."

Grace looked around the dimly lit room. She knew where she was from Rose's sketches. "Seventeen rooms," she said.

"How did you know that?" Luther asked.

"My mother's Moleskine."

"Where's Marty?"

"He's outside. We —"

"Hold it!" Luther said, with a look of panic. He pointed up at the shadowy ceiling. "This is Grace O'Har — uh, I mean, Grace Wolfe and Dylan Hickok, but you probably already know that."

"Who are you talking to?" Dylan asked, looking up at the ceiling.

"We're being watched and listened to," Luther said. "I'm not sure who's on the other end, but they're kind of like a genie. If you need something, all you have to do is ask, and it shows up in one of the rooms. Well, not everything. About an hour ago, I asked for a couple of cheeseburgers, but they haven't materialized yet." He looked up at the ceiling. "But I'm still hopeful."

"You mentioned Laurel," Grace said. "But you didn't say anything about Wolfe."

"Butch took him someplace else. Haven't seen him since I got down here."

Grace looked up at the ceiling and decided that if they were listening, it was time to reinforce her lie about Marty. "We don't know where Marty is," she said. "We were trying to get away from Yvonne —"

"Yvonne's in Brazil?"

Grace nodded. "Along with some military thugs. They were after us and we got separated. We found your tracks and figured that Marty would follow them, too, if he found them."

"Maybe they stuck him with Wolfe."

"That must be it," Grace said, knowing it wasn't. She was pretty certain that Luther knew it, too, and was playing a game for the camera and the genie.

"Follow me and I'll take you to the other inmates."

Grace and Dylan followed.

As soon as the sun set, Wolfe began the tedious and painful process of sawing through the plastic flex-cuffs. Luckily, the knife had just enough serration for the job.

Having worked with captive animals for most of his life, Wolfe knew a great deal about cages. He knew how to build them. He knew how to take them apart. But before he began disassembling his cage with the knife, he fed the bearcat. He wasn't sure why, aside from the fact that the bearcat now expected Wolfe to feed him.

By the third meat toss, there was a shift in the bearcat's behavior. His aggression seemed to melt away as if it had never existed. He rubbed his shaggy head against the wire mesh. Wolfe took a chance and hand fed him a piece of meat. The bearcat took it gently, without so much as a growl.

"Progress," Wolfe said. "I'm betting you're not nearly as fierce as you look." He slowly put his hand out and touched the bearcat's mane. The bearcat leaned in closer. Wolfe scratched him behind the ear.

"Big, tough, mutant bearcat."

Wolfe glanced back at Nine. He was watching the scratching

intently from his platform. Wolfe tossed him a piece of meat, thinking Nine would ignore it, as always, but the chupacabra surprised him. He sniffed it, then gulped it down in spite of having his own pile of meat untouched in his own cage. Wolfe tossed him a second piece of meat. Nine gobbled it down as eagerly as the first, then took a small step toward the wire mesh.

Wolfe smiled. "Who's training who? If you think I'm going to scratch *you* behind the ear, think again. Wish I had time to see what you're up to, but I have to go."

He split the rest of the meat between the bearcat and Nine, then grabbed his knife and started unscrewing the brackets holding the front mesh in place.

Violet stared at the girl following behind the odd boy named Luther.

"She's exactly like me," she said.

"She looks like you," her father said. "But she is nothing like you."

Another lie, Violet thought. But she was used to this. Her father had been lying to her since the day she was born. They were watching the young people on the monitors as they moved from room to room.

"Who's the boy with Grace?"

"Dylan Hickock. Another bad person."

He didn't look bad to Violet. None of them looked, or acted, like bad people. They looked like people she wanted to get to know — people she wanted to talk to face-to-face.

"The boy Marty you told me about? The son of Timothy and Sylvia?"

Her father shook his head. "He is still at large. By now he may be dead. The forest beyond where we live is a very dangerous place."

"But I can keep the ones that are here?"

"For now, but not forever. You'll be leaving our little paradise one day soon, and you cannot take them with you."

Her father had been telling her this for years.

"To the Ark."

"Yes, to the Ark."

She pointed at the screen. "What will happen to them?"

Her father shrugged. "No one lives forever." He gave her a wink. "Well, almost no one lives forever."

"You and I will live a long, long, time."

"Yes, we will."

She watched as the newcomers entered the room with the others. Sylvia and Timothy ran over and threw their arms around the girl who looked like her.

Grace had wondered what her reaction would be upon seeing her former parents alive and well. Her doubt came from the fact that they had lied to her for her entire life. She understood why they'd done it, but on some level she was still angry about it. She needn't have worried. As soon as she saw them, she burst into tears, returning their hugs, shocked at how thin and frail they were. She could feel every bone in their bodies and was afraid she would hurt them if she squeezed too hard.

Laurel Lee was next. Grace hadn't seen her since Noah had flown her off the *Coelacanth* and taken her to the Ark. Laurel was sitting at a table with Ana. Grace ran over and gave her a hug.

"Bittersweet," Laurel said, returning the hug. "It's wonderful to see you, but I wish it wasn't here."

"What are you doing?" The table was covered with scraps of paper.

"We're working on a lexicon of the Trips' language in case we get a chance to communicate with them."

"The Trips?"

"Triplets. Luther came up with the name."

"Actually, Wolfe came up with the name," Luther said.

"Anyway," Laurel continued. "I think I've come up with a pretty good vocabulary. Why don't you and Luther pull up a chair, and I'll show you what we're doing."

Grace loved languages and was eager to see what they were up to.

Luther, not so much. "I'm sure it's fascinating, but I think I'll continue my rounds. Last loop, I scored two new people. Who knows what I'll —"

"I think you should take a load off your feet," Buck said, stepping into the room.

"Maybe in a little —"

"We talked about this," Buck said.

"Oh yeah, that's right," Luther said, reluctantly pulling out a chair next to Grace and sitting down.

Laurel pushed a piece of paper across the table. "This is what I've come up with so far."

Grace looked down at the paper and tried to hide her surprise, because it had nothing to do with the Trips' language. It read:

We are escaping in one hour.

CLICK CLICK CLICK SNAP

Marty had made it past the village without being spotted and was a quarter of the way around the lake. Getting across to the island was looking unlikely. The dock appeared to be the only place with boats. He sat down on a stump to rest and figure out the best way to proceed. He was thinking about swimming across when an alligator as big as a small ship hauled itself out of the water, scaring him half to death.

"Holy crap!"

He fell backward off the stump and scrambled for the tree line, not stopping until he stumbled over an exposed root and face-planted on the forest floor. He would have broken his nose if the ground hadn't been soft. He flipped over onto his back, gasping for breath. Alligators weren't supposed to be that big. He couldn't believe he'd been about to take off his shoes and go for a swim.

Marty sat up, wiped the rotting muck out of his eyes, and got to his feet. He wasn't thrilled about heading back to the lake, but he didn't have any choice. That's where the island, the building, and hopefully his parents were. He put his headlamp on and stumbled through the forest for a hundred yards before angling back down to the lake, hoping to avoid another encounter with the giant gator. The coast was clear, but he didn't take any chances. He stood twenty feet from the shore as he scanned the lake. The village was lit up like a Christmas tree with campfires. He looked across at the island. The building was completely invisible in the dark. If he hadn't seen it in the daylight, he wouldn't have known it was there.

What's up with that?

He flipped through the pages of Rose's journal in his head with his eidetic memory. Several of the sketches had been drawn from the vantage point of a window.

So where's the light from the windows?

He slipped on the spyglasses and sent the dragonspy across the lake to check it out. Halfway across, he had another shock. An alligator launched itself out of the water and snapped a bird out of the air like a trophy trout snagging a mosquito. This meant that there was more than one giant gator, they could see perfectly at night, and they were hungry. Marty wasn't sure if he'd be safe on the lake even if he did find a boat. He continued to the island and quickly discovered why the building was dark. Every window was covered with a steel shutter that looked like it could withstand a nuclear blast. He was about to fly the dragonspy back to shore when a light came on from someplace and temporarily blinded him.

"Whoa!"

He whipped the spyglasses off and squinted across the lake at the building. The light was coming from the rooftop. He switched to the Gizmo screen and flew the dragonspy toward the light.

The light surprised Wolfe as well, and ticked him off. He had just stepped outside of his cage and was angry that he hadn't even thought about there being motion detectors, which had no doubt triggered the lights. The birds and monkeys were shrieking louder than any alarm. The animals that couldn't shriek were roaring and growling and rattling their steel cages, including the bearcat and Nine. Wolfe looked up at the cameras. Three of them were pointed right at him like guns. No use trying to hide. They'd track his every move. What he needed was some kind of weapon besides the now very dull egg knife. Butch would be there any moment. Wolfe broke a branch off a tree and tested it for heft. It wouldn't be much use against Butch's gun, but it was better than nothing. He proceeded to smash every surveillance camera within sight with his crude weapon.

Now what I need is a distraction. Something to occupy Butch's attention.

He looked at the bearcat.

Marty was looking at the bearcat, too, over Wolfe's shoulder, wondering what the heck it was, and what Wolfe was doing with the beast. It looked like he was trying to jimmy the door open and let the thing out, which seemed insane because the beast was trying to eat the stick and Wolfe's arm. If he wanted to let it out, it would be easier to use the key code, but of course Wolfe didn't have the key code. But Marty did, if, as he hoped, the key code was universal.

He buzzed Wolfe's head with the dragonspy. Wolfe was so preoccupied with keeping his arm attached to his shoulder that he didn't notice. Marty tried again, this time aiming for Wolfe's left eye, veering away at the very last second just before he poked it out. That did the trick. Wolfe reeled back and stared at the bot hovering inches in front of his bearded face.

"Can you hear me?" he said.

Marty flew the bot up and down.

"I don't have much time to talk because Butch is probably on his way up here to kill me. The others are locked up on the lowest level. Including Sylvia and Timothy . . ."

Marty burst into tears and missed the next several sentences, but he didn't care. His parents were alive. He knew exactly where they were from Rose's sketches. They were in one of the seventeen rooms on the lowest level of the building. He wiped the tears away and tuned back in.

". . . the bearcat loose. I don't think he'll hurt me."

The bearcat, as Wolfe called it, looked like it was going to kill him. Marty flew the dragonspy down to the keypad and tapped it.

"You know the code?"

Marty nodded the dragonspy up and down.

"One?"

Marty went through the yes/no routine, and after a short period of time he was able to give Wolfe the combination. Wolfe punched it in using the end of the stick, which didn't seem nearly long enough to Marty. There was an audible *click* as he tapped in the last number. The door popped open about an inch. Wolfe backed away. The bearcat stopped snarling and stared suspiciously at the gap.

There was another *click*, but it was not from the gate. The click was the sound of a hammer being pulled back on a pistol. The pistol was held by Noah Blackwood. It was pointed at Wolfe's head.

"Drop the stick."

"Shoot me."

The bearcat burst through the door snarling. Wolfe and Blackwood reeled backward.

Marty didn't get to see what happened next because there was a third *click*. It didn't come from the Gizmo speaker. It came from a few inches behind him. He turned. Butch McCall was pointing a gun at him.

Marty hit the OFF button. The Gizmo screen went blank.

"You think I'm stupid?"

Actually, Marty was one of the few people who didn't think Butch was stupid. "Hardly," he said. "You're the one who managed to sneak up on me holding a gun. Did you see my headlamp?"

"No. I saw your little flying robot when I grabbed Grace and Dylan, and I figured you set me up and got inside. I've been stalking you for hours. Saw you freak out over the gator."

"That wasn't a normal gator," Marty said.

"That was one of the small ones."

"They don't bother boats?" Marty asked, knowing that the longer he kept Butch talking, the longer he would live.

"Not usually. But it's a little dicier at night when they feed. The trick is to keep the boat moving. If you stop, you're dead."

Two shots rang out from across the water. Marty jumped.

Butch glanced over at the light on the island. "Only two people with guns inside the compound," he said. "Me and Blackwood. I'm here. That leaves Blackwood. I'd say your uncle is gone. What'd you see with that flying bot?"

"Noah was pointing a gun at Wolfe." Marty saw no point in lying, or in telling the complete truth.

"Well, there you go," Butch said. "I thought Noah had something more dramatic in mind than just shooting him. He must have gotten tired of having him around."

Marty hoped this wasn't true.

"Where's your boat?" Marty asked.

"Not far."

Marty didn't like Butch's noncommittal attitude. He looked across at the island. "So my parents are over there," he said.

"That's right, but you're not going to see them."

"Why not?" Marty asked, but he already knew the answer.

"Because this is the end of the line for you," Butch said. "Believe me, I'm doing you a favor. The others are nothing more than lab rats. As soon as she gets done studying them, they'll be sacrificed."

"She?" *Keep him talking*, Marty thought.

"Violet," Butch said. "A clone. A replacement for Rose, and Grace, since those two didn't exactly work out. Noah got it right with Violet. She's as scary as he is."

Marty doubted Butch would be talking this way if Noah was there. *Keep him talking.*

"What does she look like?"

"Like Rose and Grace. Spitting image."

"How old is she?"

"Eight. And I know what you're doing!"

"What?"

"Getting me to talk so I don't pull the trigger."

"Busted," Marty said. "But you can't blame me for wanting to connect all the dots before —"

Something ran out of the dark toward them. Butch pointed

his pistol at the noise. Marty was about to make a run for it when he realized that the something was the hatchlings.

"Stop!" He hit Butch's arm.

The shot went wild. Butch backhanded him, knocking him to the ground. The stray bullet didn't slow the hatchlings down. They ran in and started snapping around where Marty lay.

"What's the matter with them?" Butch shouted.

Marty got to his feet. "I'd guess they're hungry."

Snap!

Marty dodged. "You didn't have to knock me down. I saved your life. If you shot a hatchling, Noah would kill you." He backed away toward the lake.

"No, you don't!" Butch grabbed him by the collar and backed away with him.

Snap! Snap!

Marty felt water pour into his tennis shoes.

Snap!

Butch dropped the gun, swore, and grabbed his wrist. Marty took several steps away from him. The hatchlings followed him.

SNAP!

Butch screamed. Marty and the hatchlings were splattered in blood and gore. A giant gator had bitten Butch nearly in two and was hauling the pieces back into the lake.

Marty ran toward the tree line with the hatchlings close behind. When he got there, he put his hands on his knees to catch his breath and throw up. Fortunately, he'd only witnessed bits and pieces of Butch's demise. The hatchlings seemed to have lost their appetite as well. They were staring at the lakeshore, no longer snapping.

"I'd stay away from the shore if I were you," Marty said.

He felt something tickling his leg. He reached into his pocket and pulled the Gizmo out. Ted Bronson was making a video call.

"You got the comms working," Marty said.

"I didn't do anything. They just starting working. Tell me what's going on."

"Butch is dead."

I AM YOU

The explosion was much bigger than Buck had said it would be. The room shook and tilted, then the portholes blew out.

"Water!" Luther shouted unnecessarily. Everyone could see the water shooting into the room, which was going to change the plan that Laurel had slipped to them across the table on little scraps of paper.

Buck had made a fertilizer bomb to blow the door to the corridor in the chicken room. Doc, who was not nearly as sick and weak as he had pretended to be, was going to lead Jake, Buck, and Flanna through the blown door first with crude weapons to fend off anybody waiting for them. When the corridor was clear, the others would follow. Grace's job was to lead them to the stairs. She knew exactly where they were because of her mother's sketches.

"We're all out of here together!" Doc shouted.

Ten people. Grace fell into line near the front behind Doc and Jake. Doc was carrying a long lead pipe he had torn from the wall. Jake was carrying a claw hammer. Not much defense against blowpipes, bows and arrows, and clubs.

The explosion had knocked out all the lights in the other rooms. Luther moved up to the front with the flashlight app on his cell phone. The chicken room was in shambles. The door to the corridor was gone, along with half the wall. They had to clamber over debris to get to the pitch-black corridor. They made it to the elevator, which was closed.

"The stairs are farther down," Grace said.

"One good thing about it being dark," Luther said. "They can't see us."

"But they can see your light," Buck pointed out. "Hurry it along."

They reached a door marked TREPPE.

"Stairs," Grace translated.

"There's a keypad and the door's locked," Luther added, shining a light on the pad.

"I think I just heard the elevator door open," Sylvia said.

"Quiet," Doc said. "Cut the light. Hug the wall."

Voices echoed down the corridor. They were not speaking English. Flashlights came on. Everyone held their breath. The lights started moving away from them.

Luther's cell phone rang.

Doc swore. The lights reversed course.

"Hello? . . . I'm glad to hear it, but we've got a little problem. Can't really talk right now. We're trying to get out of the basement, but the doors are . . . Really? Talk to you later."

"That was Marty." Luther turned his light on the keypad and punched in 6-6-2-4. The door clicked open. The stairway was lit.

"Go! Go! Go!" Doc started pushing people through the door. He stumbled through last with two arrows sticking out of his shoulder.

Jake wedged the claw hammer under the door a split second before the Trips slammed into it. The door held.

"Your arm," Flanna said.

"I'm fine!" Doc insisted. "Let's get up those stairs."

Grace trotted up next to Luther. "Marty was on the phone?"

"Yeah. He's on his way to the island in a boat. I didn't catch everything he said, but I think he said Butch was dead."

They reached another door.

"One more floor up to ground level," Luther said.

"We have to find Wolfe before we leave," Grace said.

No one said anything.

"I'm not leaving without him," Grace said.

"I'm with you," Luther said.

"Me, too," Laurel said.

"We aren't going anywhere without Wolfe," Doc said. "We'll find him together." He was being helped up the stairs by Flanna and Jake. The arrows were still dangling out of his shoulder and he was actively bleeding.

"Not until we get those arrows out and patch you up," Flanna said.

They reached the ground level. Buck pushed past everyone to the door. "I'll pop out and see if the coast is clear." He was gone before anyone could object.

Flanna and Jake made Doc sit down on the steps. Laurel knelt down to help them by yanking the arrows out before Doc could object.

"Ouch!"

"Sorry." Laurel looked at the tips. "Doesn't look like they've been dipped in poison. Can you make a fist?"

Doc made a fist and shook it at her. Everyone laughed, breaking the tension to some degree. Flanna tore the sleeve off his shirt and bound the wounds as best as she could.

Buck came back through the door. "I don't see anybody. There are a lot of rooms to —"

The door beneath them opened and footsteps pounded up the steps. The group filed through the door quickly. Buck grabbed Doc's lead pipe and rammed it under the door.

"It's not going to hold for —"

The pipe went flying as the door burst open. Six angry Trips stepped out, weapons up. Behind them, six more Trips stepped out of the elevator.

Laurel shouted something at them. The Trips glanced at each other, but did not lower their weapons. She repeated whatever she had said, with the same results.

"I told them we were friends and that we meant them no harm. At least I think that's what I said."

Another shout came up from behind the Trips nearest the elevator. They immediately lowered their weapons, as did the Trips near the stairs.

"What you said was, 'You are no friend of ours.' "

The Trips parted, letting through a little girl and Travis Wolfe. Wolfe had a bloody gash on the side of his head. Grace cried out when she saw him, but she couldn't take her eyes off the little girl. Nor could anyone else.

"Who are you?" Grace asked, feeling her legs go weak.

The little girl smiled. "I am you."

THE O'HARAS

Marty jumped out of the inflatable, followed by the hatchlings, which had clambered aboard just as he was pulling away from shore. Surprisingly, they had ridden in the boat pretty well considering he had headed to the island at full throttle, afraid to slow down because of the giant gators. He ran up the steps to the building and punched in the code with his free hand. In his other hand was Butch's pistol. He wasn't sure what he was going to find on the other side of the door, but he was ready for whatever it was. The hatchlings shot past him through the opening. He followed with the pistol pointing the way. A couple of dozen people stood in the corridor. Half of them were covered in jaguar spots. The other half were covered in welts and gashes. The hatchlings had made a beeline to Luther and were dancing around him.

Wolfe walked up and gently took the pistol out of his hand.

"Where's Noah Blackwood?" Marty asked.

"Dead," Wolfe answered. "Killed by one of his own mutants, but it was a close run thing. Noah got a couple of shots into him before it tore his head off."

Marty barely heard what Wolfe was saying. He scanned the people in the dark corridor. Jake and Flanna were cleaning up

Doc's arm with a first aid kit. Laurel was trying to speak to a group of Trips. Buck and Ana were sitting down, leaning against the wall. Grace was smiling, holding the hand of a little girl who could have been her sister. His parents were rushing toward him.

My parents.

He dropped to his knees and wept as they wrapped their arms around him.

IT'S BEEN TWO WEEKS . . .

. . . since Noah Blackwood and Butch McCall died. No one is sorry. In fact, most people don't even know that Noah Blackwood is dead. He's been on TV almost every day conducting interviews about the merger between his Arks and Northwest Zoo and Aquarium. Not even the director of NZA knows that the Noah Blackwood he's dealing with is a copy by the name of Mr. Zwilling. Al Ikes set it all up. The government thought it was best to keep Noah Blackwood's dealings over the past sixty years quiet. Zwilling was more than happy to cooperate. The alternative was going to prison forever.

I got a chance to meet Zwilling about a week after Noah died. Al flew him down to explain to the Trips that there had been a change of leadership inside the compound. Dr. Lansa is now in charge . . . at least temporarily until things settle down. Zwilling couldn't have been nicer. He's like Noah, but without the evil. He's going to retire at the compound once the Arks are transferred to NZA. All he really wants to do is take care of the animals. Zwilling the Zookeeper. And there are plenty of animals to take care of on the rooftop, minus the bearcat. Noah shot the bearcat twice before it killed him. Wolfe tried to save the bearcat, but its injuries were too serious. Nine is still alive, though, and I spend as much time with him as I possibly can. Wolfe says Nine is not to be trusted or touched . . . ever. But yesterday I scratched him behind the ear. I told Marty about it this morning and he gave me a big lecture about risk taking (what a joke), then asked if he could try his hand at scratching the chupacabra.

Marty spends most of his time in the kitchen cooking for everyone, especially Sylvia and Timothy, who are fattening up nicely. I don't think it will be too long before they take off on another adventure. The longest they had ever stayed in one place was when they were prisoners of Noah Blackwood. And they are restless.

When Marty isn't cooking, he's arguing with Luther and Dylan over their new graphic novel. I've asked him a couple of times what happened to Butch on the lakeshore. All he'll say is that Butch got "chomped" by a giant gator. I'm wondering if that scene will make it into their book. Luther has made a few sketches of the alligator taking Butch, which is one of the things they argue about. Marty tells Luther that his drawings are not even close. Then Luther insists that Marty draw it. Marty shudders and says he can't.

Luther's parents paid a visit to the compound a few days ago. They arrived by helicopter and were here for about three hours and spent most of the time talking to Wolfe and Ted about business. Luther begged them not to send him back to OOPS, and they acquiesced after Wolfe promised to hire a tutor for all of us. Luther and the hatchlings are delighted with the decision. The hatchlings actually sleep with him at night. Once a day he takes them to the mainland to hunt and get exercise. I usually go with him to visit Laurel, who is living at the Trip village along with Jake, Flanna, Buck, and Agent Crow.

Dylan gave me his story to read. I know all about D. B. Cooper, Sasquatch, and what happened on Mount St. Helens. Agent Crow arrived a week ago, along with Ted Bronson. They were both limping a little from bullet wounds in their legs. We thought that Crow would arrest Buck and haul him back to the States, but instead they greeted each other like old friends. Crow said that while he was in the hospital, he had officially retired from the FBI and had no legal authority in Brazil, or anywhere else. He wanted to know what Buck's plans were. Buck said he was going to spend the rest of his life down here at the compound. There's plenty of work to do with the Trips and at the jaguar preserve. Crow asked if he could join him. Buck was happy to have him.

Ted, Ana, and Wolfe headed back to Cryptos Island this morning. Ted wanted to get back to his inventions. Ana is on to another investigative story now that the Noah Blackwood saga is wrapped up, which she has been forbidden to write a word about. And Wolfe? He'll be back after he checks on things on the island. He asked if I wanted to go with him, but I told him no. I didn't want to leave Violet behind, and she's not ready yet. We've been inseparable since the moment we met. And we may be with each other for a very, very long time.

We are sitting next to each other by the pool on the roof, scratching in our Moleskine journals, trying to make sense of our lives. . . .

Dylan just joined us. He sits down and says nothing. He knows better than to disturb us while we're writing. There's another reason why I didn't join Wolfe on Cryptos Island. Violet glances up from her journal and gives me a sly smile. I feel my face turn red. She knows. I wonder if Dylan knows?

In a moment I'll put my pen down, and he and I will talk about everything, except us. . . .

ACKNOWLEDGMENTS

This book would not have been possible without my editor at Scholastic, Anamika Bhatnagar. You are the best! And a big thank-you is due to my wonderful agent, Barbara Kouts, and to the fabulous art director Phil Falco, who designs these books. Thanks also to Ellie Berger, David Levithan, Ed Masessa, Robin Hoffman, Lizette Serrano, Emily Heddleson, Antonio Gonzalez, Charisse Meloto, Elizabeth Starr Baer, Megan Bender, and everyone else in the Scholastic family. But the biggest thanks, as always, goes to my wife, Marie, the kindest person in the room,

ROLAND SMITH is the author of numerous award-winning books for young readers, including *Cryptid Hunters*, *Tentacles*, *Chupacabra*, and the Storm Runners trilogy. For more than twenty years he worked as an animal keeper, traveling all over the world, before turning to writing full time. Roland lives with his wife, Marie, on a small farm south of Portland, Oregon. Visit him online at www.rolandsmith.com.